THE AUTHOR

Edith Templeton was born in Prague in 1916. Both sides of her family were big estate owners in Bohemia. (Her father, who was a doctor of technology, received, when leaving school, a gold medal from the Emperor Franz Joseph for being the best finalist in the whole Austro-Hungarian Empire.) Edith was educated at the French Lycée and then at the Prague Medical University for three years and, after several short stays in England, she settled, at the age of twenty-two, first in Cheltenham and then in London. She married Dr Edmund Ronald, for twenty years a brilliant cardiologist in India, physician to the King of Nepal, first European to enter its royal palace, and *éminence grise* in that country. While with him in Calcutta, she met Nehru, the Dalai Lama and the Panchen Lama and, of course, quite a few maharajahs. She has since lived, apart from her first four years in Vienna and afterwards her native city, in Salzburg, Lausanne, Torremolinos, Estoril and Italy. During the war she worked for the American War Office, in the office of the Surgeon General, and from 1945-6 was a captain with the British Forces in Germany as Conference and Law Court interpreter.

Although she started writing at the age of four – her first story being published when she was ten – Edith Templeton's first novel, *Summer in the Country*, was not published until 1950. Its success was followed by *Living on Yesterday* (1951) and *The Island of Desire* (1952) – all three are being published by The Hogarth Press. She is also the author of several other volumes of fiction, as well as many short stories and magazine articles, having been a regular contributor to the likes of *Vogue*, *Harpers* and the *New Yorker*. She has one son and now lives in Bordighera, on the Italian Riviera.

THE ISLAND OF DESIRE

Edith Templeton

Dans ton île, ô Vénus, je n'ai trouvé debout
Qu'un gibet symbolique où pendait mon image...
Baudelaire, *Un Voyage à Cythère*

New Introduction by
Anita Brookner

THE HOGARTH PRESS
LONDON

Published in 1985 by
The Hogarth Press
40 William IV Street, London WC2N 4DF

First published in Great Britain by Eyre and Spottiswoode Ltd 1951
Hogarth edition offset from the original British edition
Copyright Etta Trust Reg., Vaduz
Introduction copyright © Anita Brookner 1985

British Library Cataloguing in Publication Data

Templeton, Edith
The island of desire.
I. Title
823'.914[F]   PF6070.E4/
ISBN 0 7012 0574 1

Printed in Great Britain by
Cox & Wyman Ltd
Reading, Berkshire

INTRODUCTION

The Island of Desire was Edith Templeton's third novel, following the immensely successful and accomplished comedies of manners, *Summer in the Country* and *Living on Yesterday*. When it was published in 1952, certain critics found it slightly shocking, not only because it deals with the anarchy of erotic love, but by the very fact of this subject being aired at all. The 1950s were the last years of English *bienséance* and nothing was allowed to mar the even tenor of fictional entertainment. *The Island of Desire* was reviewed in the same batch of novels that included, according to the predilections of the reviewer, Han Suyin's *A Many-Splendoured Thing*, Nancy Spain's *Out Damned Tot*, and Margery Allingham's *Tiger in the Smoke*. Edith Templeton's novel was praised, but with some reserve; it was regretted that she had abandoned her 'charming' comedies of manners, and it was even felt that the bitter verse from Baudelaire's *Un Voyage à Cythère* from which the novel takes its title and which is quoted on the title page was in bad taste. The prevailing feeling seems to have been one of discomfort, as if to write about love in this way might be all right on the Continent but would not quite do in the quiet English suburb where Edith Templeton was living at the time. Her Bohemian background was referred to more than once, as if this could be the only explanation for a story universally perceived as subversive.

Edith Templeton, for all that she was married to an Englishman, was still a Czech through and through. Her first four years had been spent in Vienna, her girlhood in Prague, and it is the *beau monde* of these two cities which forms the social context against which the story unfolds. The perceptions that the novel contains and even celebrates have about them a cruelty and a sadness, have, in addition, a sort of inescapability, which make the novel equally shocking today, though for a different reason. For although in the 1950s it was thought that the society of central Europe could be called to account for such decadent goings on and that such things need never happen here, it was indeed here, in England, in the Sixties and Seventies, that all manner of frantic and uninhibited sexual encounters were promulgated, to the riotous enthusiasm of all concerned. Such indiscriminate and whole-hearted experimentation would have been viewed with an impassive eye in central Europe, certainly in the *beau monde*: it was, to use the dismissive word beloved of the snobbish characters in *The Island of Desire*, decidedly *canaille*. Therefore, although *The Island of Desire* celebrates a form of self-discovery and of recklessness, this self-discovery is arrived at warily, it is experienced as shock and, even more important, it is described in the briefest and most circumspect of terms. The conclusion drawn is epigrammatic rather than celebratory, and there is matter here for thought rather than for exhibitionism.

The story is a fairly complex one, although it follows the general theme of a young girl's sentimental education. Franciska Kalny is docile, well brought up, and completely overshadowed by her dreadfully worldly mother. Mrs Kalny, in the rare intervals between having her hair done and consorting with men other than her husband, is apt to hand out advice which the innocent Franciska is far from being in a position to receive: 'One can never tell what a man is like till one has gone to bed with him. One can get a tremendous surprise in this way, good or bad. Remember this for life, Cissy.' The girl is bored and uncomfortable at home, for she is beginning to get in her mother's way. For this reason, and because she is indeed very innocent, she is flattered when one of her mother's guests, Hugo Ling, a disaffected journalist, begins to pay her some attention. Such susceptibility is, however, misguided and Mrs Kalny is not the sort of mother to console her daughter for any kind of social tiresomeness. Her solution to Franciska's indiscretion is to send her off to Paris, theoretically to complete her education but in fact to get married as soon as possible, for she cannot come back to Prague until she has repaired her error of taste, the solecism which has caused her to be banished.

When we next meet Franciska she is indeed married, to an English husband, and living in Paris. Mrs Kalny, completely unreformed, is on a visit, and it is quite clear from their first exchange that it is Mrs Kalny who is living like a young girl – like a young girl in Paris – while Franciska is a grave and burdened young matron. The burden is soon revealed to be her husband, Johnny, always referred to as Mr Parker. This alerts us to the fact that he is beyond the pale. Mr Parker is a dreadful character. He hates quite a lot of things: women (although he loves his mother), filthy foreign muck, Gay Paree, the French language (to which he refers as 'the lingo'), and all other car drivers, for he is in the motor business himself. The extent of this mésalliance is revealed to Franciska not by her mother-in-law's wall-to-wall carpets in Coventry (for in Prague only Persian rugs are acceptable) but by Mr Parker's curious excitability when either Franciska or indeed he himself looks at another man. The reader will by this time have worked out exactly what sort of a marriage Franciska has contracted. She, however, cannot at first allow herself to understand that Mr Parker is 'impossible' and succumbs instead to migraine, her mother's ailment, and, imperceptibly, to an inherited remedy.

Franciska does not recognize herself as an adult, and as her mother's daughter, until the very last page of this succinct and mordant novel. The manner of her recognition and the knowledge that it brings with it should be reserved for the reader's own enjoyment. And although it closes the story, it is in fact the beginning of a life, and thus has a resonance beyond the words on the page. The reader may be invited to ponder on his or her own experience, the truth of which may have been kept a secret. For these are secret matters, despite the misleading openness of contemporary propaganda, 'therapy' 'counselling', and similar manifestations. Hence the quotation from Baudelaire:

Dans ton île, ô Vénus, je n'ai trouvé debout
Qu'un gibet symbolique où pendait mon image . . .
– Ah! Seigneur! donnez-moi la force et le courage
De contempler mon coeur et mon corps sans dégoût.

In addition to being sexually shocking – for to the timid it is only acceptable to write about sexual matters in terms of hilarity or outstanding success – the novel is socially shocking. Mrs Kalny and her daughter are snobs of the old school. They are snobs not in the English sense of coming from a recognizable class but in their intuitive knowledge of what is possible, what is impossible, and what is *canaille*. This is why Franciska gets all Mr Parker's signals wrong: because he is handsome, moneyed, and living in Paris, she assumes that he is possible. It is only when she comes up against his mother's fitted carpets, his petulant temper, and his hysterical disgust, that she realizes that he is *canaille*. It is to be wondered whether she ever realizes why he is impossible. Even Mrs Kalny is not quite sure, for she has never met anything like him before. For Mrs Kalny, men fall into much more easily distinguishable categories. Either they are rich, ghastly and useful, like the millionaire Feldman (' "Aren't you sorry, Mama, after all, that you did not marry Feldman? He is terribly rich, you know." Mrs Kalny replied: "Every day I am sorry. Every night I am glad." '); or they are fun; or they are impossible. Mrs Kalny could hardly be called promiscuous, for she is in fact very discriminating. But it takes a lifetime to become a Mrs Kalny, and Franciska will have to dedicate her own life to acquiring anything like her mother's expertise, even though she has the benefit of her mother's excellent advice: 'Remember this for life, Cissy. There are four professions where the men are not men: the tailor, the doctor, the waiter, and the hairdresser.'

Although it might be thought that Mrs Kalny herself is, for English readers at least, quite impossible, attention should be paid to the undercurrents of feeling in this otherwise memorably unsentimental novel. The reader, if alert to the mood of the story, will recognize a tenderness, a mute tribute, in fact, to a very unpromising and unaccommodating mother, as well as a sadness for the girl Franciska's innocence and the amount of time she wastes in getting rid of it. But as the whole novel is about the loss of innocence, about the getting of wisdom, the reader is bound to feel some sadness, for what is lost, even well lost, can never be repossessed. That, after all, is the meaning of experience. The other emotion for which the new reader should be alert is a sense of dignity. For if what is lost can never be repossessed, then anyone who lays wrongful claims to innocent feelings is seen to commit an error of taste, to become *canaille*, in fact. A case in point is the hairdresser, Sylva, who assumes that all men desire her, pursue her, and are virtuously repulsed by her. As these virginal attitudes are unbecoming and inappropriate in an adult woman, and a woman, moreover, who dislikes men, the author shows us that they are also undignified. For the cardinal virtue of this book is honesty. Only the truth of situations is acceptable, and all the rest can easily be perceived as subterfuge. Subterfuge, of course, is *canaille*. For anyone who finds this attitude as refreshing as it is rare, *The Island of Desire* will be a delightful discovery.

Anita Brookner, Bordighera – London 1984

PART ONE

CHAPTER 1

'When did you come home last night?' asked Mrs. Kalny, in an off-hand voice, and in order to prove to her daughter how little importance she attached to her question she went on sorting out buttons in an old painted box, without looking up.

'Oh, I don't know really,' replied the young girl.

'Don't you?' still very casually but already the movements of her fingers gave her away, for she jerked her hand so violently inside the box that mother-of-pearl, metal and wood knocked together and produced a sound like the evil thunder of tiny wardrums. One button shot out and rolled under the chair. The young girl did not speak.

'No answer is also an answer,' said Mrs. Kalny pleasantly in the same voice she had used before. She paused to draw breath. Twice she moved her lips as though the words she wanted to say were too horrible to be pronounced. At last she was ready:

'Very well, then. In this case, let me refresh your memory. You say you don't know, but I do. It was half past four in the morning.'

The young girl showed no signs of being surprised or upset. 'If you knew all along, why ask me?' she muttered.

'Better and better. First you lie to me and then you are impertinent.' She gave her daughter a last indignant glance,

7

took up the box again which she had placed on the dressing table a few seconds before delivering her accusation, and began to rummage gently among the buttons. The eagerness with which she had pursued this occupation until the young girl had entered the room, was gone from her countenance. Indeed, one could see from the random way in which she turned them over, that she had already forgotten which buttons she wanted to sort out and for what purpose. She bent over the box with a kind, gentle look, gazed at her daughter for a second with eyes glittering with annoyance and then, resuming the gentle expression, she returned her attention to the box, as though to say: 'My daughter is impertinent and causes me nothing but worry, but you, dear buttons, you appreciate me.'

A few moments later she was already bored. The young girl made ready to leave the room. She called her back, willing to pay the price for a measure of company.

'Where are you off to, Cissy? You don't have to change yet. Tired?'

'A bit.'

'Was it worth it?'

'Not really.'

By now, Mrs. Kalny was all friendly curiosity. 'Tell me,' she said, 'were there any nice men at the party?'

'Not really.'

'Not even one?'

Franciska twisted her lips. 'The handsomest man was the waiter,' she replied. She moved to the door and, wrenching the handle with a violence that was uncalled for, added in a toneless voice: 'As usual.'

Mrs. Kalny, alone once more, felt contempt mixed with astonishment at her daughter's words. The longer she considered them, the more bewildered she grew over the young girl's apparent lack of enthusiasm and she would have liked to shake her head over it. But this she did not dare to do, because the pins which fastened her curls would have pricked her at the slightest unwonted movement of her head and the veil tied over her hair to flatten it, would have tightened painfully and cut a red streak across her forehead. She would have liked to frown but refrained from doing so, as she knew that this was a bad habit which traces premature lines on the brow. So she remained outwardly calm, compelled by the discipline demanded by the constant care of beauty, which in its way is no less ascetic than the discipline of the soldier or the nun.

Thus, like so many other fashionable ladies before her, Mrs. Kalny modelled herself in the likeness of the martyrs in those old pictures, who exhibit their arrow-pierced and racked bodies with the complacent elegance of dressmakers' models and who are the patron saints of all those who know how to suffer prettily.

For a while Franciska stood by the window in the dining room and looked down at the near-by park; at the lawn grey with rime and dirt, at the wintry shrubs standing like tangles of thorns beside the empty paths.

She had bribed the porter with a tip of two crowns when he had opened the door to let her into the house this morning; and while she stepped away from the window and let her eyes wander round the dim room, she began to reproach herself for what she had done. The truth was out, her mother knew, and although she was glad that she had received only a half-hearted chiding, she felt ill at ease for having tried to shut the porter's mouth. It occurred to her that it was a lesser crime to disobey the rules of her parents' home than to lower herself to the level of the *'canaille'*, and to enter into league with them.

In the fading light of the November afternoon the dining room looked unfriendly to her, as rooms do when they have been robbed of their usual ornaments and furniture. The chairs had been removed, the fruit bowls had been taken away and so had the square crystal decanters and the painted vases. The drawers of the sideboard were half open, revealing the empty, felt-lined grooves in which the silver was usually stored, and the shelves inside the china cupboard were bare, except for one cup. She thought that the maids had overlooked this. But as she took it out, she saw that it was cracked and put it back on its place.

Her reason told her that the room had been gutted and turned into a skeleton so that, in a few hours' time it would be reborn into a place flowered, brilliantly lit and pervaded by scent and laughter; yet she could not feel it in her heart. And although she knew that the bowls would reappear heaped with sugared fruit and raisins, that the decanters would be filled with rum and sherry, that the vases would be bearing the white lilac which had arrived after lunch, she found it as hard to believe as it is to imagine that Spring will come when one is in the midst of Winter.

She went through the hall into the kitchen and entered into one of those sudden and breathless silences which occur among uncouth people upon the arrival of a person whom they do not wish to include in their talk.

The two parlourmaids covered up their embarrassment by a hectic display of activity, stacking piles of plates and folding napkins and retreating with the fruit of their labours into the shelter of the pantry.

Soon there was only the cook and the kitchenmaid left. The cook sat by the table, turning the leaves of her recipe book and peering down through steel-framed glasses which rested on the tip of her nose, while the kitchenmaid turned the handle of the meat mincer.

'Good afternoon, Mary,' said the young girl.

'Well, Miss Cissy,' replied the cook and raised her head. She gave the young girl a look of compassion and then, as though ashamed of it, turned her attention to the book on the table. 'Why does she look at me like that?' thought Franciska, who had noticed that the cook's expression was unusual but did not understand its meaning. 'If Mama did not make a fuss, what business of hers is it?'

She said: 'Busy?'

'What do you think? With forty people coming?'

'I thought there would be only twenty,' said Franciska who had not thought anything at all.

The cook shook her head. 'Forty people and Mr. Feldman on top of it.'

'Feldman?'

'Yes. At the last minute. He announced himself, Mr. Feldman did.' And the cook, who by now had decided to give up all pretence of reading, took off her glasses and laid them across the open page of the book.

'But I did not know he was in town.'

'We none of us did. Madam your mother didn't know either, or she would have told me in time, and that's why I've got to be standing here now, with all the rest of the work on my hands, standing here in the last minute, mincing meat,' replied the cook and leaned back in her chair with an air of comfortable suffering while, at the same time, in the person of the kitchenmaid, she was 'standing up and mincing meat', as she expressed it.

'I did not know he was invited,' said Franciska.

'He wasn't invited, he invited himself. He doesn't care if we have a party or a–I mean, a party, anyhow.'

'A party or what?'

'Oh, I don't know, Miss Cissy. I suppose I meant to say a wedding. And it wouldn't be such a surprise either, what with the goings-on in this house. Coming home at four in the morning. I don't envy madam your mother. I'd rather keep watch on a bagful of fleas than guard one young girl. Oh, well, if he is a nice young man—'

'Oh, you don't know what you are talking about,' said Franciska. 'There was no particular young man last night. And Susy's mother was with us the whole time and there was quite a crowd of us anyway.'

'That may be as may be it doesn't stop me thinking my own thoughts,' said the old woman. But while her tone of voice was arch and bantering, as she considered fitting on such an occasion, she made–Franciska thought–the wrong kind of face with it and the young girl felt a similar, though deeper uneasiness as when, a few years ago, something had gone wrong with the clock in the hall and the hands had pointed to eleven while it had struck five.

'I'm getting the coffee ready, Miss Cissy. You'd better go in and have it with madam your mother. You'll need it to be lively for the party.' And with this, to show that she was not willing to enter into further talk, the cook put her glasses on with gingerly movements; she was not yet used to wearing them and bore them with distrust.

'Did you hear what I said?' she asked the kitchenmaid as soon as Franciska had left.

'Mm.'

'When I said party, I nearly said funeral. Thank God, I've got my wits about me.'

CHAPTER 2

EVERYONE IN the house was doing something useful, thought Franciska, except herself. The cook supervised the kitchenmaid, the other maids were preparing for the party, even her mother was doing work by sitting still and allowing the cold cream she had spread on her face to soothe her skin and her hair to set in the shape in which she had arranged it with combs and pins. She wandered from one dusky room into the other, too indolent to put the light on, brushing against a table leg or a chair, listening to the sound of shivering glass after she had knocked against a glazed cabinet.

In her room she found Louise kneeling in front of the dressing chest.

'I am laying out your things now, Miss Cissy. The dress is on the bed, I've just pressed it, so you can start getting ready and I'll give you a hand. But if you don't do it straight away you'll have to dress yourself, because I shall be too busy later on.'

Saying this, Louise unfurled a pair of stockings, looked at them critically and at the same time with reverence and then laid them over her arm. She was inclined to be off-hand with people but she always handled people's belongings with awe.

The young girl turned and looked at the bed.

'I don't want the green one, you know I don't. I'll put on the red.'

'You can't, Miss Cissy.'

'Why not?'

'Because madam will wear her red dress and your red would clash with it.'

'Oh, very well. Leave me alone.'

A bell rang.

'Somebody will open. I can't. I am too busy,' remarked the lady's maid, still bent over half-opened drawers. By now her movements were impeded, as she had draped her arms and shoulders with pieces of underwear, turning herself into a living clothes horse.

Before Louise left, she took the red dress out of the wardrobe and away with her in order to, as she said, put it aside to remove a stain. Franciska knew that she did this in order to prevent her from wearing it; the annoyance and feeling of helplessness which arose in her effaced the last trace of elation she had experienced through having escaped with so little fuss from her mother. She realised that her mother had got the better of her again, if not in person, then through one of her creatures, Louise.

Although she knew that no one exciting could have called at this hour of the afternoon, Franciska went out into the hall, where the hairdresser, a gaunt amazon, was just slipping out of her tiger coat. The yellow black-spotted fur huddled over a chair seemed not so much like a garment as like the sloughed-off skin of this sallow, black-haired woman whose savage good looks were of a startling and aggressive nature.

Franciska went into her mother's bedroom.

'Sylva is here,' she said.

'Yes, I know, isn't it dreadful?' said Mrs. Kalny absent-mindedly. 'Trust her to arrive just when we are going to have coffee. Now what am I to do with her? She can't have it in here with us, of course, and she can't have it in the kitchen and the other rooms are all upside down already, I don't think there is a single chair in the dining room. I am sure she did it on purpose.'

'Let her have it in my room,' said Franciska.

'Very well. If you don't mind.'

'I did not think you'd want her to-day, in any case,' said Franciska.

'That's quite true, I didn't. But I have had such a bad night and my nerves are worn to shreds. So I felt I'd better have her after all, anything for peace you know, and Louise gets so on edge before a party that I thought I'd at least spare her doing my hair.'

'I am sorry about last night,' said Franciska. 'I did not know I made as much noise as that.'

'You didn't. I could hardly hear you,' said Mrs. Kalny. Then, changing from the slightly wailing, absentminded tone, she said with sudden firmness: 'No, I suppose you must have made a lot of noise. Or I would not have woken up, would I?'

There was a silence.

'I wonder if I'll ever be as moody as she is,' thought Franciska. She did not know that she had not awakened her mother on the night before. Mrs. Kalny had only heard her coming in because she had been lying awake already, worrying over the probability of her husband's death. Mr. Kalny had departed from home only ten days ago, on his doctor's advice. He now bore his diseased kidneys with as much weariness and resignation amidst the oleanders and camellias which line the paths of Merano, as when he went stumbling through the slushy snow past the Bank houses on the Graben, on his way to the Stock Exchange.

Just as people with weak hearts are experts at avoiding excitement, so Mrs. Kalny, always anxious to keep her youth and beauty, had a gift for avoiding scenes and scenting possible friction. Thus she often seemed feckless to people who hardly knew her, and even, sometimes, to her own daughter. In reality her apparent changeability was due to her quick perception. She could see the possibilities of a scene before others could and she quickly adapted her actions accordingly in order to spare her nerves.

'Why can't she at least make up her mind whether I made a lot of noise or not?' thought Franciska resentfully.

Mrs. Kalny did not keep silence about the reason she lay awake at night so as not to distress her daughter, but only out of consideration for herself. She felt that being upset in herself was bad enough without having to soothe an upset young girl. Besides, she would have been ashamed to divulge the real source of her worries. Her thoughts had not dwelt very much on her husband's person but mainly on the possible state of affairs after his death. It was, in fact, ceaseless calculation over money matters which had occupied the larger part of Mrs. Kalny's night.

'Mama,' said Franciska.

'Yes?'

'Is there anybody coming this evening?'

'Nobody. Only people.'

'You have not invited Mr. Ling?'

'Why should I? Anyway, why do you ask? You don't know him.' said Mrs. Kalny.

'Yes, I do.'

The hairdresser came in, carrying the small spirit lamp and the curling irons. After having brushed two combs on to the floor to make room for her implements, she set them with a crash on the glass top of the dressing table. She slithered the lamp towards and away from the mirror till she was satisfied with its position, while the glitter from the silvery metal flashed through the darkening room. At last she seized the tongs by one handle only and spun them round and round with a savage clutter.

Thus, having announced her presence by assaults on eye and ear, she was satisfied that only a blind and deaf person could have ignored her entry into the room and she felt it safe now to offer her greetings, fully confident that they would be acknowledged.

'Madam,' she said belligerently.

She could never bring herself to say: 'Good afternoon, madam,' she either said: 'Good afternoon,' or 'Madam!' She was always very keen to show her independence and to have pronounced a complete: 'Good afternoon, madam,' would have seemed to her to be an expression of servility, on the level of the servants.

'Good afternoon, Sylva,' said Mrs. Kalny. 'You've got two combs on the floor, you know.'

'I know, madam.'

'You'll step on them.'

'I shan't.'

'You will forget they are there and you will step on them,' said Mrs. Kalny.

'Somebody else might, but not me,' replied the hairdresser.

It was not laziness which prevented her from stooping down to pick up the combs. It was, again, her way of demonstrating that she was a hairdresser, not a slave.

'Cissy, my peignoir,' said Mrs. Kalny. 'In the second drawer on the left.'

While the young girl went to the dressing table, Sylva approached Mrs. Kalny and gripped her hair net.

'What's this?' she asked.

17

'I just thought it would make it easier for you if I——'
began Mrs. Kalny.

'Ha!' said the hairdresser. 'Madam thought she could do
her hair all on her own but in the last minute she saw she
could not do without me. And a fine mess it looks too. All
the waves in the wrong places. And I am to put it right in a
minute, I suppose? Always the same story.'

She would have continued in this vein had she not been
interrupted by the maid. The coffee tray was carried in.

'You will have some coffee, won't you, Sylva?' asked
Mrs. Kalny beseechingly. 'It's ready for you in Cissy's room.'

As usual, the hairdresser could not bring herself to accept
anything with good grace, but she at last agreed to have
her coffee as a special favour to Mrs. Kalny.

'Anyway, which one do you mean, Cissy?' asked Mrs.
Kalny, pouring out the coffee and milk simultaneously, a
skill she was very proud of. 'Emil Ling or Hugo Ling?'
She pronounced the names: 'Emilling' and 'Hugoling'.

'The newspaper one.'

'Ah, that's Hugoling.'

'I met him last night,' said Franciska. 'He was with another
party at the Boccaccio and he came and joined our table.'

'That just proves what I have always told you. The
Boccaccio is a most unsuitable place for a young girl.'

'But why, Mama?'

'If it were a decent and proper place a man like Hugoling
would not hang about there.'

'He inquired after you, Mama.'

'Oh, did he?'

'He said he had been an admirer of yours years ago.'

'Is that what he said?' asked Mrs. Kalny with contempt.
She put her cup down and, turning towards the dressing
table, she glanced into the looking glass and smiled at her

own reflection. Then she grew stern again and went on drinking her coffee with composure.

'He seemed very nice, Mama,' said Franciska.

'All men seem nice at first.'

'From the way he talked about you, I thought it was rather a pity—I mean—I don't know really.'

'Did he say he would like to be invited here?' asked Mrs. Kalny.

'Yes, well, not in so many words, but very much so, just the same,' replied Franciska. 'And why don't you, Mama? He is so interesting. And not at all stuffy or on his dignity or anything.'

'It is easy to impress you when you want to be impressed,' remarked Mrs. Kalny. 'He is not interesting. He is merely insolent. That's how he got his job. But my house is not a newspaper office. And he won't set foot in it, ever. I should leave him alone, if I were you.'

'But what's wrong with him?'

'Oh, he is just impossible,' said Mrs. Kalny. She dabbed a drop of coffee from the lace edge of the silk wrapper and, still rubbing it, she added without raising her eyes: 'If you want to know, he came once to a house ball of ours, when I was a girl and he had a nail in his shoe which hurt him. So he took a Dresden cup and smashed it on the floor, deliberately, out of sheer bad temper, because of the pain in his foot. That's the sort of man he is. Never again.'

Then, rearranging the wrap over her shoulders, she said: 'I think you'd better call Sylva now. And it was one of the set of which each cup has a different flower painted on it, you know, the one that belonged to your great-great-grandmother. You shall have the set when you get married and you can thank Hugoling for the fact that the one with the cornflower is missing.'

Franciska returned to her room, got out a few of her textbooks and looked at them thoughtfully. During this, her last year at school, all written homework had been abandoned; the sole purpose of these last few months was to prepare the pupils for the final examinations.

Franciska had a very good memory and she never did any work at home at all. As usual, she decided, to do her Latin preparation in the lavatory at school, during the interval between lessons; to read up geography in the tramway on her way in the morning, and to ignore the other subjects completely, trusting to her luck and her power of bluffing.

Louise came to fetch her, saying that Sylva was now ready to touch up her hair.

Franciska followed the maid into her mother's bedroom.

'Hurry up, Cissy,' said Mrs. Kalny. She looked flushed and pretty and now that her hair, freed from the bondage of net and pins was displayed in layer upon layer of shimmering dark waves, her whole countenance was freer and happier than it had been before.

The spirit flame flickered blue under the gleaming lamp. Sylva spun round the curling tongs with a show of virtuosity and held them from time to time to her lips to test the heat. All the while she went on with one of her longwinded stories which were always the same; tales of how men tried to make her acquaintance and how she repulsed their advances.

Sitting down among the raucous exclamations, the hiss and the clatter, Franciska felt as though she were nearing a thunderstorm and while her hair was being seized and tugged first this way then that, the illusion was complete.

Mrs. Kalny, glad that the hairdresser was appeased at last and that she was in her good graces again, joined in the talk in a desultory fashion, breaking into the recital of the adventures by saying: 'Well, I don't know, Sylva, if you were right. Perhaps he was quite a decent man. You can't always tell, you know. And perhaps it might have led to something.'

'Of course it would have led to something. Ha! It's not difficult to imagine.'

Mrs. Kalny, feeling that she had done her utmost to be affable, fell silent again.

The hairdresser laid the tongs aside, blew out the flame and, with an intent look, she laid her hands on Franciska's head. Then she withdrew her fingers slowly and stepped a few paces away from the dressing table, while she gazed with solemn pride at her work, like a sculptor unveiling his finished statue.

'Thank you, Sylva,' said the young girl. She did not say, thank you, because of the attention she had received but because she was grateful that the ordeal was over.

'I hope you have not made her look too grown up,' said Mrs. Kalny.

'She is grown up, Madam, what am I to do about her? You can't get up a girl of eighteen in pigtails and bows.'

'No, no, of course not. I was only joking,' replied Mrs. Kalny hastily.

'She looks nice, very nice, the way I've dressed her,' remarked the hairdresser, still annoyed about Mrs. Kalny's words and she added spitefully: 'Anyway, it's a pleasure to do Miss Cissy, her hair is nice and obedient. If she had inherited Madam's hair, it would have taken me three times as long to get her into shape.'

She did not wait to receive any praise, as this, in her opinion would have been detrimental to her independence and so, as usual, she supplied her own praise of her achieve-

21

ment. She explained why she had arranged this curl in one place, that one in another, as though upholding unalterable laws, which though hidden to the profane, have been revealed to the initiated.

'We are going to the theatre to-morrow night, Sylva,' said Mrs. Kalny who felt that she had been listening long enough.

'Very well. I'll come to-morrow before lunch,' said the hairdresser and, stopping by the door, she compelled herself to bow very faintly and added, amidst a clatter of her implements: 'Madam.'

'Sylva is really very silly,' said Mrs. Kalny as soon as they were alone. 'She is quite wrong, you know, about what she said about men, that it's easy to imagine what's coming. One can never tell what a man is like till one has gone to bed with him. One can get a tremendous surprise sometimes in this way, good or bad. Remember this for life, Cissy.'

'Yes, Mama.'

Such remarks as these often embarrassed the young girl, because she could not help wondering how far her mother distilled her knowledge from actual experience. But although such thoughts came to her mind, she did not take them any further. She unquestioningly accepted her mother's right to chide her for coming home at an unduly late hour after a dance, even if her mother's behaviour might not have been impeccable in the past or in the present.

Mrs. Kalny too, would have seen no connexion whatever between her daughter's actions and her own. Like everyone else in her social set she believed that there were certain rules governing the conduct of young girls and others for the conduct of married women. Had anyone questioned her, she might even have said: '*Quod licet Jovi non licet bovi,*' thus expressing the conviction that bovine stupidity is transformed by marriage into a state of Olympian wisdom.

'I say, Mama,' said Franciska.

'Yes?'

'Feldman is coming? I did not know you had asked him.'

'I did not know either,' wailed Mrs. Kalny. 'I did not even know he was in town. But he rang up and asked himself.'

'But if he is coming to our reception, why does the cook make minced meat for him as though he were coming to dinner?'

'He's coming to dinner, that's the dreadful part about it,' replied Mrs. Kalny. 'I told him we had this party to-night and he said he hated parties and he was coming to dinner.'

'But how can he?'

'Oh you know what he is like.'

Louise came in and said that the manicurist had arrived.

'Oh, God,' said Franciska. Suddenly she began to giggle. 'You know what, Mama?'

'No, tell me?'

'You can rig up a tiny little table for Feldman in the corner of the dining room, for his dinner, like a cat's table for children when they have been naughty, and people will think he's somebody's chauffeur and there was no room for him in the kitchen.'

'I wish they did,' said Mrs. Kalny, too preoccupied to laugh. 'Unfortunately, you know what it will be like. They will crowd round him as though he were a two-headed calf. I suppose if he went and had his dinner sitting outside on the stairs, they'd all march out of the drawing room and stand round him, in the cold. He is frightful really, for a party. He breaks up everything.'

23

'Yes. I am going back to my room now. You know I can't stand her.'

'But you are not to change or do anything, Cissy, just now. Because when she has done my nails she will do yours.'

'I don't want her to. I want to be left alone.'

'You will have your nails done, Cissy. Please. You must learn to control yourself. Sylva said just now that you are grown up. You must get more responsible, really. Do you think I like her?'

Louise entered again, carrying the two finger-bowls filled with steaming water which always heralded the approach of the manicurist.

'She is all ready now, madam.'

'Why doesn't she drown herself in her own nail-varnish?' murmured Franciska and made a face.

'Cissy, please. Don't make it so difficult for everybody.'

'Vanity must suffer,' said Louise, who too, shared her mistress's dislike, loyal servant that she was.

'All right. Fetch me when you want me,' said the young girl to the maid and followed her out of the room.

Although the hairdresser was aggressive and often outright rude, everyone in the Kalny household respected her, because she despised gossip and was the soul of discretion. This was partly due to her independence and partly to her egoistic pride, which prevented her from taking an interest in other people's doings. On the other hand, the manicurist, who was a soft-spoken, soft-stepping and meek little woman, was loathed by all, because she was a living *chronique scandaleuse* among her clients and, although the scandalous matter which she retailed could have been quite interesting, she robbed it of its drama by her monotonous way of recounting it. Thus she carried with her only the menace of gossip without its delights.

CHAPTER 3

AT HALF PAST seven that evening, Franciska left her room, after having been 'looked at' by Louise and told to: 'go in quick, before you spoil yourself again.'

But as she did not belong to those who start a swim by diving into the water head first, but rather to those who sit on the shore, dangling first one foot and then the other, she did not make straight for the drawing room. She stepped into the hall, where the kitchenmaid, rigged up in black and white for the occasion, had been put in charge of coats and hats.

'A lot more to come yet, Miss Cissy. I still 've got all these hangers empty.'

Franciska nodded without listening. On one side of the hall where the space was reserved for the male guests, she saw about fifteen topcoats, all of sombre hues, like a row of mourning flags. But there was one among them which stood out by its princely richness, although it was no different from the others in cut or colour. Like the other coats, it was of dark cloth, but it seemed of a velvety softness. It was lined with a brown fur. 'It can't be,' thought Franciska, comparing it with her mother's sable tie. She touched it. It was sable. 'He is impossible with his showiness,' she thought.

It was fashionable for men during that winter to wear

white silk scarves underneath their coats; and a white silk scarf, heavier and glossier than any of those belonging to the others, had been stuffed into one of the pockets, carelessly, as though it were a worthless rag.

Franciska looked and drew her brows together.

'Feldman is here already, isn't he?' she asked.

'Yes miss, and he gave me such a look, I got a cramp here, straight away,' and the maid put her hand over her belly. 'I always get the collywobbles when he comes.'

'Oh, don't be silly,' said Franciska. 'If you did not know who he was, you would never think twice about him.'

She said this with as much conviction as she could muster because she knew that her mother would have replied in the same way. But she did not think that the kitchenmaid was silly. Most people who came into the presence of the celebrated man felt an excitement so strong as to affect them bodily, although the form it took varied according to their constitutions.

She went into the dining room and joined a group of people assembled round Vorel, the sculptor. She smiled and nodded silently, so as not to interrupt his story, glad to be allowed a few more minutes' relaxation.

'So there it was, I beg you to imagine it,' she heard him say. 'On one hand there was this dog, wretched no doubt, although of the best pedigree—need I assure you that he was of the highest breeding, considering who his master was?' and he paused, practised raconteur that he was, to allow his audience time to laugh. He was still young enough to indulge in impish humour and left dignity to older artists.

'——on the other hand there was this bronze bust of mine, standing on the studio floor, wretched too, because it had been commissioned and then refused. And lastly,

26

there was I, doubly wretched, because I tried to laugh it off and did not know how. But what could I do? The dog had turned art critic, to put it delicately and all I could think of was, that such things will happen in the best of families. But the story has a happy end. I never wiped the bust after master and dog had left, I forgot all about it and it developed a most exquisite green patina—really beautiful, I wish I had it here and could show it to you—and I managed to sell the piece to a rich Rumanian.'

'Whose bust was it?' asked several people at once.

'It was the portrait of a professor of philosophy. Now, please, dear people. No more questions.'

'I am sure it was old Kern,' said a man near Franciska. 'Who else could it have been? And old Kern deserves it. What a clever dog.'

'I don't agree with you. Forget the dog,' said someone else. 'Kern is very sound and he's got quite a following. This last book of his——'

The dog enthusiast stood his ground: 'First of all, he pinched the whole theory from his assistant lecturer, so you can hardly call it his book, and secondly, it was all old stuff hashed up.'

Several other people joined in with their opinions and as none of them had read the book in question or knew anything about the trends of modern philosophy, the ground was established for a long and heated discussion.

Vorel and Franciska, both bored, left the group and walked a few steps together.

'If somebody had asked the name of the Rumanian,' said Franciska, 'they would now be tearing each other to shreds about Rumania.'

'Exactly. But leave them to it. They are so uninteresting. They've all got eyes and mouths and noses and all the usual

27

and necessary things, but none of them has got a face. Whereas you——'

'Oh, nonsense,' said the young girl, 'I've got a good hairdresser, that's all.'

'I suppose you are young enough to believe it,' said Vorel. 'But seriously. I'd love to model you, you know. I had a talk with your mother, this evening, and she said that it depended entirely on you. I would not need many sittings, I think. I've got you more or less in my head already.'

Franciska listened with a smile, convinced, that he had also in his head the price he would ask for the bust.

'Not now,' she said. 'I must study for my finals, you know. But once I'm through with school – next year, I promise you.'

'Oh, why worry about those wretched exams?' asked Vorel in a disparaging tone. 'Anyway, you are doing so well at school, always at the top of the class, your mother told me. I wish I was as sure of everything, as I am about your passing brilliantly – my life would be a lot easier.'

'No, really, I must not fool about just now. I shall have to go to several balls when the season starts – I'd much rather go to odd parties and dances instead, but I have to do the balls, because Mama would never let me off and I shall have to do some cramming besides. I don't see how I could fit it in with the rest.'

'So much determination in such a pretty head. What will you do with all this learning? Do you think anybody will ever ask you about the succession of the Cæsars?' said Vorel, still pursuing his prey.

'No. But I've got to pass, because I want to read for a degree afterwards,' replied Franciska.

If he had continued with his line of talk and asked her why she wanted to obtain a degree, she could not have answered, nor could she have told him what subject she was going to choose. As it was, although she had a facility for learning, she was not particularly interested in anything nor did Mrs. Kalny expect her to be. She did not realise herself that by her determination to go to University, she was expressing not only her desire to get out of the orbit of her mother, but also to achieve something which her mother had never done and thus to exclude her mother from the rivalry in which, since her adolescence, she had been caught.

She said: 'Don't worry. I've promised. Next year.'

'I don't believe in putting things off. Next year, anything may happen.'

'What on earth should happen?' asked Franciska. She felt slightly annoyed at his persistence, because she was quite aware that he cared neither for her as a pretty girl nor as a pretty model and was only out to obtain his fee.

'You may be tired and faded from all this learning, and instead of calling my work "head of a beautiful young woman," I shall have to call it "character study" and you know what that means; if I say that someone has character in his face, it means that I have scraped the barrel of my flattery."

"I'll risk it," said Franciska and left him, laughing.

Vorel gazed after her with anxiety, which, on his pleasant young face, took on the look of yearning.

He was an outsider among the other guests and as his living depended on the crumbs which those wealthy people chose to throw him, his wits were sharper than theirs. Already he felt that this might be the last reception he attended in this house. And as to the work he had been promised for the coming year, he knew that it would never materialize; for, just as dead men tell no tales, they also do not pay bills.

29

CHAPTER 4

'REALLY, THIS is impossible. You cannot expect me to listen,' said Mrs. Kalny.

They had gone to the so-called 'Wintergarden,' a glass-roofed, glass-walled balcony, filled with evergreen plants and potted camellias. It lay at the narrow end of the music room and was separated from it by glass doors.

At this early stage of the party, when the guests were inclined to cling to the buffet and cluster near the door of the drawing room to view new arrivals, it was not likely that anyone would enter.

She spoke in a low nervous voice and twisted her fingers. At each of her small restless gestures the folds of her dress of shot taffeta changed from red to mauve, from mauve to red and the foliage at her back rustled as she brushed against it every time she moved her shoulders.

'Rubbish. What's impossible? Would I tell you anything that's impossible? Has Feldman ever told you anything that was impossible?'

'It was impossible at the time.'

'Rubbish. Eh! I said then already, pack yourself together and the girl, that man is no good to you, I would not like to be in his shoes. And I said then, if you do stay with him, you'll be lucky when his health folds up, because his bank account will have folded up already and it's better to die in

bed than in jail. Eh!' And with this Eh! which he delivered
in his creaking voice, Feldman made a disgusted gesture as
though throwing something away. The large diamond
flashed on his finger.

'I couldn't leave him then. There was no reason for it.'

'Rubbish. Of course you could. If Feldman tells you, you
can. Don't play the Holy Virgin, I said, nobody will thank
you for it, they've got one in every church, don't put the
Saints out of business, I said. But you would not listen to
Feldman. But now listen to Feldman, he never lets you
down.'

Mrs. Kalny looked at the floor. Her eyelids flickered as
though she were fighting against tears.

Feldman smacked his lips, which was one of his dis-
agreeable habits.

Although he appeared to be unmoved by her distress he
did not seem impatient. This vigorous, elderly Jew, uneducated and ill bred, who still spoke with a strong Polish
accent, was used to advising Royalty, Cabinet ministers and
great financiers. He, to whom people of all walks of life
turned in circumstances of sorrow and disaster, knew that
one still debates over a decision, long after one has made up
one's mind, just as the eel, already cut up and in the frying
pan, will still wriggle.

He called himself a graphologist because his extraordinary
powers of foreseeing people's fate were generally brought
into play when he looked at their handwriting. He did not
claim to possess any scientific theories and his achievements
were often of such a nature that they earned him the name
of charlatan, mountebank, clairvoyant, miracle man, according to people's dispositions.

He could, for instance, by looking at a person for a short
time, give a perfect counterfeit sample of that person's

handwriting. On the other hand, when being shown the handwriting of an absent man, not known to him, he would get up, walk about the room, and by gestures and ways of speech and intonation, give an amazingly faithful imitation of that man's personality.

Sometimes, inevitably, he failed to 'see'. But even then, he did not fail by stating anything which was not true, but by overlooking important things and concentrating on trifles. His reputation was enormous, both in Europe and in America. Numerous books had been written about him. At various Universities physicians and scientists had made experiments with him, giving him blank envelopes with samples of handwriting inside them. He had put his hands on the envelopes and had 'seen', and had remained, as before, inexplicable and unfathomable.

In spite of it all, when it came to directing his own life, he floundered about like everybody else. He could not tell what was in store for himself. Several times he had fallen victim to swindlers, when investing large sums of money, thus proving once more the truth of the proverb that the cobbler's children go unshod.

Mrs. Kalny sighed and looked up with a pretty flutter of her lashes. She wrung her hands.

'But what am I to do?' As she put a hand to her forehead, the glow of the rubies of her rings was reflected in her shimmering nails.

'Feldman is telling you what to do. Just listen to Feldman. I'll be staying here for two weeks. Then I go to Paris to give some lectures. Then I go to America for two months. I'll book the passage for you to-morrow.'

'But you are mad, Feldman. Now that my husband is ill, I can leave him less than ever.'

'Eh! Rubbish,' and the hand flew through the air, the

diamond flashed. 'Feldman doesn't ask you to leave your husband. Feldman asked you that twelve years ago. But now I only ask you to marry me, because he'll be dead in a fortnight, you know that as well as I do, it is not a great achievement to know it.'

'Yes, yes,' said Mrs. Kalny, with little grief, but great anxiety.

'Now, you marry me, and you'll be all right. Every year I come and tell you. You will wear pearls and diamonds and go in silks and satins.'

He still used the common fortune teller's stock phraseology, although he had been a celebrity for years, and had rubbed shoulders with people of the highest distinction on two continents. It did not occur to him that his words were ludicrous. Mrs. Kalny had possessed pearls and diamonds all her life and if she did not wear silks and satins, it was only because velvet and taffeta were more fashionable that year.

'And my daughter?' she asked. A strong rustling of the foliage behind her betrayed how uncomfortable she felt.

'She's grown up, she'll go her own way. She is going it already. You don't know, of course. Parents never know.'

'Oh, God. It's all so worrying. What am I to do with her? I must marry her off as fast as I can. But not to anybody. It must be somebody.'

'It doesn't matter. She'll get married soon enough,' said Feldman and smacked his lips and moved his nutcracker-jaws.

'Do you think so?' asked Mrs. Kalny eagerly.

'Well, I don't see why she shouldn't. Pretty and well brought up.' He fell silent, and seemed to gaze into abysses. It was obvious that he refused to be drawn out, that he either did not know what was going to happen to Franciska, or that he knew and preferred to steer clear of unpleasantness.

Whatever his reasons were, Mrs. Kalny, always thirsty for flattery, took his silence as a compliment. She felt that he was too much taken up with her, the mother, to give a thought to the daughter. She put her scented hand to her hair and gave a little laugh.

'Well,' she said, 'I am very touched. You have always been a faithful friend, the most faithful I have ever had. But now I must see to my ghastly guests. Do you think you will be able to bear them? I hope they won't pester you too much. And I've got some sort of dinner for you. Minced veal, the way you like it.'

She moved to the door, anxious to be gone before anything might happen. She dreaded the possibility of his kissing her, not because she thought him repulsive but because she was afraid that he might ruffle her hair and disarrange her make-up.

'Ah. Minced veal. Thank God for it,' he exclaimed with emotion and took her hand. 'I can't stand this filth, this messed-up food everywhere, which they give me at the Imperial here and at the Majestic there. When I come to the Crillon the *maître d'hotel* doesn't even dare to show me the menu any more. Filth. Rubbish. Eh!'

'That's what I thought. Poor Feldman,' said Mrs. Kalny, advancing a further step and opening the door.

'Poor? What's poor about me? If you marry me, you won't have to stand about in a verandah like this, planted with three lettuces. I'll give you ten hot-houses with palms in them as high as mountains and you can have ostriches running up and down the trees.'

It was at this point that Franciska came up to them. The great man had his back turned towards her and above his

34

head, grey and stubbly like a frosty field, she could see her mother's face, smiling and distressed.

'Look at Cissy. Hasn't she grown since you saw her last time?' and Mrs. Kalny withdrew her hand from his and put her arm round her daughter's shoulder. She was not given to demonstrations of motherly fondness in company, not since her daughter had been a little girl and such displays had made a pretty picture in the drawing room. But now, this gesture was a welcome escape from the great man's attentions.

He turned and looked at Franciska. Already the titter, provoked by his misguided botanical and zoological illusions, froze in her throat. She felt that he could read her inmost thoughts.

'How are you, Mr. Feldman,' she said.

'She hasn't grown,' he replied, ignoring her greeting. 'What d'you want her to grow for? She is exactly as tall as her mother and that's the best thing she can be.'

He turned to the young girl: 'Your mother is getting prettier and younger every year. She looks younger than you do.'

Then, as though he were guessing that he was flattering the mother by wounding the daughter, he took a jeweller's box out of his breast pocket and gave it to Franciska. 'That's for you from Feldman,' he said.

Franciska knew that it would be an expensive trinket of vulgar taste and was relieved when he cut short her polite exclamations with a creaking: 'It's nothing. Just rubbish. Eh!'

In the beginning of his ardent, though intermittent wooing of Mrs. Kalny, Feldman, ignorant as he was of social conventions, had presented this lady with pieces of magnificently ugly jewellery which had always been refused and returned to him. Thus, in the end, his only way of showing his devotion and of courting the mother was by giving presents to the daughter and in this he had persisted faithfully.

In the attic above the Kalnys' flat there was still the peacock made of real peacock feathers which opened and closed its tail when wound up. There was also a stuffed polar bear, standing upright, containing a musical box within its now moth-eaten body. These and other toys, manufactured for the children of millionaires and Indian princes, had provoked Mr. Kalny to shake his head and give a look of silent horror; Mrs. Kalny to shrug her pretty shoulders, and Franciska to experience a fleeting feeling of pride. They had been put out of sight as soon as the famous man had left, as neither of Franciska's parents had thought for a moment that their daughter might enjoy them. The only pleasure they had ever given was to the maids.

The young girl followed her mother and Feldman into the drawing room. She was still filled with resentment. In the music room she talked to several of her mother's friends, who told her that she had grown and not grown at all, that she was a perfect lady and that they still thought of her as a little girl, that she was the living image of her mother, that she looked exactly like her father, that she did not look like either of her parents but took to an amazing degree after her grandmother, was asked whether she enjoyed school, was pitied because it was taken for granted that she loathed school, was expected to remember events which had taken place before her birth and, at last, was hissed at by Louise who told her to leave the room at once and straighten her stockings.

All this, although she was well used to it, did not increase her good humour.

She returned to the reception rooms and engaged in conversation with Horak, a man of about forty-five, who tried to preserve his own youth by voicing the thoughts which young people are supposed to think.

'What a collection of pompous old fools,' he said to her. 'And they talk down to you as though their age were a merit.'

'But sometimes it is, isn't it?' asked Franciska. 'Isn't it true that a woman only becomes interesting once she is over thirty?'

He raised his glass and looked at it as though he could see the answer there.

'That's just the foolishness they like to believe,' he said. 'As you know, there is no fool like an old fool and how can a woman who was a young goose become anything else but an old fowl?'

They laughed. He raised his glass again and drained it. He continued;

'On the contrary I should say that when a woman is still young and pretty, one does not notice her stupidity but when she is old, there is nothing else left and then, God help her.'

Franciska was getting bored. For a while he had served her well enough to restore some of her lost self-confidence, but now she realized that he did not talk to her because he found her interesting, but that he merely used her as a prop for his own youthful feelings, just as before, others had used her, to get a commission for a portrait or to pay her mother compliments.

She asked: 'Is what you are drinking nice?'

'It is quite nice. Quite nice whisky. Shall I bring you some?'

'I am not allowed to drink it,' said the young girl.

'Really, aren't mothers the limit?' exclaimed Horak. 'Why should someone dictate to you, only because they are twenty years older than you are, and certainly no wiser? Why should you respect your mother only because she is your mother? You did not ask her to bring you into the world, did you?'

In the end, Franciska took a few sips of whisky; she did not like the taste of it and she had no desire to drink it. She was convinced that Mrs. Kalny's rule was justified, for Mrs. Kalny was not against drinking because it is sinful but because it leaves ugly marks on a woman's face.

As it was, Horak's words of youthful revolt were so touching that she did not want to disappoint him. Franciska's action pleased him greatly; it seemed to him a symbol of youth casting aside the bondage of the older generation. Franciska thought that this casting aside of bondage would have been more complete if Horak had encouraged her to drink the whisky in full view of Mrs. Kalny. Instead of which he took great care to screen her with his back. Thus, it became one of those revolutionary gestures which never touch the authorities against whom they are directed, but which, nevertheless, give a glow of pride to their perpetrators.

'Now let's have a look at the circus,' said Horak who had for the last few minutes been casting glances towards the drawing room. At first, Feldman had still been visible, seated on a sofa in a bay, surrounded by a crescent of people who had dragged their chairs into the proximity of the great man; viewed from a distance it looked like the pattern of the Turkish emblem; the crescent with the star. Now, the largest part of the vast room was already thick with people and more were constantly joining them.

Franciska, gazing at the spectacle with a frown, was

reminded of those clusters of bluebottles which one finds on one's path when walking through the summery countryside. And the voices which she could hear only faintly from where she stood, reminded her of the buzzing activity of these flies when they converge from all sides on their disgusting prey.

She glanced at her companion. It was obvious, that the excitement which Feldman induced wherever he went, had already invaded him. Yet, ashamed of it and wishing to remain detached, he adopted an air of cynicism.

'What a collection of old fools,' he began. 'Just watch them, he's got them eating out of his hand.'

'He always does,' said the young girl.

He laughed. 'I wonder, was it wise of your mother to invite him? I bet their blood pressure is soaring sky high and with these old dodderers you never know. Anything might give them a stroke. I wonder what it's all about?'

'I suppose we might as well go and see,' said Franciska. 'Of course, you know, it's partly scientific,' she added, apologetically.

'Scientific fiddlesticks,' replied Horak, and made his way towards the crowd with great speed, so that the young girl had difficulty in keeping up with him.

They squeezed themselves against a window. They listened. They heard the creaky voice: 'So there you are. And she fell on her knees and wept and said, Feldman how did you know? Feldman, you are a miracle. Feldman, you saved my life.'

'I don't think he'll perform, he is only telling stories,' whispered Franciska.

There was an outburst of exclamations.

The great man smacked his lips and the people were

offended by his ill manners. He moved his hands with the expressiveness of a guttersnipe, the big diamond on his finger flashed and they were revolted by his vulgarity. His keen and unpleasant glance travelled over them and made them quail beneath it. Yet they surrounded him, fascinated against their will, filled by a disagreeable and gripping excitement.

'There is Helvik, look at Helvik,' said Franciska's companion. 'He's got something to show him. Now isn't it just like Helvik, trying to get something for nothing? No wonder he is so rich. I once saw him, at a dinner party, putting his tongue out at a doctor because he wasn't feeling well and thought he'd squeeze out a gratis consultation. I suppose he had been drinking his own coffee by mistake.'

Helvik was the owner of a chain of tea-and-coffee shops. He had so many of them, that they had become part of the face of the town and were in their way as characteristic as the unfinished Gothic tower of the cathedral on the hill. As his shops were always situated in corner houses, it was said of him: 'Helvik is like a dog; he has a business at every street corner.'

'I don't think it's anything serious,' said Franciska, 'Mr. Helvik does not look worried.'

'No, he doesn't. Funny. Look at him. Grinning away at Feldman. What's the joke? I wonder,' and Horak, dragging Franciska with him, edged nearer and nearer, till they came to stand at the very tip of the crescent which surrounded the 'star'.

It was true Helvik looked mischievous, as he handed Feldman a piece of paper which had obviously been torn from a notebook. Gazing at his countenance, Franciska was reminded of the expression on her cousins' faces, when they used to offer their governess lumps of sugar that remained floating on the top of the coffee, or, worse, laxative pills disguised as chocolate bonbons.

Helvik bent forward, holding the paper with pointed fingers like a man presenting a tit-bit to a dog.

'I find your stories most–fascinating, Mr. Feldman. But the proof of the pudding is in the eating, isn't that so? I've got something here, the handwriting of a friend of mine–I don't think you will be able to make anything out of it. Still, if you would care to have a look? Only I don't think——'

Feldman had a look. And although no handwriting of any kind could be seen, only a few thin and wavering pencil lines which formed no recognizable pattern of any sort, the great man seemed to gaze into abysses. Then it was all over. The nutcracker jaws worked, there was the smacking of the lips.

'Let me see, let me see. Ah!' and he lifted his disagreeable eyes towards Helvik.

There was a pause. Nobody spoke. Nobody moved.

Then Feldman said: 'What a sorry creature. Yes. A being, who is a prisoner far, far away from his homeland. He is very sad. He has a deep longing to be back in his native country. That's all I can tell.'

Helvik's face was swarthy. He could not blanch. But a sudden pinched sharpness appeared round his nostrils and lips. There he stood, an overgrown schoolboy, fat and sheepish.

Horak muttered: 'Do you call this fortune telling nowadays? He has not put himself out very much, I must say. If that is what his art boils down to. I suppose the wheels only go round when they are lubricated with thousand-crown notes. Ha ha, serves Helvik right.'

There was a silence among the guests, but its quality

41

had changed from the hush of tension to one of disappointment.

Helvik said: 'It was my pet monkey. He played with a pencil one day. He died of pneumonia last week.'

'Ah, well, there you are,' exclaimed Feldman. His jaws worked. His hands flew upwards in a triumphant movement, the diamond flashed, and people's eyes, dazzled, followed its course.

'I am quite overcome,' said Helvik. 'I don't know what to say. I am sorry if I ever doubted your——'

'Sorry, why be sorry? What did I tell you? Feldman is always right. Feldman is wonderful. Feldman never lets you down.'

'Really, Mr. Feldman, you are priceless.'

'Of course I am. I had not asked for money in the first place. Eh!' and he made a gesture as though dashing something to the floor with great contempt.

Franciska, watching, wondered whether Feldman despised the stinginess of Helvik or whether he wanted to make it apparent that he would quail at the mention of money in a gathering of this kind.

Everyone around her showed signs of tension. Voices were more highpitched and shrill than before, and the blood rushing to the women's faces contrasted with the rouge they had rubbed on their cheeks. They talked in a feverish, reckless, desultory fashion. Somehow it reminded the young girl of her mother's bridge parties when, after the finish of a game, the players indulged in mutual reproaches and showed an embarrassing lack of control in their behaviour.

Only Mrs. Kalny, who stood near Feldman, kept her serene hostess's smile as though taking it for granted that the breath of the beyond which had invaded the room for an instant was part of the drinks, the sandwiches and the flower arrangements of her party.

Horak had joined a few men who stood round Helvik, asking detailed and irrelevant questions about the coffee merchant's monkey, as though some enlightenment might be gained from that quarter.

A lady, offended to have witnessed a happening which she could not understand, approached Franciska and said peevishly: 'Did you know that Helvik had a monkey? It's the first time I've heard about it. And what did he keep him for, in any case? It's sheer affectation.'

Franciska, without attempting to make an answer, fled into the music room.

CHAPTER 5

THE PARTY had continued till well after midnight; and although the next day was a Sunday, Franciska had not been allowed to sleep late and had been called by Louise.

Mrs. Kalny who occasionally suffered from migraine, had found out by experience that prolonged sleep after late nights predisposed her to this complaint, and because of this she enforced those rules upon the young girl which she had found beneficial for herself. And although Franciska had never yet experienced migraine, Mrs. Kalny took it for granted that, as Franciska was her daughter, she would sooner or later follow in the footsteps of her mother's suffering. If anyone had told Mrs. Kalny that it was just possible that Franciska would never have migraine in her life, she would have regarded it as an impertinence.

When Franciska joined her mother over the morning coffee, she did not dare, as usual, to criticize her mother, but protested instead against Louise's action.

Mrs. Kalny answered: 'Remember this for life, Cissy. An English lord once wrote a whole lot of letters to his son, with precepts for all sorts of situations. And in them he put down what I am always telling you: if you have had a late night, get up as usual on the following day and then go to bed exceptionally early.'

'But I always have to get up early, Mama, because of

44

school. So really to-day she could have left me alone and in bed and in peace.'

'It has nothing to do with Louise. I told her to wake you up. And don't try to make me feel sorry for you because you were tired already yesterday from the night before last. That's entirely your own doing. If you feel wretched, keep it to yourself. I'm not interested.'

Sometimes, Mrs. Kalny was of the opinion that people were only to be pitied if they met with suffering while following the path of honour and duty. On other occasions she was ready to commiserate indiscriminately with anyone, but this happened only when she was in good humour. And if she showed herself adamant this morning it was because she felt uneasy about her last night's talk with Feldman.

'I can't see the sense of it,' said Franciska. 'Why shouldn't one sleep when one feels like it? Who was this English lord in any case?'

'Oh, I don't know, I can't remember everything,' wailed Mrs. Kalny. Already she had forgotten her mood of sternness and was giving way to self-pity. She added: 'His son was illegitimate but in spite of this he collected the letters and published them in a book. So you can see how clever they were.'

Franciska felt indignant over the stupidity of her mother's argument but she kept silent and let her eyes roam over the stacks of plates ranged on top of sideboards and side tables ready to be put away.

The parlourmaid came in to clear the breakfast things. She looked softer and more pleasant than usual. Although parties gave a lot of work, she loved them, partly because they satisfied her craving for excitement and partly because of the tips.

'It isn't fair,' said the young girl to herself, following the

45

maid with her eyes. 'She gets something for staying up late and working. And I stay up late too, and can't even get any sleep on the next day.'

Louise entered. 'The doctor's on the phone, madam.'

'For me?'

'Yes, madam.'

'Oh, God, what can he want? I did not call him up, did I, Louise?'

'I suppose it's something to do with Father,' said the young girl.

'How can it be?' said Mrs. Kalny and gave her daughter an exasperated look. 'Your father is there, in that place and the doctor is here. So how could he know anything?' and she gathered her morning coat with abrupt movements and left the room in a hurry.

'What's the matter, Louise?'

'I don't know, Miss Cissy. The doctor didn't say. Now get up and get out. The room must be put in order. Mr. Feldman is coming for lunch.'

'Why? Again?'

'Because he's been invited. And you are not to put on anything blue because madam will be wearing her dark blue wool. I should put on a skirt and a blouse if I were you.'

Franciska would have liked to say something rude but nothing occurred to her. She left the room. Louise's words always annoyed her because they brought it home to her again and again that she merely existed in the maid's eyes as a sort of living dummy, created for the purpose of serving as a foil to her mother.

She went into her room and rang for Louise. 'Get my bath ready, will you?' and then, after a long pause she added: 'please.' This was an insult of long standing which never failed in its effect. But the maid, who knew quite well what the doctor's phone call had been about, felt too solemn to give her usual, snappy answer of–'Somebody will run it in for you. I'll tell them in the kitchen. But I can't. I'm much too busy.' Instead, to Franciska's astonishment and disappointment, she said meekly: 'In a minute, Miss Cissy, just one minute,' and she went out as Mrs. Kalny came in.

'You shouldn't order her about so much, Cissy,' she said with a sigh. She sat down for a moment with a blank stare in her eyes. It seemed that she had sat down not because she was tired of standing but because the chair just happened to be in her way.

'She orders *me* about the whole time,' said Franciska, 'and she is getting beastlier every day.'

'Yes, I know. But she is very efficient.'

'Why are efficient people always beastly, Mama?'

'Oh, I don't know. You ask the silliest questions, really. But she is getting a bit–difficult, that's quite true. Oh God, how I wish she had a man. When they are on the tiles all night, they are so much better tempered during the day. And they work so much harder. You would not believe the difference it makes.'

Franciska did not answer, as she was not supposed to know what difference it did make.

Mrs. Kalny rose, passed the mirror and threw a glance a herself.

'Feldman is coming to lunch,' she said after some meditation. 'Try and look nice, will you? You do look so pale. I wish you didn't look so pale. You will try to look nice, won't you?'

'Yes, Mama,' said Franciska.

Officially, as became a young girl of her class and up-bringing, she was allowed to use powder and eau-de-Cologne but no paint or scent; and Mrs. Kalny adhered to this rule.

But sometimes, on important occasions, she encouraged her daughter to put on rouge, without actually saying so. And this was her way of hinting.

'Mama, I'm going to Susy's before lunch. And then in the afternoon again. Can I take your sable tie?'

'Take it, but don't tell me about it,' said Mrs. Kalny. She then began to ask some questions about the new villa on the outskirts of the town which Susy's parents had bought recently. A few minutes later she returned to her bedroom, to get dressed, and said to her maid; 'Louise, if I had to go away for a few days, which suitcase would I need? And do you think I could manage without a trunk? I suppose two suitcases would be all right, don't you think?'

To which Louise replied: 'Poor madam.'

And although Mrs. Kalny had just uttered a lie and the maid knew it, the two women looked at each other sadly and at the same time with great composure.

Mrs. Kalny did not wonder whether she might have to go away; she knew that she had to, the doctor had made the situation quite plain to her. According to a telegram which he had received on Saturday night from the resident surgeon of the nursing home in Merano, Mr. Kalny was not expected to live till the end of the week.

But Mrs. Kalny was determined to see Feldman at lunch. Therefore she was not willing to acknowledge the meaning of the message because, had she done so, she would have had to leave at once upon receiving the doctor's telephone call. She had already decided on her plan. She would ring up the doctor in the afternoon and inquire again about the telegram under the pretext of having been too distressed to grasp its meaning. This would give her time to pack and take the night train to Innsbruck which, she believed, had the best connexion for Merano.

CHAPTER 6

FRANCISKA ARRIVED at eleven o'clock at the house where Susy Graber lived.

In the hall, still pervaded by the smell of new paint, she tried to linger as long as possible, hoping that her friend would come to greet her and see the splendour of her fur. Instead, Susy's mother appeared.

'Susy is waiting for you upstairs,' she said. 'It's really dreadful the way you young things have to work. Wouldn't it be better if you had a tutor for the last few months? If you and Susy got together and perhaps two other girls, it would not be so very expensive, would it? Have you had news from your father?'

'Not for the last three days. But I think he likes it there.'

'Well, that's the main thing. That's all that matters, isn't it?' said Mrs. Graber anxiously.

'She worries about Father,' said Franciska to herself. 'I didn't know she was so fond of him.'

While she accompanied Franciska upstairs, Mrs. Graber said:

'You know, we haven't got any more rooms now than we had before, in the old place. It only looks as if we had.'

Mrs. Graber always tried to conceal how affluent she was. This she did not out of modesty, but because she was miserly and therefore afraid that people might ask her for loans.

49

She belonged to those who put on their worst and oldest clothes when they go to see a new doctor or lawyer. And as she tried to avoid paupers like the plague, she was constantly on the look-out for signs of decline in the financial status of her acquaintances. It is never easy to judge from outward signs; all signs are treacherous. And as Mrs. Graber was a stupid woman, she was often deceived.

'Is your father in a hotel or in a pension?' she asked, anxiously rubbing her hands together.

'In a nursing home,' replied Franciska.

'Ah. And is he treated by the resident doctor or does he have outside advice as well?'

'I don't quite know. I think both.'

'Oh, well, he should be all right,' said Mrs. Graber, beginning to give her inopportune questions the semblance of solicitude. Then, stopping by the door on which the pale lacquer was still so fresh that it shimmered like melted wax, she delayed the young girl with a further avid question: 'But you had a specialist here, didn't you, when your father's illness began?'

'We had four of them, at different times, apart from our family doctor,' replied Franciska. And while Susy's mother looked suddenly quite pleased and said cheerfully: 'Did you really?' she gave the doorknob an impatient twist.

Mrs. Graber finally released her, after having urged her again not to hesitate to employ a private teacher if the girls should feel the need for one. Reassured that Mr. Kalny was going to die richly and in style, she had no further fears that she might be saddled with having to pay the entire fees of the tutor.

Susy, in her mother's boudoir, had pushed a settee, a chair and a few small tables close to the walls. This, she had told her mother, was in order to gain some room where she and Franciska could pace up and down; it helped them to concentrate on their work. She had not added that the work might include the trying out of some new dance steps with Franciska. She had also obtained from her mother the promise that an *aperitif* would be sent up to them during the morning, to strengthen their nerves. And lastly, so that their nerves might not be weakened again, she had begged her mother to enforce a complete silence in the house.

All this, Susy did quite knowingly and callously. She was, like most of the girls in the school, not at all grateful for receiving a good education. And as she was driven by her parents to pass the final examinations she intended to make the most of it and play on their ambition. Since Mrs. Graber herself had never passed examinations of any kind, it was easy for Susy to surround the matriculation with mystery and awe and use it as a way of blackmail. She was much more observant and calculating than Franciska and whereas Franciska merely grumbled half-heartedly, Susy turned it to good advantage.

'I've got out the fifteen questions on the French revolution,' she said to Franciska. 'I'll ask you first and you tell me and then you ask me and I tell you.'

They settled down to work, speaking in low monotonous voices and without ever finishing their sentences. It sounded as though they were reading out to each other telegrams written in a code taken from the history of the French revolution, with a meaning still hidden, as yet to be deciphered.

After the son of Louis XVI had, for the second time, been put in charge of an obscure cobbler, Susy, instead of going on, said: 'I say, did your feet hurt after Friday night? I had blisters all over mine.'

'I didn't. I had my old gold sandals. My mother won't
let me wear satin slippers for dances, I'll get them only for
balls. I felt so terribly shabby in my sandals and Mr. Ling
said they looked pretty and he didn't understand why it's
shabby to wear gold and silver shoes for evening dress.
And then he was very astonished when I told him and said
something about our senseless luxury and he can't think
how we can breathe in it. Do you understand? I don't.'

They looked at each other, speechless. It was common
knowledge to them that evening shoes made of gilded or
silvered leather or gold brocade could be worn with dresses
of any colour and therefore worn on many occasions. Real
elegance demanded that silk slippers dyed to the same shade
as the evening dress, should be worn; so that one had to
have as many pairs of shoes as one had dresses.

'Do you think he is in love with you?' asked Susy. 'He
talked to you the whole evening.'

'Yes, he did,' said Franciska. 'But not in that way. But
he said he would like to see me again and talk to me. So I
don't know.'

'And will you?'

'I'd like to. But I can't invite him home because my
mother can't stand him. And if she said I could invite him,
I wouldn't just the same. You know what would happen.
So what's the good of it.'

'Thank God my mother doesn't run after men,' said
Susy. 'That's at least something.'

'Yes, but then, yours is dowdy and mine isn't and she lets
me wear silk stockings, even at home and nice underwear
because she has them herself and she says you shouldn't
stop the mouth of the threshing ox. She isn't mean, like
yours.'

'That's true,' said Susy. 'Mine is so mean that she will

buy me expensive clothes but not good underwear because you can see the clothes and you can't see the underwear.'

'Yes, but then, your mother is stupid and you can tell her anything. Mine is not really clever, but she is clever in patches and it isn't so easy. She knew when I got home on Friday night.'

'There you are. I had no trouble at all.'

Franciska said: 'I saw a wonderful nightgown, with black lace the other day. My mother said it was frightfully unsuitable for a young girl.'

'Would you wear black lace on your wedding night?' asked Susy warily.

'Yes, definitely,' said Franciska.

'Well, I wouldn't,' remarked Susy with a superior look. 'Do you know why?'

'No?'

'Because it isn't virginal enough. You'd have to have something white. Or pink.'

'Yes, you are right,' and Franciska frowned. 'My mother says that she can understand very well why girls want to run away from their husbands on the wedding night. Do you understand it?'

'No,' said Susy. 'But some girls faint. Would you undress in front of him?'

'No, I'd go into the dressing room,' said Franciska.

'But if you didn't have a dressing room?' asked Susy. 'What if you got married to a man who had a two-room flat?'

Franciska began to shriek with laughter and Susy joined her, pleased with her own joke.

'Really, Susy. Oh God, you are silly,' gasped Franciska.

'Yes, but only in the head.' This was one of the standing witticisms among them, and it never failed in its effect.

'Would you marry Mr. Ling?' asked Susy, who never liked theoretical discussions, not even of the scabrous order, but preferred to choose practical instances.

'He wouldn't be right. He has a big job but he has not got any money of his own. And then, his family is not very good.'

'Do you know,' said Susy, 'when we left the Boccaccio, he pulled his trouser leg up because his sock had slipped and he had a beautiful leg. I didn't know men could have beautiful legs. Did you?'

'I saw it too,' said Franciska.

'Do you think he's got hair on his chest?' asked Susy, again with a wary expression.

'I can't tell.'

'Would you like him to?' asked Susy.

They were shaken by fits of laughter.

At last, Franciska made a reply which was very fashionable among her school friends at the moment: 'Ask the horse, it's got a bigger head than I have.'

Franciska, returning home at one o'clock first went into the kitchen where she witnessed the end of a row between the cook and the hairdresser.

Sylva always got a veal steak on Sundays because this was her favourite dish and she had complained that it was not sufficiently browned. The cook, who knew this to be true, was as indignant as one always is on similar occasions. She gave the hairdresser to understand that she was colour blind and advised her to brown the steak with some of her hairdresser's dye. She concluded that Sylva might spare some of the stuff left over from the occasions when she tinted her own hair.

There was an uproar. Sylva ran frenzied fingers through her hair to show that it was naturally black down to the roots. The cook, without glancing in her direction, took the steak and threw it into the fire.

The young girl stood near the door, watching, and feeling envious. Like all well-brought-up young people she had been taught to repress outbursts of emotions and to her, tears and rages seemed a luxury.

Then she went into the drawing room where she found her mother and Feldman. After a curt greeting the great man turned his back on her, put an elbow on the table in front of him and shaded his face with his hand, as though to make it quite apparent that he did not wish to include her in the conversation. Thus he remained till the meal was announced.

The food was, as always when he was invited, very expensive and very dull, almost tasteless. Feldman liked it that way, as highly spiced, hearty and coarse dishes recalled to him his poor childhood. Also, he preferred everything hashed or mashed, not because he had bad teeth, but because he thought this was more refined. He did not understand wine and therefore Mrs. Kalny, who was not disposed to waste anything, gave him a cheap *Graves*, insipid and without body.

The cook had put so much cream and egg yolk into all dishes that the savoury, which was asparagus *purée*, tasted and looked almost like the sweet, which was chestnut rice. Franciska ate in silence and listlessly without following the talk. She thought of Mr. Ling. From time to time, when Feldman looked at her, she felt guilty and her heart shrivelled.

She was not experienced in the ways of men, just as she could not yet interpret the fluttering of her own senses. Had her mother, in her stead, been spending an evening with Ling, she would have known after an instant whether he was interested in her as a woman or not. Franciska could not tell. It was true, she had the feeling that Ling had merely enjoyed talking to her and nothing else. But now, when she recalled Friday night, she could not recall it without remembering the remarks Susy had made on this very morning and so she was inclined to believe that Ling had really paid court to her. That he had not done so outright was probably due to a reticence inspired by the difference in their ages, she thought.

Then her attention returned to Feldman. 'Why does she bother with him so much?' she asked herself. 'What's the good of it? She can't accept any presents from him. He is not nice enough to flirt with and he's unpleasant altogether. Perhaps she wants him to pull strings for her or for some friend? But then, she would have told me already. She can never keep anything to herself.'

In the late afternoon, when Mrs. Kalny created the frantic atmosphere of running and fetching which preceded her departure, the young girl realized for the first time that her father was going to die.

Hardly anyone experiences on such occasions the appropriate emotions. But the distress aroused by one's own, inappropriate feelings often produces a sadness which helps to save appearances. It was like this with Franciska. The first thought which occurred to her, upon her mother's departure was, that now that she would be alone and without supervision, she would be able to see Ling. Afterwards, a feeling of loneliness invaded her which grew into despair. She began to see a new purpose and meaning in her mother's attentions towards Feldman and what she saw did not please her. She was sad about her father's nearing end, but her sadness was largely due to self-pity. She was apprehensive when she tried to imagine her future life, from now on to be laid entirely in her mother's hands, those hands which were restless and half-hearted in caressing and punishing alike.

Mr. Kalny had never concerned himself overmuch with his daughter's well-being, but he had nevertheless exerted a beneficial influence by acting as a brake on his wife's erratic behaviour. It was impossible to tell how well or ill informed he was as to her infidelities. But it was certainly due to his sobriety and good sense–the good sense of the mediocre–that nothing scandalous ever transpired and that Mrs. Kalny had acquired the reputation of an *allumeuse*, which was flattering, instead of that of a society whore, which was not.

CHAPTER 7

On the third day of Mrs. Kalny's absence a letter arrived from Merano and in it Mrs. Kalny had put the pressed gentian blossom which she had picked, so she wrote, on the previous day while climbing the Vigiljoch. Franciska, who had been handed the letter when she returned from school for lunch, put the blue flower on the cloth beside her plate and did not take her eyes off it while she waited for the next course.

As soon as Mrs. Kalny had left, a strange peace and harmony descended on the servants and with it a slackness, which they did not try to conceal. For instance, the parlourmaid had immediately discarded the white gloves she used to wear when waiting at table. The cook, in turn, did not arrange the meat and vegetables on separate dishes, but lumped them all together on a large platter. Franciska noticed it but did not dare to reprimand them.

Her mother's absence, instead of strengthening her sense of independence, had increased her feeling of helplessness. She knew that she lacked authority with the maids and that instead of becoming a sort of deputy-mistress of the household, she was being pushed about more than ever, given to understand that she was a nuisance and never asked for her wishes or consulted for advice.

The parlourmaid entered with the meat and the young

girl, in order to hide her resentment, kept her head bent low. She ate the braised beef which had been warmed up from the night before, another reminder that it was not worth the cook's while to prepare fresh dishes for Franciska's sake only.

Afterwards she went to her room, took some of her textbooks out of a drawer, put them back again and sat down at her desk.

She tore a leaf out of an exercise book and began to scribble on it.

CHAPTER 8

HUGO LING had chosen this small, shabby coffee house because it was frequented by students only. Also, as it was situated on the Karlsplatz, which lies at the centre of the University quarter, and far away from the big business houses and fashionable shops, it was unlikely that Franciska would meet any of her own or her mother's friends.

He had not made this choice in order to safeguard the young girl's reputation. It had been done entirely for his own sake and while he looked out on to the square bordered by bare-branched lime trees, he quoted to himself a line by Heine:

> Blamier mich nicht, mein schoenes Kind,
> Und gruesse mich nicht unter den Linden.
> Wenn wir erst beieinander sind,
> Dann wird sich alles andre finden.

He then glanced through the evening papers which the waiter had brought him, in such a way, that he could see the door out of the corner of his eye.

When Franciska stood by his table he jumped up like a man who has been taken by surprise.

Franciska had again put on her mother's sable tie. It was not a showy piece of fur, nor were her hat and coat conspicuous in any way. Yet she was conspicuous among these chatting, smoking, coffee-drinking young people; that air which is undefinable and yet unmistakable, the air of one whose appearance is the fruit of other people's labours, the air of isolation which derives from being dependent upon servants, lay on her as visibly as the bloom lies on the grape. In the Boccaccio, Hugo Ling had hardly noticed it. Now it overwhelmed him and filled him with bitterness. He told himself that it was contempt; in fact, it was envy.

He ordered black coffee for her and white coffee for himself and offered her a cigarette with a taunting expression, aware that she was not allowed to smoke. She took it, blushed over her clumsiness in getting it lit and began to draw at it, careful not to inhale.

She looked him full in the face for the first time since she had sat down and was again fascinated and bewildered by the white ruined face from which life had burnt away the flesh and left lines that seemed like scars. His countenance which spoke of thought, struggle and disorder, belied his conventional and elegant clothes, the well-kept hands and well-groomed black hair.

'Well?' he asked, 'What is the news of your father?'

'I think it is very serious. But perhaps it isn't. Mama writes that the weather is beautiful and that she is going for tours in the mountains.'

'Fiddling while Rome burns,' he said. 'Like all of you. And what are you doing about it?'

'What can I do about it?'

'But don't you see how useless you are?' and at the word 'useless' his eye glittered. 'That comes from having money. Money is hateful.' He said this quite sincerely. Like many men, he hated money when it was in other people's pockets.

'Your whole family is useless. Your mother has never done a stroke of work in her life. And she cannot even fill her rôle as a wife properly. She goes out there–Bolzano,

61

isn't it? or Merano or what have you,' and he pronounced the names of the towns hesitantly and with contempt, as men do when they speak of places of ill repute of which they have heard but want to make it quite clear that they do not know them personally.

'Merano,' said Franciska, without looking up.

'Very well. She goes out there in order to be with your father. But does she sit at his bedside? Does she nurse him? Does she concern herself with him? Far from it. She takes it like a gift, like a holiday.'

'There are nurses and doctors there and everything.'

'That's not the point. You understand quite well what I mean. At least, I hope so. I had thought you were intelligent.'

Ling used to stick to a rule when dealing with women; he treated the pretty ones as though they were clever and the clever ones as though they were pretty, working on the assumption that one always wants to be what one is not. In Franciska's case, he saw that she was pretty and had the impression that she was intelligent. But as she was very young and as young girls did not appeal to him, he made the mistake of not thinking of her as a woman at all, and it therefore did not occur to him that she might like to be treated as one. Franciska would have loved to be told that she was attractive. At home, the people surrounding her only looked at her hair, her nails, her clothes with professional interest and found fault with them. The young men she met at dances and parties paid her court but she knew that it was done for the sake of her social position only and that it did not matter to them what she looked like, so long as she was her parents' daughter. To be told that she was intelligent was nothing new to her and she did not take it as a compliment because neither of her parents

62

attached any importance to it; in fact, in their eyes it was no merit at all.

'But my mother does work, in her own way. She is always very busy,' said Franciska, not out of a desire to defend her mother but because she felt that it was tactless of him to criticize. She did not really believe what she was saying and yet, it was true. Mrs. Kalny could not have done a day's work of her kitchenmaid without collapsing with fatigue. But the kitchenmaid could not have gone through the strain of dressmaker's fittings and endless hours of entertaining or attending at parties, without dropping dead.

'Even if she does work, it's no good to anybody,' said Ling. 'But that's not the worst of it. Your mother and your father and their like and the generations before them have been suppressing the working people of this country for—for—well, anyway, for as long as they have been in power.' He paused expectantly.

The young girl frowned. She had never heard an opinion like this before and she found it very boring, as it did not concern her in any way. She never thought of her father as being in a position of power or of suppressing anybody. As far as she knew, he was well liked by the employees in the town office and by the staff of the factory. This, she thought, was the way it was. Her mother suppressed the servants, that was true, but the servants in turn also suppressed her mother and herself and if Ling could have seen the way Louise used to snap her head off and would sometimes tyrannize even over Mrs. Kalny, he might have realized that he was talking nonsense. She had never thought of it before, but now that she did, she found that both were right; the hammer and the anvil.

'Of course,' continued Ling, 'I would never talk like this to your parents. The rot has set in too deeply there, they just wouldn't understand. But I should have thought that you, surely would see it the right way. Aren't you feeling ashamed of yourself? Wouldn't you like to do something real, something worth while?'

'But I am working. I am studying for my finals,' said Franciska.

He laughed soundlessly.

'And in any case, I am still too young for work. I mean, real work.'

He said : 'What about all those youngsters who start to work at fourteen. What about all those children who have to support their parents. Aren't they working?'

'I suppose so,' said Franciska.

'You suppose so. But I know.'

There was a silence during which he tried to catch her eye with a reproachful stare.

'He was much more pleasant in the Boccaccio and on the phone,' said Franciska to herself. 'Perhaps Mama was right and he is impossible. What if he smashes a coffee cup again?'

Ling saw that she was not impressed with his words. He decided to be more drastic in his expressions.

'Your people have been ill-treating the workers of this country for generations. You have been feeding on their blood. I don't know how you can sleep at night. Don't you hear the blood dripping down the roof of your house?'

The young girl was irritated by this. She felt his words were fanciful, tactless and altogether in bad taste. Whether they were true or not, did not worry her, because she knew that he himself did not believe a word he had said. She had been brought up without a governess since she was six years old and in the constant vicinity of her mother, watching her mother's behaviour in and out of the drawing room, she had learnt to discern between the expression of true feelings and those which are assumed for other people's benefit. Hypocrisy wears many coats and colours but the young girl was so used to observing it, that she could recognize it as easily as Mrs. Kalny could recognize a Paris model, even if it had been copied clumsily by a little seamstress. She knew that, while Ling spoke of dripping blood, he was thinking of something quite different.

'We aren't ill-treating anybody,' she replied. 'I know, it looks like it, from the outside, but we aren't really, you know. When I was a child I always thought it was terribly unfair that we had lobster and salmon and the servants never got it. But they could have had it, if they had wanted to, my father says that everybody in our house must get the same food, only they won't touch it themselves, they just don't like it. Our cook for instance, lives on coffee and bread and butter; it's all she cares for.'

'I cannot know all the peculiarities of all the cooks in the country,' he said and tried to laugh. 'You must not take everything I say so personally. I should have thought you'd understand me better.'

He crushed his cigarette and changed to a lighter tone of voice.

'I know of course, that you do understand me. I am never deceived in people, I can always tell. And I realize of course that you have to stand up for your parents, no matter what you think about them——' and he gave her a look which was meant to be penetrating. 'But now, take your school, for instance. This useless, silly, snobbish school of yours. We had such an amusing little talk about it the other day in the Boccaccio. I enjoyed it so much. Now do you remember what I asked you to do?'

'Yes,' said Franciska. 'Did you really mean it?'

'I always mean what I say, you should know me better than this.' He did not care any more what he was saying. 'Ten more minutes,' he thought, 'and if it doesn't work, I'll have to try somewhere else.'

'But it was nothing really, what I told you. It couldn't interest anybody,' said Franciska.

'It is of the greatest interest to everybody—well, in any case, to me,' he added hurriedly. 'You are so very interesting you know, I always thought so. And then, if it is any good—and I am sure it will be—it would give me such a pleasure to be of assistance to you. I am always on the look-out for young talent, naturally.'

'I have written something the way you suggested it,' said Franciska. 'But it is not an article. I wouldn't know how to write one. It's just a poem. Very silly, really.'

'All the better. If it is silly, it's only because your school is so silly. And that's what I want to—to emphasize. Have you got it with you? Please do let me have a look at it.'

'It won't be any good to you,' said Franciska as she took the folded paper out of her handbag.

For the first time since she had met him at the coffee house she felt that he was genuinely interested in her. The ardent look in his eyes, the eager tone of his voice, could not be mistaken. 'He is so different from all the young men,' she thought. Her previous boredom and irritation had vanished.

He took the paper from her. 'This is perfect, quite perfect,' he murmured. 'And you've got the bit in about the central heating. That's wonderful. It couldn't be better.'

'I can't see anything very wonderful about it,' said Franciska. 'I only put it in because you were so interested. We've got central heating at school, that's all.'

'But it isn't all, it's terribly important—I mean, interesting, it's so witty, the way you put it. I am delighted. I cannot tell you how delighted I am.'

Franciska had written the poem in the mock heroic style; a vehicle popular in her form for writing skits on teachers' foibles, meant to be passed round from hand to hand. It was neither a difficult nor original way of letting off steam and she was not the only one in her form who excelled at it. The coupling of Homeric expressions with everyday, modern words always produced an exhilarating effect among her schoolmates. But nobody had ever before called her compositions witty, interesting or perfect.

'He must be in love with me, or he wouldn't praise it so much,' she said to herself, as she watched Ling putting the paper in his wallet.

'I shan't publish it in the daily paper,' he said. 'It's much too good for it. I'll put it in the Sunday issue. Quite wonderful. But don't tell anybody about it, will you? I want it to appear as a surprise, spontaneously. For your sake of course. Give everybody a surprise. No, don't say anything, I know what I am doing. Let me handle it. You do trust me, don't you?'

He called the waiter and paid.

'You want it published under your own name, of course, don't you?'

'I had not thought of it. I didn't think you'd like it,' said Franciska. She added: 'Perhaps it would be better not to——'

'But why not? You have not said anything against anybody. You have not mentioned any person in particular. There is no libel in it. How could there be? Don't you think I know all about that sort of thing? Surely you don't think I would publish anything which might be ill advised? You should know me better than this.'

He fell silent. There was a tension in his countenance which made her feel uncomfortable. 'He is terribly touchy,' she thought. 'He might yet break a coffee cup.'

He said lightly: 'No, really, there is nothing to worry about.'

It had not occurred to her that there was anything to worry about. Now that he had mentioned it, she began to wonder.

'And you stand by all you say, don't you?' he said, still lightly and absentmindedly while he sorted out a few coins in the palm of his hand.

'I don't know what you mean,' said Franciska. 'Why shouldn't I stand by it? It's all true – I mean, I haven't made anything up.'

'Of course not. That's what I meant. That's – what – I – meant.'

And without giving her another glance he handed the waiter a tip.

CHAPTER 9

AND WHAT did you have? Coffee and whipped cream?' asked Susy Graber and she looked at Franciska in such an eager and searching manner as though hoping to find traces of past delights in her friend's face.

'No, that's childish. I had black coffee,' said Franciska trying to sound unconcerned.

'Yes, that's true,' said Susy. She was impressed yet regretful. It was considered to be 'grown up' not to eat whipped cream, because both Mrs. Kalny and Mrs. Graber abstained from it, since they were afraid of getting fat.

'And what did he have? Go on.'

'He had white coffee.'

'And anything to eat with it?'

'No.'

'Do you know why?' asked Susy. 'Because he was feeling passionate. When men feel passionate they can't eat. And they go white in the face. Was he white in the face?'

'Yes, very white,' replied Franciska hesitantly as though yielding a shameful secret.

They were standing at the end of the corridor on the first floor which gave on to the school yard. Behind them, between the double windows stood rows of jam jars with specimen plants in them or animals' insides, pickled in spirits and labelled in the crotchety handwriting of the natural science teacher.

Now the natural science teacher herself, an upright, cold beauty of about forty, appeared at the head of the stairs and moved in their direction. The girls turned their backs to her, as though contemplating the exhibits in the window. They felt that the delicate nature of their talk might be discerned in their faces.

'Do you think she is a virgin?' asked Susy.

'Yes, definitely,' replied Franciska.

'But Mademoiselle Blanchard isn't,' said Susy. They did not refer to the teachers by nicknames, as the younger pupils did. This too, was an expression of their being 'grown up.' 'Did you hear what she said yesterday? She said, *Monsieur le directeur et moi, nous nous entendons très bien.* You know what that means, don't you?'

'Did she really? I didn't hear it.'

'Yes. You ask Gerty. But now go on. So you got there and he was already waiting. And what did he say? Did he kiss your hand?'

'No, he didn't.'

'That's because it was in a public place,' said Susy soothingly. 'Now what did he say?'

'I can't tell you. He asked me not to.'

'Is it serious?' asked Susy. 'But you won't marry him, will you?'

'Don't be silly. But I really can't tell you any more about it,' said Franciska with great firmness. If the meeting between her and Ling had developed in the way outlined by Susy, she would have had no hesitation of disclosing the secret to her friend. But as she felt that the rendezvous had taken an unexpected course and therefore been unsatisfactory, she had not the courage to say what had happened.

'So he doesn't want to marry you,' concluded Susy, who knew that Franciska could not have kept this to herself. 'Then he wants it without. Or do you think he just wants to cuddle you? Did he say I shan't do anything you might regret later? That's what they say when they mean just cuddling.'

'My mother is frightfully against kissing and nothing else,' said Franciska. 'She says it's agony to a man. Do you understand it?'

'No,' said Susy.

Then, as usual, she turned away from abstract speculations and applied herself to a concrete example.

'And when will you see him again?' she asked.

'He did not say anything. He did not ask me,' replied Franciska and for the first time during their talk in the interval between classes she expressed her thoughts. She said: 'You know, I don't think he is in love with me. Otherwise he would have wanted to see me again, wouldn't he?'

'But he must be in love with you, Cissy. Why should he have wanted to see you in the first place?'

'Yes, yes,' said Franciska. She agreed with her friend. Susy was right, without doubt. If a man wanted to see a woman there was only one thing in his mind—what else could there be? But there were variations of shading in that one thing and it was those variations with which Susy concerned herself. And if, for instance, one was to call that thing 'red'; then Susy's speculations as to Ling's intentions had ranged from pale pink to deep scarlet. The young girls were colour blind because they could not see that life around them was not confined to this one colour only. Their blindness derived from their education which could have been expressed: 'A woman is a poor creature; what can she give but herself?'

71

And yet, although Franciska believed the same as Susy did, she was worried and doubtful about her meeting in the coffee house on the Karlsplatz. Only those are good liars who believe in what they are saying at the moment they are saying it; only they can be convincing. Ling was not a liar. He was merely, at times, a hypocrite.

Franciska, as she stood now half-turned away from Susy's avid glance, contemplated a desiccated plant in a jar and recalled again, as she had done so many times before, Ling's words. Again she felt a falsity in them, contrasting with the reality of his thoughts. She recalled also his hurried goodbyes and how he had hardly glanced at her while making them.

Her vanity was hurt and she began to invent all sorts of excuses to explain his behaviour; they were more or less plausible and even ingenious. Only, as always on such occasions, the right explanation did not occur to her.

'I suppose he is in love with me,' she said. 'But in a queer and unusual way. That's because he is queer and unusual himself.'

'Yes, he is queer,' said Susy. 'He wasn't in evening dress at the Boccaccio. That just shows you, doesn't it? And he didn't take Seltzer with his whisky either. Look, there is Gaby. She's been downstairs again to eat sausages. Isn't she dreadful?'

'Yes, isn't she,' said Franciska. 'And on Sundays they eat at a restaurant.'

In a part of the passage on the ground floor the school beadle put up a trestle table every day and sold hot sausage rolls and chocolate wafers during the big interval at ten o'clock. It was considered to be in bad style to buy any of these snacks. The girls from 'good' homes always brought their sandwiches with them. And when a girl was given

72

money by her parents to buy her own food downstairs, it was not considered a sign of affluence but of sloth. It meant a badly run household, few servants and lack of care. Also, those pupils who had rich parents, like Susy and Franciska, were never given any pocket money at all and did not want to have it either. All their needs were catered for at home and direct contact with money was thought to have a coarsening influence on the girls' natures. For similar reasons, it was not 'decent' to eat at a restaurant because this too, was an indication that one's cook was inefficient and could not produce festive fare.

'Let's go before she gets near us,' said Susy.

The bell rang. The girls did not return to their classroom but went towards the staircase, to descend to the gymnasium.

'I won't do any gym to-day,' said Susy. 'I can't stand the temporary. Come and sit out with me, do.'

'But I did a fortnight ago. It's too soon.'

'But then we still had Matzka; the new one doesn't know. Just tell her you can't exercise. She won't look under your skirts.'

'I wish Matzka would come back again soon,' said Franciska. 'I would not have cheated with her. But the new one deserves all she gets.' Then, more to please her friend than out of real curiosity, she added: 'Do you think she is a virgin? She is bandy-legged, you know.'

'And how,' said Susy. 'And with that frog face. She is not just an ordinary virgin, let me tell you, she is hermetically sealed.'

They ran down the stairs giggling.

Susy and Franciska usually refrained from making spiteful remarks about the teachers' appearances; that too, was part of being 'grown up'. And if they let themselves go on this occasion it was because the temporary gymnastic teacher

73

had jarred on them from the beginning. She had, for instance, lectured them against wearing corsets and girdles. She had told them to forget that they were women and to disregard their monthly complaints. Pains like these, she said, were purely imaginary.

As the two girls went into the cloakroom where the lockers were kept containing their sports clothes, they were met by several of their friends who were in great agitation.

'She told us to put up the net in the yard,' they screeched, 'and it's raining.'

'Wasn't I right?' said Susy and pinched Franciska's arm. 'We are well out of it.'

'Playing netball in the rain,' said Franciska. 'It's the limit.'

'She is a revolutionary, that's what she is. She must be, if she thinks the girls will play out there in the rain. I told you she was a revolutionary.'

This was Susy's strongest word for expressing contempt. And as she had used it already on several occasions before in connexion with the gymnastic teacher, other pupils had taken it up and made it into one of the fashionable expressions.

Now one of them shrieked: 'I can't find my left gym shoe. A revolutionary must have taken it. Can't you see it any where?'

'Ask the horse, it's got a bigger head than I have,' answered another.

'I'll tell you what, Cissy,' said Susy as they entered the gymnasium and made for a row of chairs ranged against the piano. 'When you see him next time, have coffee and whipped cream. Perhaps he doesn't like you to be grown up, some men like them young and girlish and then, after all, why shouldn't you have something nice? One cannot live on passion, can one?'

74

CHAPTER 10

THE SERVANTS who, like dogs, have a sixth sense and
know what is going to happen to their masters before it
has happened, changed in their behaviour towards Franciska
during the second half of the week. They treated her with
awe and solicitude, approached her on tiptoe and asked for
her orders in a hushed voice. Franciska understood and
went through her days with becoming melancholy.

She forced herself to think of her father's approaching
death and tried to measure the depth of her sadness. To her
distress, she found no tears. Then, still determined to weep,
she resorted to a trick in order to produce them. Like a
woman who, in the arms of an unloved man, imagines she
is being embraced by her lover and thus creates a show of
feeling which deceives the man whom she is with at the
time, so Franciska recalled the most grievous experiences of
her past and when her eyes began to water, she told herself
that she was weeping for her father. She believed that if
she practised this subterfuge often enough she could rely on
weeping at the right moment when it would be expected of
her.

On Friday, while she was at lunch, the family doctor
rang up to say that he would like to call on her during the
afternoon. The parlourmaid, who felt that the honours of
the house rested in her hands, removed the Paisley shawl

which covered the grand piano in the music room and replaced it with the white, long-fringed silk cloth reserved for parties. This was nonsensical, as she knew that the doctor would remain in the drawing room during his call, but it served to heighten her anticipation of the excitement which she was determined to savour to the last drop.

Franciska received the doctor standing in the bay, on the same spot where her mother had stood when Feldman had exhibited himself at the party.

'How are you, Doctor? Won't you please sit down?' she said with the intonation her mother used, when receiving someone not well known to her, who paid a formal visit.

'Thank you,' said the doctor and remained standing. 'I had a telegram from your mother this morning. She asked me to tell you – it's bad news – but I don't think it will come as a great surprise to you – not that this makes it any better of course——' he paused, hoping that the young girl would guess the meaning of his words and break the news to herself, so to speak.

Franciska, who had expected him to behave in a more picturesquely solemn fashion, felt annoyed at his sober way of speech, which was not different from his usual, everyday manner. She bent her head and began to pluck at the tassels of a cushion.

The doctor did not mind witnessing a death, but he hated his patients to 'die on him', for the sake of his reputation. That was why, whenever possible, he would send them to a health resort, where they could die, conveniently, under the care of someone else. This manœuvre, although it made things easier for him, nevertheless, placed him in a dilemma. Sometimes the family of the deceased reproached him for having misjudged the patient's condition, if they held the naïve faith that health resorts exist for the purpose of restoring health. It was this knowledge which made the doctor awkward on occasions when he had to break the bad news and gave him the air of dithering and contradicting his own statements.

'The death of your father occurred during the night,' he said. 'That is to say, in the morning, really. At about one o'clock. Not that it makes any difference, unfortunately. It was a rapid end, which was fortunate for his sake. There was nothing to be done of course, any more. Although everything was done. I hoped that the end would come quickly—I foresaw it—but one can never be quite certain, of course. It could have been very prolonged and drawn out.'

There was a silence.

Franciska was so angry that she did not even try to weep. She said to herself: 'If he had to tell Mama, he would have done it properly. With me, nobody bothers.'

Mr. Langer, the surgeon, who had also been consulted before Mr. Kalny's departure, was shown in. The doctor had arranged for him to call, as he thought it would ease the situation. The surgeon was an energetic man who believed in the virtue of speed. Also, as he was only called in on special occasions, he did not have to worry about being tactful and keeping on good terms with the family.

'What did I tell you?' he exclaimed cheerfully, turning to the doctor. 'Miss Kalny is bearing up well. I admire her courage. Don't you admire her courage?'

When people did not weep, he always said he admired their courage. When they did weep, he said that he respected their grief.

'Your father was a hopeless case, anyway,' he continued.

'He was a wonderful man,' interposed the doctor quickly.

'A wonderful man, but hopeless just the same,' said the surgeon. 'I said to him only a month ago, Give me a nice

77

cancer of the bladder any day, that's something, I could operate it. Still, there it is. We can't pick and choose.' And he made a sweeping gesture as though to indicate that people who could not be operated upon had no excuse for wanting to live.

'That doesn't make it any better for those who are left behind,' said the doctor, who was anxious to curb the surgeon's high spirits.

'He was hopeless and I told him so.'

'Mr. Langer means that your father's kidneys were hopeless,' said the doctor as though interpreting a foreign language to Franciska.

The surgeon threw him an impatient and reproachful glance as though to say: 'Now look here, who is telling the story, you or I?'

They continued in that vein, the one deprecating Mr. Kalny's kidneys, the other praising his character.

A few minutes later they departed together, leaving Franciska in a mood similar to that of an actress, who, after having prepared and dressed herself for the part of Ophelia, is led on to the stage to find a modern drawing-room farce in progress.

CHAPTER 11

IT IS always a bad sign when ceremony and usage are discarded all of a sudden. For instance, when a woman, who has hitherto never allowed herself to be seen in a state of unbecoming undress by her husband, suddenly does not care any more when and how he sees her, it means that he has ceased to attract her as a man.

Or when tradespeople suddenly drop their respectful attitude towards a customer, it means that his credit has come to an end.

Similarly, when the head of the school asked Franciska to see him in his study, he did not chide her as a headmaster usually chides a pupil who has misbehaved. Nor did he show the pompous indignation he was wont to display on such occasions. Instead, he talked to her as though she were his equal. The young girl was too inexperienced to know that this, in itself, was an indication of the end and that, if he did not bother to behave for her benefit as a headmaster behaves towards a pupil, it meant that in his eyes she had already ceased to be a pupil and he therefore had ceased to be the headmaster, as far as she was concerned.

Franciska had stayed in on Saturday, as Louise had told her to stay at home. Louise had given this advice partly because she thought it proper as an expression of grief and partly because she required the young girl's presence in

79

order to fit a mourning dress which she hurriedly made up from an old black frock of Mrs. Kalny's.

On Saturday midday those acquaintances of the Kalnys who had the same family doctor as Franciska's parents and who had therefore heard the news, rang up, said what is usually said on such occasions and asked Franciska if they could do anything for her, in a way which made it plain that they did not intend to do anything. Some, more practical than others, questioned her about the arrangements for the funeral and speculated to what charity they should give their donations; it was a tradition in the Kalny family to prefer these to flowers. As Franciska could not answer any of their questions, the calls were kept short.

In the afternoon her Aunt Hilda rang up, addressed her as 'poor little thing' and invited her to spend the Sunday with them. Franciska accepted, was forced to accept, because of her lack of *savoir faire*. When one declines an invitation it is essential to produce one's excuse quickly. Franciska, not yet versed in this practice, failed and was caught.

Aunt Hilda and Uncle Victor were always referred to as 'distant relations' by Mrs. Kalny although they were not as distant as Mrs. Kalny would have wished them to be. But although their lives did not move amidst the solid, patrician elegance which surrounded the Kalnys, Franciska's mother would have seen them more often, had they behaved as she expected them to behave. She would have forgiven envy and spite which, after all, is a sign of admiration, but she could not forgive their cheerful, unobservant and unappreciative attitude when confronted with the impressive splendours of the Kalny household. Victor was capable of admiring Mrs. Kalny's dress in the same breath as that of his wife. Hilda did not think that certain ornaments were necessarily beautiful because they decorated Mrs. Kalny's rooms. And they both, instead of acknowledging the superiority of Mr. and Mrs. Kalny's style of living, only pitied them both because they considered them to be the slaves of their numerous servants and acquaintances.

Franciska shared her mother's contempt without ever asking herself whether it was justified; and as she was convinced that Hilda's and Victor's judgment could never be right, she was not put out when, on the Sunday, they spoke about the poem which had appeared in the paper, with an unpleasantness which she could not comprehend.

'Did you really make it up yourself?' asked Uncle Victor. 'I am not asking this because I think it is so good, far from it, but because it is so bad. It looks to me like something the editor has made up himself and done badly on purpose, so that it looks like the real thing. He should have really put in some spelling mistakes, to make it more convincingly school-girlish. But how on earth did he get hold of your name? That's what I can't understand. I should sue him if I were you. No, don't laugh. I am quite serious.'

'But I did write it myself,' said Franciska. 'And he liked it very much.'

'Of course he liked it,' said Aunt Hilda soothingly, 'or he would not have printed it.'

'Of course he printed it because he wanted to print it,' said Uncle Victor. 'But why did he want to print it? Who wants to read that stuff, about sandwiches with *paté foie gras* and central heating and lost gym tunics which are blamed on revolutionaries?'

'Perhaps it is much better than we think,' said Aunt Hilda. 'Perhaps it's *avant-garde*. They do things like this in Paris.'

'But we are here and not in Paris and Ling edits the paper

81

for us and people like us. I am amazed, I must say. I'm not talking about the poem. Cissy isn't a genius, but then we don't expect her to be. But I can't understand the paper. I always knew newspapermen were uneducated, but I didn't think they were illiterate.'

'He did not say it was good, I know it isn't,' said Franciska. 'But he said it was so amusing.'

'Did your mother see it?' asked Uncle Victor. 'She used to know Ling, didn't she?'

'Yes, but that's a long time ago.'

'She doesn't see him any more?'

'No, and anyway she was away in Merano.'

'I give up,' said Uncle Victor.

'But how did you get to know him?' asked Aunt Hilda, who, like most women, was more interested in the tangle of human relationships than in isolated facts.

'That's not interesting, that's neither here nor there,' said Uncle Victor. 'She met him at a party, I suppose. Where else could she have met him? Perhaps he had sweaty hands, so she didn't want to dance with him and so she had to talk, and she talked about her school because she had nothing else to talk about. Well, I can only say that you'll be lucky if people think the poem is just stupid. I think so myself, but then I am your uncle and I'm kind.'

CHAPTER 12

FRANCISKA HAD arrived late at school on Monday morning. She was unnerved because she knew that the girls would offer their condolences and that it would be embarrassing for her and for them. But only two of them came to shake her hand; one of them was Susy.

'I say, my father and mother are furious with you,' she murmured, while she pretended to express her sympathy. 'I wanted to ask you over yesterday, but they wouldn't let me.'

The bell rang.

Franciska sat down. She was not astonished. Mrs. Graber was always given to feeling neglected and the young girl imagined that Susy's mother felt slighted because she had heard about Mr. Kalny's death in a roundabout way and not from Franciska herself.

She got out her Virgil and opened it at the Georgics, at the chapter which deals with advice to bee-keepers.

The Latin master came in. Nobody took any notice of him. While he looked through the absence book, Franciska turned to the girl behind her and whispered: '*Examen examinis* means the tongue on the scales and also the swarm of bees. Isn't it crazy?'

The girl began to titter, then she suddenly stopped herself and grew embarrassed. She shook her head and glanced significantly at the teacher on the daïs, as though to indicate that she did not dare to make herself conspicuous. Franciska thought this nonsensical, as the Latin master was not concerned about discipline and was only keen on getting his charges through the finals, safely, and with the highest possible honours.

'I suppose she thinks that I must not laugh because I am in mourning,' she said to herself. She did not know that her position was such that it was an embarrassment for any of her schoolmates to be seen sharing a joke with her.

The teacher got up from his platform and stepped down into the room. He went to Franciska, held out his hand and said without looking her in the face: 'Miss Kalny, I want to express my sympathy for you in your bereavement, will you please go to the headmaster now, he wants to see you.'

He said it all in one breath and hurriedly, as people do when they have to say something which it is their duty to say, but want to indicate at the same time that what they are saying has nothing to do with their own convictions and opinions.

When the headmaster received pupils, he would sit at his desk, with the bust of Cæsar on a pedestal of black-veined marble on his right and the globe on its mahogany tripod on his left, as though relying upon this frame to lend him the dignity required for his office. Now, he was pacing the room. His hair was dishevelled, as though he had been running his fingers through it repeatedly.

Franciska, who had wanted to greet him as soon as she entered, stopped at the door, silent with fright, as she looked at him. It sometimes happens that in a familiar room a wallpaper painted with roses, reveals, when looked at in a certain way, hags and monsters, formed by the blank spaces between the pattern. It was with a similar shock that

Franciska beheld the headmaster's new face which she could discern between the lineaments she was accustomed to see; the greying hair still touched the large-lobed ears, the golden pince-nez was posed as always, on the same fleshy nose.

He stopped walking up and down and moved towards his desk. But, as though his new face had also brought with it new movements, he sat down on the corner of the table top, instead of taking his wonted seat behind it. In this position his head was on the same level as the stony face of the Roman. Before she had entered the study, Franciska had been convinced that the headmaster had called her in order to express his sympathy on her father's death. Now she said to herself: 'He is angry about the poem. And Ling said, nobody would mind. But why should he mind? There is nothing offensive in it.'

The headmaster said: 'Do you know any of the boys at St. Stephen's?' St. Stephen's was a school situated in the same part of the town as Franciska's school.

The young girl was startled by this question and relieved.

'So it isn't about the poem,' she thought. 'Ling was right, nobody cares.'

She replied: 'No, I don't.'

The headmaster said: 'What are their names?'

It was an old trick of his; when confronted with a misdemeanour, he would ignore denials and make it appear that the guilt of that particular person was already established beyond doubt.

'I don't know,' said Franciska.

'You mean, you don't know several of them, you only know one? Well, what's his name?'

'I have never known anybody who goes to St. Stephen's.'

The old, familiar tactics had restored to the headmaster

his old, familar appearance. Now it vanished again and the large ear lobes and the gold pince-nez stood like disused signposts in a strange landscape.

He held his head. 'All right,' he said, as though apologizing for she knew not what. 'I thought you didn't. Otherwise you would not——' He shook his head as though saying: 'What's the use?'

For a while he was silent. His shattered features might have inspired pity, had the young girl seen them on their own; but seeing them, as she did, next to the ironical calm of Cæsar's countenance, they inspired only disgust.

'Did Ling ask you to write the poem?' he said.

'Yes,' said Franciska.

'He didn't use pressure to obtain it?'

'What could he have done?' asked the young girl, astonished.

'Did he offer you payment for it?'

'No,' she replied and thought: 'He should have done, I suppose. But then, it was not really good enough.'

'As bad as I thought,' said the headmaster and added: 'Did he ask you in writing that you should send him the poem?'

'No,' said Franciska.

'You have nothing in writing from him at all, no suggestion about the poem, or anything?'

She shook her head.

'That's all there is to it,' and the headmaster slid off the desk. He said lightly: 'It may interest you to know that you have come nearer to breaking my neck than all the authorities have done for the last fifteen years. My neck may be broken already, for all I know. No, don't——' and he held up his hand in the way he used, when he met pupils in the passage and wanted to cut short their salutations.

'You had better go home now. For your own sake, too. I can't expect to maintain discipline like this, can I?' and he looked at her not indignantly but in a business-like manner as though discussing a problem with an equal. 'At least I will be able to say that I have sent you away.'

The young girl felt her blood turning to ice.

'I am sorry,' he said. 'I am not sending you home as a punishment. You will be punished enough, more than enough. I don't know how much, myself. I wish I did. Well, you can go now. Goodbye,' and he added in a friendly voice: 'And go straight away, don't wait for the interval. Much wiser.'

As is usual on occasions of profound distress, the mind seems to separate itself from the heart and leads a life of its own, observing details with a minuteness and accuracy which is all the more horrible, as these details are trifling and irrelevant. Thus, Franciska, on her way back to the classroom, noticed cracks in the walls showing like the skeleton branches of wintry trees and stains on the doors, shaped like the map of unknown continents; all things she had never seen before.

She gathered up her school books and took her hat and coat from the peg with trembling fingers, while she listened to the halting speech of one of the girls: '*nec casia liquidi corrumpitur usus olivi*. And the oil, the oil, the use of the cinnamon——'

'Oh, God,' she thought, leaving the room. 'And the use of the liquid oil is not vitiated by cinnamon, any fool would know it.'

It was at the sight of her coat, hung over one arm, that the terror returned, and a darkness, which she had not known to exist, rose inside her and veiled her eyes for an instant. As she came almost to the bottom of the stairs, a voice shouting: 'Kalny, Miss Kalny,' made her turn. She was filled with apprehension.

Matzka, the gymnastic teacher, followed her down the stairs, smiling. She laid a hand on her shoulder.

'Just the girl I wanted to see,' she said. 'Wasn't it splendid of you? And so clever. I always said you were a clever girl. The temporary was no good, I knew it from the beginning, but I didn't know she was so bad that she couldn't even tidy up the lockers and keep them padlocked. How many tunics were lost? Tell me? And all so nicely put, in hexameters, too. I did not think it could be done.'

'I don't know, really,' murmured Franciska.

'Well, never mind, we shall soon see. I'll put some order into things in no time. But I am so pleased, really. Bye-bye.' She passed, smiling, and waving a muscular arm.

Before the young girl could think over Matzka's words, the school beadle came out of his quarters, carrying a tray on which strings of rounded and pink sausages lay coiled like enormous chains of corals. He stopped right in front of the young girl, so as to block her path.

'Well, miss,' he said with a grin, while Franciska, in bondage to her new awareness, was forced to behold the gums above the decaying teeth and the stubbles on his upper lip. 'You've shown them up well and proper. My fingers are too greasy, so it would never do, but I'd like to shake hands with you, I would, and no mistake. I've always said the girls get spoiled with their sandwiches from home, no wonder they are green-faced misses. If they'd eat what I sell, they would be much better for it, no mistake. You've got your head screwed on the right way, not like most of the misses. Good luck, I say. Good luck.'

The young girl forced herself to smile and waited till he had cleared the way.

Outside it was drizzling with snow and the chill on her face and neck made her realize that she had not yet put her coat on. She laid down her scrip to get her arms free.

'Miss Kalny. My dear Miss Kalny. What a sight for my astonished eyes!' said a dry, refined woman's voice at her shoulder. It was the headmaster's secretary, an aristocratic old maid.

At the first sound of her name, Franciska's heart contracted. She still could not understand the nature of her guilt. But already the knowledge that she was guilty had taken root in her, so that she expected something unpleasant from every encounter. Already she had lost the confidence of the young animal which has never yet been hurt. She had become grown up in half an hour, and even if she had, from now on, taken whipped cream in her coffee, referred to people by their nicknames and indulged in all the other traits of 'childishness' which she had up till now so assiduously avoided, she could not have re-entered the lost paradise.

She straightened the collar of her coat and adjusted her hat and, forcing herself to turn round, she said: 'I am sorry, Miss Rehak, I did not see you.'

'What do my astonished ears hear?' continued the secretary and cocked her head. 'Has the head sent you home? T . . . t . . . t . . . How very naughty of him. He should show the revolutionaries where they get off. But I suppose he got into a panic. Not very nice, getting into a panic, is it? I wouldn't. I'd snap my finger at them. And so should you. You'll be back in a day or two, mark my word. And you don't mind? No, I thought not. How very clever of you not to mind. Now I must get back or he'll tear my head off. His sort—you know what I mean—they are all the same. When something goes wrong they can't control their temper. Not very nice, is it? I don't care any more, I'll retire next year. I'll go and live with my cousin and her cows near Podebrady. She is an utter bore but her cows are perfect darlings. But then, they are pedigree, of course.'

She shut her lips tightly and gazed into space. Then, an aggressive expression came into her face for an instant and the tired blue eyes shone with a fresh brilliance. 'And talking of cows, Miss Kalny, my dear—you'll forgive my language but I feel these things very deeply, you know— that friend of yours, that little Susy Graber, has a mother who is a perfect pest. She rang up this morning and complained to the head about that darling poem of yours. She said that she didn't give Susy sandwiches with *pati foie gras* every day, only when there was some left over from parties. She said she did not have any money to throw about. And the head was so angelic to her—on the phone, I mean. He'd do anything to please the parents, he'd let them dance on his head if they wanted to. He thinks of nothing but his fees, he's got the mind of a grocer, if you ask me. Not very nice, is it? If he could, he'd sell geography by the pound and Latin by the pint. But I've watched him for so many years at it that my astonished eyes simply refuse to be astonished any more. When I retire, I'll write a book called "Thirty Years with Headmasters! Their Beliefs, Customs and History." Now, I must really fly.'

And the secretary gathered up her skirts, which she still wore long, after the fashion of her youth, and swept away.

Franciska walked through an alley into the Jungman street, across the square and into the Lindt arcade, which gave on to the main boulevard of the town.

In one corner of the arcade stood the beggar who, several times a week, at noon, used to prostrate himself in a feigned epileptic fit, in order to attract alms. It was doubtful whether these were given to him by the passers-by out of pity or in gratitude for a gruesome performance; the family doctor, who had witnessed a fit on one occasion, had told Mrs. Kalny that it was done very well and with great accuracy of detail. 'Then he deserves all the money he gets,' had been Mrs. Kalny's reply.

Franciska, looking at the beggar, remembered this and for the first time since this morning, her thoughts went to her mother. 'Thank God, she is away,' was the first thought. But then, there were the maids to be considered. If she was not allowed to go to school for a few days, they would become suspicious. The winter had already set in and she could not spend five hours every day in the park. Neither could she kill time in a coffee house; she had no pocket money and besides, it was not a suitable thing for a young girl to do. Nor could she spend the time with any of her mother's friends because they were not to know that she was in trouble. The beggar came to her mind again. 'I'll be ill,' she thought. 'If he can put it on, so can I.'

She was walking towards the lower end of the boulevard. The snow was melting underfoot, but on the border of the pavement where thin-stemmed lime trees grew out of round patches of earth the snow clung to the clods.

On the corner of the boulevard and the Graben were the large show windows of a draper's. The shop had only recently been opened. The young girl stopped.

As in all cheap shops, every inch of space was used for display. It looked as though a tide of purple and one of pink had flooded the window, had intermingled their waves and had, before receding, been frozen not into ice but imitation silk and velvet. 'How the servants would love it!' thought Franciska and she quickly moved on, ashamed that she had allowed herself to linger in front of wares which

91

were beneath contempt. 'Damn the maids,' she said to herself suddenly. 'I'll stay at home quite simply and they can think what they like. I'm not going to pander to the *canaille* again. Last time I wasted two crowns on the porter and those I had to borrow from Rudy, that idiot, and Mama knew just the same and I could have spared myself the trouble. By the time Mama gets back from Merano, it will have blown over, and if the maids tell her then, it won't matter any more. She wouldn't care in any case. The *Mandrake Root* thing was much worse and she never turned a hair.'

She entered the Graben, stopping from time to time in front of shops which were familiar to her and where she knew the exhibits would not offend her taste.

The Mandrake Root was a book, a salacious fantasy, a kind of racy, modern fairy tale, written by a German novelist in a style which mingled obscenity with mysticism. It described the life story of a devastatingly beautiful and heartless young woman who had been conceived from the seed of a hanged murderer and mothered by a whore. This book, the sale of which was banned, was considered at Franciska's school to be a treasury of information. It was lent to Franciska by her Aunt Hilda, who had said: 'You'd better read it now, while it's forbidden and you can still enjoy it. Later on, you'd get no pleasure out of it.' The book had gone from hand to hand, till one of the teachers had pounced on it and, being young and eager, had taken it to the headmaster.

The headmaster, to whom the appearance of *The Mandrake Root* was as familiar as the annual school fête at the end of the summer term, had informed Mrs. Kalny. He always informed the parents of the culprit on such occasions, because he preferred to let them go to the trouble of being scandalized, instead of going through the motions himself. Mrs. Kalny had been very annoyed for a few minutes. 'Really, Cissy,' she had said, 'that sort of reading is stupid, because it gives you wrong ideas. You get things like: "and he picked her up in his arms and carried her to the bed." It's idiotic. In real life you'll damn well have to walk to the bed yourself.'

Franciska recalled the incident and her spirits rose, but only for a moment. Her new trouble was different. At the time of *The Mandrake Root* she had never been told to leave the school. 'But what can they do to me?' she thought. 'Perhaps the head has to send me home to appease people like Mrs. Graber. But then, he did not call it punishment. He said that was still to come. He did not know himself what would happen. I suppose he said it to scare me. If he doesn't know, who should? He was talking nonsense.'

Thus she tried to cheer herself up. To her the headmaster was the highest authority in the school. She did not realize that he, too, was under the supervision of still higher authorities. But although she could not imagine what was going to happen and why, her own perceptions told her that he had not tried to frighten her; he had been much too frightened himself.

She turned into the Herrengasse where the offices of the newspaper were situated. The porter eyed her sullenly and with impertinence and told her that the editor never came in before four o'clock in the afternoon. Although she realized that she could call again, at the right hour, and see Ling, she felt that this failure to see him right away was a fresh sign of her guilt. In this she was not altogether wrong. Ill luck, like success, has its own way of propagating itself and affects even those circumstances which are beyond control.

93

She turned back into the Graben and went home.

Again and again, during her way home, she went over her interview with the headmaster, without gaining any understanding. She also recalled the words of Matzka, the beadle, the secretary, and all that she understood was, that none of these underlings had grasped the nature of her offence. Neither did they care for her welfare. They had made use of her poem to air their own particular grievances.

She was too ignorant to realize that this, too, was a sign of how serious her trouble was. Ill-starred happenings are always seized upon by the small fry who have an axe to grind and who never comprehend the real nature of the event; just as, on the other hand, they will acclaim a hero, not for his valour, but for the sake of the advantages he will bring them.

At home she found a letter from her mother. Mrs. Kalny wrote that she would return at the end of the week, after the funeral in Merano.

There was also a message from Feldman, asking Franciska to get in touch with him at the Esplanade.

She rang up the hotel. It was obvious to her that his request sprang from some gossip which must already have reached him. But although she was always seized by a dis-agreeable excitement at the thought of coming face to face with him, she was not afraid to talk to him on this occasion, when she quailed at the thought of seeing anyone else. She felt that this ill-bred elderly Jew had a quality which was absent in all the other people she knew: he was human.

At first, on the telephone, one insipid voice gave way to the other. Then the rasping voice came through. 'This is Feldman speaking,' as though anyone who had ever heard him could have been in doubt. 'Feldman wants you to have lunch with him to-day. At twelve-thirty. At the Esplanade. Right. Goodbye.'

'It's a disgrace your going to the Esplanade and you haven't got a black coat yet,' said Louise, who came in, after having listened at the door. 'Still, I suppose you'd better go. Miss Cissy. I see you've got no head for school and it will take your mind off your poor father'.

Franciska was amazed at this. The maid had given her permission in so many words to go out to luncheon, as though she had been appealed to, whereas in fact the young girl had never asked for her opinion. Yet, she felt too depressed to continue her daily war with Louise and she nodded and followed the maid into Mrs. Kalny's dressing room, where some black gloves and a black handbag were found for her.

Feldman's secretary, a smooth empty-faced young man, who had all the graces in which his master was lacking, met her in the hotel lounge and kissed her finger tips in order to indicate that he knew that the young girl was a friend and not a client. 'Please don't order any wine with your lunch, Miss Kalny. Mr. Feldman has several important interviews this afternoon.' He withdrew, still facing her, walking a few steps backward.

She waited for some time, listening to the purring of a lift in the distance, interrupted by the clanging of the lift doors. Then, after the doors had clanged once more she heard Feldman's voice: 'Eh, rubbish. How am I to tell you? Has the horse got a handwriting? Throw your money out of the window instead.' After a pause, she could hear him again, sounding less far away: 'Go and back Pukkah Belle. What? What does he tell you? He tells you? Nonsense. Feldman tells you. Pukkah Belle or nothing. Why don't you buy your wife a new hat instead? What's wrong with your

wife? What? Well, you can't have everything in life. Eh.'
And now she could see Feldman coming round the reception desk, towards her.

'You don't look well,' he said and his unpleasant glance
made her breathless.

'No, I know.'

'But then, why should you look well? You've got nothing
to look well about. When is your mother coming back?'

'On Saturday, I think.'

'I shan't see her then. I'll be in Paris on Saturday. Come
and eat now.'

He went in front of her, preceded in his turn by the
manager.

The dining room was almost empty. They sat down at a
table in a corner.

'It's a fine mess,' he said. 'What d'you want to write
poems for? Leave it to poets. They've got to, they haven't
got any money. Now, what will you have? Soup? The soup
is good. Feldman tells you it is good.'

'Yes, please, Mr. Feldman,' said Franciska.

The waiters left them.

'Now don't get desperate, listen to Feldman. Don't weep
about the school. Leave it alone. When you've missed the
train it's no good running after it. What d'you want to go
to school for? You've gone long enough. You are a pretty
girl. They can't make you any prettier in school. What more
do you want?'

He smacked his lips and looked at her.

She said: 'Do you mean—you think they won't let me go
back? The headmaster said I was to stay away for a few
days.'

'Eh! Rubbish. He said, she said, anybody said. He's got
to say. It's his job to say. He doesn't know himself. Of

96

course, you won't go back. I've spoken with them today at the Ministry.

'At the Ministry? At the Ministry of Education? They know about it?'

'Yes. They are very glad. It's a treat for them.'

'Then they won't punish me?' asked Franciska.

'They won't do anything to you. They'll only throw you out and that doesn't hurt. There are much worse things in life. Feldman tells you, you listen to him. The Minister says he'll have to punish you on top of it, to save his face. I say to him, why punish her, let God the Almighty punish her. Be grateful for what you've got, I say to the Minister, play with it, take it to Parliament and leave the girl alone. You've got the St. Stephen's scandal and you've got this scandal, so count your blessings and make the best of it.'

'It's a scandal?' asked Franciska, to whom this word was more familiar than the other words.

He turned the palm of his hand upward, above his empty soup plate, as though presenting on it something unpleasant which could be concealed no longer. 'They call it scandal. Feldman doesn't call it a scandal. Feldman says it's rubbish,' and he made his contemptuous gesture as though dashing something to the floor.

The young girl agreed with him. How could a poem be a scandal? She glanced at him silently while he, in order to hide his vexation, rearranged some forks and spoons by his plate with unnecessary clatter. Then, forgetting that he was in a luxury hotel instead of the taverns of his native Poland, he took up his napkin and began to polish the cutlery, as though not trusting to its cleanliness.

He had wanted to prepare her for the shock of being expelled from her school, and this he had achieved. But he had not the heart to tell her that she would not only be expelled from her own school, but be excluded from all further education, whether school or university, in the entire republic.

An omelette with chicken livers was brought and the young girl watched Feldman while he cut a roll in half and then began to eat the omelette with knife and fork.

She broke her roll with her hands and ate her omelette with a fork only. 'His table manners are impossible,' she said to herself. 'Mama could never marry him.'

They both ate in silence, interrupted by the smacking of his lips.

'Mrs. Graber complained to the head about it,' said Franciska. 'She is the mother of a friend of mine. She was so annoyed about the poem. Do you think she went to the Minister?'

'Nonsense. Don't think about Mrs. Graber. Who wants to know about Mrs. Graber? If she is the mother of your friend and complains about you, then your friend isn't worth an apple of horse manure. Don't see your friends any more. You'll find new ones. Eh.'

Franciska had believed him when he had told her that she would not be allowed to return to school. Now, his words seemed to hint that the society which made up her mother's set was going to exclude her as well. She found that incredible. She was too young to realize that everything has its conventions, even scandals, that there are happenings which, although scandalous, can be forgiven, whilst others cannot. Society would have forgiven her if she had had a love affair with a married man and caused a divorce. It would have forgiven her if she had run away with someone's chauffeur and produced an illegitimate child.

It may be sad to lose a husband; it may be disastrous to lose a chauffeur, but they can, and have been, replaced.

But people will not tolerate anything which bears an adverse criticism on their way of life, because this threatens the roots of their existence, especially when those roots have already grown thin from constant attacks from without.

The omelette was followed by slices of fried brains, one of the dishes favoured by Feldman because they were soft and tasteless.

'But I did not mean to do anything wrong,' said Franciska. 'I did not mean to offend anybody. If I had known, I would have never done it. I did not do it on purpose.'

'Has Feldman said you did it on purpose? It was bad luck. If you are unlucky you break your finger while picking your nose. Purpose is rubbish. Eh!'

'But at the Ministry——'

'Nonsense. They know you did not mean anything. But it fits in with the rest of their filth and that's all they care about. But why worry? Leave the filth merchants alone.'

The young girl who would have liked to ask many more questions felt that the great man was hiding behind his barrier of crude words and commonplaces. And as she tried to find a subject related to her trouble which had not been mentioned yet and where, therefore, she might get fresh information, Ling came into her mind. She said: 'The newspaper. Do you think they knew what was going to happen?'

His jaws worked and he gave her a glance that made her shudder. It contained all the suffering, the treachery, the cruelty of thousands of years and with it, a matter-of-factness which revolted and impressed her. He had stood eavesdropping behind many doors of life. He knew, but he did not condemn. Nor was he amused.

He looked down on his plate again and went on eating while the young girl bent her head to hide her mortification. It was her worst moment.

For a while her throat ached from suppressed tears. He took it for granted that she, in her distress, would not finish what was on her plate and he told the waiter to clear away and to bring fruit and cheese.

She resented that he had not asked her whether she had finished. 'He treats me like a child,' she thought. She did not know how kind it was of him, not to have asked her. She still could not trust herself to speak; she knew that her trembling breath would choke her voice.

Feldman, too, did not say anything. He had peeled an orange and was eating it with disgusting, sucking noises. He knew that whatever he might say at this moment would sound self-righteous and insincere and would give no consolation. And although any talk would have been unbearable to the young girl, she was irritated by what she mistook for his lack of *savoir faire*. 'He has no conversation,' she said to herself. 'He is impossible.'

It is a part of the irony of life that the performance of a virtuoso is ignored or only little appreciated by the ignorant, because they are deceived by its apparent lack of effort. Thus, for instance, when an eminent throat specialist had once painted Franciska's throat with iodine, she had felt no discomfort and had thought nothing of it. The next day, when the family doctor performed the same task, it had been painful and she had thought with respect that the family doctor had been much more thorough than the specialist.

Feldman had seen more kinds of grief than most of his contemporaries. As he was, in his crude but very practical way, an expert in human emotions, he considered it to be best that he should break the bad news to Franciska rather than anyone else. He had gone to great trouble in making his preparations. It was torture to him to eat in a public dining room and he always had his meals served upstairs in his suite. But as he thought that the constant presence of the waiters and their heartless servility would force the young girl to remain calm, he had decided to use the dining room for her sake.

Also, he never ate more than one course at midday when he was working, in order to remain alert for the rest of the day. But to-day he had eaten dish after dish in order to prolong the meal and thus create a source for frequent pauses and distractions in the conversation. Also, he had only told her a part of the bad news, knowing too well that she could not have borne the whole truth at once.

Franciska felt that he was holding back some facts of which she was as yet ignorant and it made her angry. 'He can't be bothered with me,' she thought. 'I am nothing to him but my mother's daughter. He can only talk about himself.'

He was still sucking a slice of orange.

She said, imitating her mother's polite tone of inquiry: 'Has anything interesting happened to you recently, Mr. Feldman?' She thought: 'Anything rather than to listen to this. If he talks, he'll stop eating.'

She was wrong. Ill-mannered as he was, he proved to her that he was capable of talking and eating at the same time.

'Ah, yes,' he said and his hand, bespattered with orange juice, moved upward with a flash of the diamond. 'The day before yesterday I come into the Esplanade and I walk through the lounge, to the lift. In one corner I see a man with a beard, he reads a newspaper. I turn back from the lift and I go to the manager and I say to him, Is this man over there staying in the hotel? He says yes. I say, You'll have trouble with him, why don't you turn him out? He'll commit suicide to-night. The manager says, Am I to turn him out because Feldman says he'll kill himself? I can't run my business on hunches. I say, watch him, you'll have trouble. He says, How can I watch him, am I to knock at his door every five minutes because Feldman says I should watch him? So I go upstairs. In the morning the manager comes and says, Feldman, if I had only listened to you. He hanged himself and now I've got to deal with the police and the mess. Feldman, you are a miracle. Feldman, how did you know?'

Although Franciska was worn out, she was caught again by the old spell. 'You are a miracle,' she said.

He smacked his lips. 'What's the good of being a miracle? Who wants a miracle? They only listen when it's too late. When Christ heals the sick, the doctors don't like it, it puts them out of business. When Christ makes five thousand loaves out of five, the bakers don't like it, it puts them out of business. When Feldman sees a suicide, the manager doesn't like it, it puts him out of business.' He dipped his fingers into the bowl of blue glass in front of his fruit plate. One of the rose petals floating on the water caught in his ring.

'Eh,' he said, shook his hand and wiped it on to the tablecloth.

'Oh, God,' thought Franciska, 'I hope Mama doesn't marry him. If she does, the maids won't stay. He is impossible.'

He lit a cigar without asking for her permission. 'Charming,' she said to herself. 'The perfect gentleman.'

The secretary approached their table and stopped a few paces away, as though to show that he was not only a secretary but also the soul of discretion.

'All right, I'm coming,' rasped Feldman. 'Well,' he said,

more softly, turning to Franciska and at the same time rising from the table, before she had done so. 'Remember what Feldman tells you. Listen to Feldman and don't pay any attention to anybody. They are all busybodies. Get yourself a nice young man, or two or three and if your mother says you shouldn't go out with them, say that Feldman says it's all right.'

The young girl tried not to wince at his coarseness and said: 'Thank you very much for your kind invitation, Mr. Feldman.' She said it without much conviction, as Mrs. Kalny had once told her: 'Never thank a man too much for what he's given you. One never gets enough out of men, in any case.'

'It was nothing, eh.' The diamond ring flashed. He was gone, followed by his secretary.

Feldman returned upstairs to his suite to give his first consultation on that day without having taken the rest he always had after his meal; he had to start work straight away, because the luncheon had taken up too much of his time.

The young girl walked through the dining room into the lounge, feeling outraged and superior. She had yet found another fault in the great man's behaviour: he had not seen her out.

'Really, I don't know why he wanted to have lunch with me,' she thought. 'He does nothing but blow his own trumpet the whole time. And perhaps he wants to impress Mama by being attentive to me. My God, his table manners. I thought I'd die.'

In fact, Feldman had not 'blown his own trumpet' loud enough, but had been of remarkable modesty. He had not mentioned that he had wasted the whole of that morning in his endeavours to obtain an introduction to the Minister.

That he had intervened on Franciska's behalf, he had mentioned, but in such a way that it had barely obtruded. This was a pity; had he stressed these facts more, there might have been a chance of her forgiving him his bad table manners.

She left the Esplanade and walked along the street that borders the lower part of the Stadtpark.

It had turned colder since midday and it was now snowing so hard that the ducks had left the pond and were walking in the shelter of those artificial rocks which are raised on the far side of the water.

She was still in reasonably good spirits; the irritation caused by Feldman, still burnt within her and masked her despair. Also, without knowing it, she was sustained by the vitality which the great man imparted to all those who came into his presence, and which was felt by so many people bodily and as something unpleasant.

At the point where several paths unite into one walk which leads into the street, she met the beautiful Mrs. Reiser, who was holding a *marron glacé* between her gloved fingers. A few steps behind her trotted her son, a boy of eight. He was dark, pale and fragile like his mother. He had none of the robust, pink-skinned, chubby good looks which pass for prettiness in children, yet he was dressed as though he conformed to that type. It hurt Franciska to see his beauty framed in English tweeds.

'Isn't it dreadful?' said Mrs. Reiser. 'Come and stand with me in a doorway, Cissy. Come on, Kurti. As soon as we cross the street you can have it. I have to lure him like this, from step to step. Isn't it lucky he likes *marrons glacés*? If he didn't, I'd never get him out for a walk in bad weather.

'Yes, very lucky,' said Franciska.

They walked to the other side of the pavement. Mrs. Reiser slid her hand under the young girl's elbow. She loved walking arm in arm with other women; they acted as a foil to her beauty.

Franciska braced herself for what was coming. It came.

'Aren't you a naughty girl? Now, why did you do it? I went to the school myself. And so did your mother.' She paused and smiled reproachfully; her teeth, small, narrow and white, looked like grains of rice.

Mrs. Reiser wanted to convince the young girl of the excellence of the school. She could have told her that, as it was one of the very few private schools still existing in the new republic, it was forced to maintain a level of excellence well above that of the other State-supported schools, as it subsisted entirely on the parents' subscriptions. She could have told her that it was the most up-to-date, the best-equipped school in the capital, the only school, for instance which had central heating and shower baths. And she could have told her that the teachers had better degrees than those required from the average schoolmaster. All this, Mrs. Reiser dimly realized, but she did not think it was worth while mentioning. She brought out her strongest trump card in favour of the school: she herself had been educated there. This, to the beautiful Mrs. Reiser was a proof beyond all others that the school was the best of its kind in the whole world.

'We adored the school,' she continued. And smiled again, this time fondly reminiscing. 'And the way they taught us. Wonderful. You will not believe it, but my favourite subject was Greek. My husband says it's a most unusual favourite for a girl. Don't you think it is remarkable?'

No doubt Mrs. Reiser's preference for Greek would have appeared less remarkable to her husband, had he known that the Greek teacher at that time was a young man of a pleasantly saturnine countenance.

'Making fun of my old school,' said Mrs. Reiser dreamily and she peeled off one glove and waved it in front of her breast in the way she had used to flirt her fan at the balls of her girlhood.

'But I like the school,' said Franciska.

'Then, why did you do it?' and the beautiful Mrs. Reiser tapped with her glove on Franciska's cheek; a gesture that would have warmed most men's hearts, but was wasted on the young girl.

Why indeed? The headmaster had not asked her because he had been preoccupied with his own plight. Feldman had not asked her either, because he knew too much about human nature; he had realized that her poem was not directed as a protest against the school but at something quite different. In his crude way he might have expressed it by saying: 'She hit the sack and meant the donkey.' Why indeed? She could not tell clearly herself. She could only see the core of her humiliation. She saw Ling, facing her across the coffee table; his cold look while he sorted out the coins in his hand and gave a tip to the waiter. She saw Feldman's eyes and his fingers, distorted behind the blue glass of the bowl; the rose leaf wiped off on the tablecloth.

'I don't know,' she said. It was true. She did not know at this moment. She only knew that, whatever explanations she might give, she could never admit that she had been taken in by Ling and ill used.

'Very well. Don't tell me. Keep it to yourself,' said Mrs. Reiser. Her smile still played round her lips but her eyes were peevish. She was not annoyed because the young girl had withheld the information she had asked for, she was not really interested. What annoyed her was, that anyone could be recalcitrant face to face with all her charm and beauty. As though to reassure herself, she turned her smile to her son, who smiled back at her.

Later on that day she told her husband of her encounter.

'I should not have asked her,' he said, rubbing his hands cautiously. 'One never knows how one can get involved. But I should like to know something more about it myself just the same. This poem was a brilliant coup, brilliantly timed.'

'Really? I never thought of it in that way. And how can it be a coup?'

'But don't you see? It comes just at the time of the coal strike when there is so much ill feeling already. And that links up with this other business——' he stopped to rub his hands and placed them behind his back.

Mrs. Reiser knew this gesture. It meant that her husband was going to start a lecture on some issues touching the Government and the State. She dreaded his prolixity. She left the room with the pretence of seeing if Kurti had got his supper.

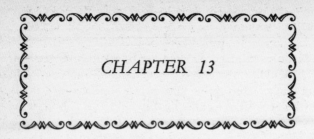

CHAPTER 13

THE NEXT few days, until her mother's return, were spent by Franciska mainly at home.

Ill luck brings isolation. The flat had become to her a fortress doomed to be sacked and any persons entering it, were bound to bring bad news. Whenever the telephone rang, she asked the maids to answer it.

She was forced to tell Louise that she was in disgrace at school and would have to stay away for some time. The maid had already heard some rumours, from sources which she did not specify. To Franciska's surprise, she took the young girl's side and showed herself indignant about the headmaster's attitude. Like so many soured, dutiful people, Louise had a wonderful capacity for loyalty. Grievous happenings especially brought out her staunchness, because they satisfied the bitterness inherent in her nature and filled her with a satisfaction all the keener since it was not marred by envy.

Sylva called, blazing and belligerent in her coat of tiger skin. She regaled the young girl with a story of a man, who, after beholding her crossing into Foch street, had followed her all down the Weinberge to press his advances: 'I get to the museum, never looking right nor left and the miserable worm still crawling behind me.' She took a deep breath while rolling a strand of Franciska's hair round the tongs, with a baleful expression, hinting that the worst was yet to come.

'But, Sylva, how could you tell, if you didn't look round?'

'One can always tell. He was lecherous down to his footsteps.'

She withdrew the tongs, laid them down and took up another pair from the spirit lamp where they had been heating. 'I get to the statue and see a policeman standing by the horse. So I go up to him and I say – after all, that's what he is there for – so I say, Look here, there is a man following me and he's making a nuisance of himself. So the police looks me up and down and I think to myself, Never mind how much he looks me up and down, I'm not one of those women, I don't care, and then——' and the hairdresser raised her head and looked in the mirror in front of her, as though wanting to watch herself in her moment of tragedy re-lived – 'then he pinches me in the cheek and says: And I don't blame him either. That's men for you. The republic will come to a bad end with all this debauchery going on.'

She put the tongs down, applied the brush and arranged Franciska's hair in three vertical curls on each side of the face.

'You look lovely and sleek now,' she said. 'The black hair and the black dress. Quite Spanish. They say the King of Spain too goes about pinching women, and not in the cheeks of the face either.'

'Would you have minded, Sylva, if it had been the King of Spain?' asked Franciska.

The hairdresser laughed with contempt. 'Pinching is pinching, all the world over, Cissy. It's disgusting. And then, with the police, I would not have minded so much if it had been in a room, but it was in public. The way the men run loose in this town. They'd have to build a roof over the whole of Prague to make it decent.' She raised the lamp and blew the flame out.

Franciska had listened to the tale with enjoyment, like one listens to descriptions of exotic countries which one will never visit. She did not connect the men figuring in Sylva's stories with any men she might ever meet, any more than a person who takes a walk in a wood in Europe expects to come upon a tiger. According to Mrs. Kalny, such incidents only happened to menials, never to women of her own set: 'Men are very sensitive. They know exactly with whom they can try it on and with whom they can't.'

For similar reasons the young girl did not bother to examine the laws of decency as laid down by the hairdresser. As they would not have applied in her own case, she accepted them unquestioningly as part of the servants' turn of mind, just as she had turned away from the display of cheap silks in the shop window, after the first glance.

She laughed. And then, suddenly the knowledge of her guilt pierced her with a fresh, renewed sharpness as always happens when a grief, forgotten for a moment, returns to the heart.

Sylva left without making any allusions to the disgrace; either out of delicacy, or because she was too much taken up with her own adventures. To her own surprise, Franciska resented the hairdresser's silence.

'She cannot understand that sort of thing,' she told herself. 'She could only understand if I had been caught cuddling with one of the teachers.' For she had already begun to lie to herself about what had happened. The thoughts about 'cuddling' which she blamed on to the hairdresser, had not been absent from her own mind before and during her meeting with Ling in the coffee house and during her talks with Susy.

There are women, who, after having failed with a man, will rather blame him for impotence than blame themselves for lack of attraction and ability to rouse him. The women in such cases are always unattractive and unsure of themselves. Franciska was not unattractive but she was inexperienced, and therefore unsure of herself. She was willing to admit having intentionally betrayed her own school and her own society rather than to disclose the true motives of her connexion with Ling.

Already she chose to forget how he had bored her while talking about the patricians and the workers, and how she had revived at once as soon as he had praised her poem and in doing so, had shown an interest in herself and herself only. Her tragedy, as she imagined it, lay in the fact that he had flattered her in order to wheedle the poem out of her, knowing full well the disastrous fruit it would bear. She could not deny this. But in order to allay her deepest humiliation, she retained the pattern of the truth, but changed its colours. She denied to herself the thoughts of 'cuddling' and replaced them by feelings of contempt for her school and her friends, feelings which, until now, she had never experienced. She pretended to herself that she had always been critical of the school, had expressed this in the poem and had simply been fooled by Ling as to the consequences of her criticism.

She had quailed at Feldman's crudeness when he had advised her to 'get a nice young man. Get yourself two or three', as a remedy for her distress. Also, she had failed to see the link between the poem and the 'nice young man', because she did not allow herself to see it.

The forces of 'cuddling' were stronger and deeper within

her than any other feelings. Like all emotions, they wore many masks. Before she had written the poem, she had been too blind to recognize them; now that she could have recognized them, she refused to do so. In this lay her real tragedy.

CHAPTER 14

MRS. KALNY returned on Saturday, dressed in mourning and with a short black veil on her hat. 'Those long, trailing crapes are impossible,' she said. 'They destroy the whole line of one's dress.'

She was full of complaints as to the inefficiency of the dressmakers in Merano, but there was no strong indignation in her voice; she knew, as she said, that in a case of sudden death one has to bear one's cross with resignation.

'The main thing with black is to make up more vividly,' she told her daughter. 'And don't forget your ears. You must put rouge on the ear lobes, that's very important. You can't yet, you'll have to stay pale. But remember it for life.'

'Yes, Mama,' said Franciska.

'Your hands are a sight. Didn't you have the manicurist while I was away?'

'She did not turn up. So I did not send for her.'

'Funny. Why didn't she? Is she ill or what?' said Mrs. Kalny and without waiting for a reply she told Louise to bring out a certain black dress from the dressing room and to see if it could be altered.

Franciska had never thought that the manicurist might be ill. She had taken her absence – and quite rightly – as a further proof of the spread of the scandal and of her guilt in the eyes of society. Sylva had called, but she was of an inde-

113

pendent nature. The manicurist had been afraid to enter a house which, for all she knew, might be ostracized by her other patrons. There are always people who act as barometers in the social climate and the manicurist was one of them.

Franciska, after walking home on Monday afternoon from her lunch with Feldman had expected to find herself in the middle of a storm of indignation, curiosity, abuse and reproaches. Instead, she met with silence from all sides, which showed that people considered her beneath abuse. She imagined that everyone she knew was against her. She did not realize that this was the case in a very few instances only and that most of her friends and acquaintances had merely withdrawn because they were cautious and afraid of compromising themselves. What hurt her most in this respect was that her closest friends, like Susy Graber and a few others, had not made any attempt to get in touch with her.

The reason for this lay mainly in their age and partly in Franciska's good looks. Had Franciska provoked the same sort of scandal a few years earlier, at, say, fourteen, or at a much later stage in her life, she would have found loyalty and support among some of her friends. But one cannot expect to find friendship where the spirit of competition is prevalent and in a small and exclusive circle, made up of girls of nearly marriageable age, there can be no question of loyalty. In a few months' time, after the matriculation, all mutual friendliness was bound to vanish and school mates would be turned into rivals in the space of time required to put on a ball dress and long white gloves. Had Franciska been dull and plain, there might have been a chance for her being re-admitted into her circle. As it was, there was none.

The evening meal was the first occasion when Franciska

and her mother were alone together. Mrs. Kalny talked in a desultory fashion between courses, mainly in a wailing tone of voice.

'We shall have to give up the car and the chauffeur. There is no sense keeping it on, now.'

The young girl knew that this was absurd, as Mr. Kalny himself had never used the car and always went on foot.

After the fruit had been put on the table and the servants had left the room, Mrs. Kalny said: 'It's no good your asking me any questions, Cissy. I have not seen the lawyer properly yet. But I don't think you should go on with your riding lessons. It's very hard luck on you. But I can't help it.'

'Are we going to be hard up, Mama?'

'I don't think so. Not really.'

'Then why can't I go on with my riding?'

'Because people would think that we were living above our means.'

'But they did not think so before?'

'Oh, leave me alone, Cissy. You don't understand.'

Mrs. Kalny fell silent. The young girl could not grasp the meaning of her mother's words. She did not know that her father, shortly before his death, had withdrawn most of his capital from his business and had tied it up in such a way, that it would benefit his family and be inaccessible to his creditors. This was why Mrs. Kalny had implied that from now on, they would have to appear less well off than they really were.

'But we shall be all right, Mama?'

'Yes, of course. They have got a new junior partner at the lawyer's office. He is very presentable and he is very keen on sports, but not too athletic, thank God. Don't ever go to bed with an athletic man, Cissy. They look very good but all their strength goes into sports and there is nothing left over. Remember this for life.'

'Yes, Mama.'

The fruit was taken away and the cloth was changed. They remained seated at the table. The young girl pushed back her chair, so that she was outside the circle of light thrown by the lamp.

'They had beautiful apples in Merano,' remarked Mrs. Kalny. She suppressed a yawn.

'Mama,' said Franciska, 'You will be terribly angry with me.'

'Oh, God. Yes, I'm sure, I will be very angry. Now tell me, I shan't bite your head off.'

'I've got myself into a dreadful mess.'

To Franciska's surprise, her mother dropped her wailing voice and said quickly and calmly: 'With Ling?'

'Yes. How did you guess?'

Mrs. Kalny moved one shoulder impatiently and bit her lip.

'You are a fool. You might have waited another year or so. It's no good getting married and thinking you'll have some fun because you won't.'

'It's nothing to do with marriage.'

'Better and better. What do you expect? If you throw yourself away.'

'But I didn't, Mama.'

'Well, what did you do? You must have done something. You did not read the Bible together did you?'

'It's nothing like that, Mama. I only met him once and——'

'Once is quite enough. You'd be surprised how much damage can be done in two minutes. Now, for Heaven's sake tell me, I shan't bite your head off, I've told you before.'

116

'I will tell you, if only you will let me talk,' cried Franciska. 'I met him in a coffee house, that's all.'

'What do you call a coffee house?' asked Mrs. Kalny coldly.

'A coffee house. With tables – and – and coffee.'

'Don't shout,' said Mrs. Kalny. 'Look,' she continued and brought her chair nearer to the table. 'Don't get into a panic. It's too soon yet to tell anything, but what has been done can be undone.'

'I didn't do anything, Mama, he didn't touch me. He did not even kiss my hand.'

'That's not surprising. He never had any manners,' and Mrs. Kalny lost the alert look in her eyes and leaned back in the chair.

'Well?' she asked in a tired voice 'What are you complaining about? Be thankful he did not seduce you. He'd be rotten in bed, in any case; bad manners and a tortured soul. It does not make for good love making.'

'There was never any question of that – that sort of thing. We only talked – about a poem.'

'About a poem,' repeated Mrs. Kalny. Then she pretended to grow indignant to hide her relief. 'Please, Cissy, do me a favour and compose yourself. I don't know what we are talking about.'

Franciska began to weep tears of exasperation. The way in which her mother misunderstood her, was more unbearable to her than any reproaches would have been, because her mother's attitude echoed Franciska's own hopes before her disillusionment.

'Don't play injured innocence with me,' said Mrs. Kalny and, as with this, she came very near the truth, Franciska's tears increased.

'This is getting a bore,' said Mrs Kalny. 'What do you

want me to do? Have you fallen in love with him and do you expect me to do anything about it? I shan't, you know. I would not dream of it.'

'Mama is as bad as Sylva,' thought Franciska. 'She cannot think of anything else.' Her indignation stopped her tears and, as Mrs. Kalny seemed to have fallen into a distracted silence, she was at last able to say what she had carefully prepared in her mind.

Mrs. Kalny listened with her head thrown back, so that the upper part of her face lay in darkness, while the light of the lamp lay full on her mouth and chin. It looked to Franciska as though she were wearing one of those short velvet masks that are to be seen on prints depicting the life of eighteenth-century Venice. And whether it was that this fancy made her mother appear to her heartless and frivolous, or whether her mother's countenance really expressed such emotions, the young girl felt chilled with this apparent withdrawal while at the same time her fear of receiving a chiding vanished. By the time she stopped talking, she felt that her mother had so completely forsaken her that there could be no question of any rebuke for what she had done, because one can only chide others for what one might have done oneself. When the deed of others is outside one's own capacity of action, one cannot work up any anger over it.

Mrs. Kalny asked to be shown the poem and scrutinized it with the same face with which she used to examine the cook's expense book; it was a face which showed a pretence of faith and a certainty of finding deceit.

'That's entirely your own affair,' she said at last. 'If the headmaster won't let you go to school, I don't blame him. And if your school friends cut you, I don't blame them either. Nobody likes being made to look a fool.'

'But they are fools,' said Franciska. 'And silly.'

'Possibly,' said Mrs. Kalny. 'But you don't like being cut, do you? Either you think they are silly and then you don't care what they do, or you do care, and then you have no right to think they are silly.'

This had not occurred to Franciska before. She could not protest. She could not say, not even to herself: 'I never wanted to criticize them. I only wanted to please Ling, and to rouse his interest.'

'What am I to do now?' she asked.

'I don't know,' said Mrs. Kalny. 'I have no idea.' She added: 'We shall see,' and rose from the table. 'I must go to bed now,' she said. 'I shall start receiving to-morrow. Send me Louise, will you?'

She left the room without saying good night or giving her daughter time to do so.

When Mrs. Kalny had left the dining room she had already made up her mind about Franciska's future, but she preferred to keep silent about it in order to avoid a scene. Already before the young girl had finished her story, Mrs. Kalny had assembled in her head the assets and debits of the situation.

While Louise put away her mistress's clothes, stuck trees in the shoes and stuffed the empty handbag with a ball of tissue paper, Mrs. Kalny sat down in front of the winged looking-glass, dressed only in her nightgown. This was a garment without sleeves and cut very low round the arms and in front, so that it showed the cleft which marks the rise of the breasts and a good deal of the breasts, when looked at from the side. Below the belt, delicate seams were arranged like the ribs of a leaf in such a way that they met in a pointed angle in the middle and underlined the shape of the thighs. The nightgown was not made of transparent stuff; this would have been indecent, in Mrs. Kalny's opinion. In fact, the nightgown allowed for as much indecency as was possible within the frame of decency.

Mrs. Kalny raised her arms to take the combs out of her hair. She did this slowly; all she wanted to do was to look at herself, but in the presence of her maid she had to pretend to some activity.

She thought, as always, when she contemplated the reflection of herself in becoming undress: 'What a dreadful waste. What a pity that no man can see me just now, just like this.' She always expressed her thoughts in the same words and they were words which did not express her feelings accurately. What she really felt, was something like: 'I wish I could go to bed with a man to-night. And I should, it is my right to do it; I am so desirable.'

Instead of admitting to herself her sensuality she thus denied it and shifted her desires on to the plane of mere vanity and nothing else, by implying that beauty such as hers should not waste away unseen. Furthermore, by thinking the way she did, she pretended to herself that she had no desire at all; she was merely considering the interests of an imaginary man who was wronged by being deprived of the sight of so much beauty.

She opened a drawer and looked inside it. 'Louise,' she said, 'I can't find my hairbrush.'

'It's been washed, Madam,' said the maid. 'I put it away to dry.'

While she left the room to fetch the brush, Mrs. Kalny, glad to have a moment's privacy, raised herself in her chair, turned her back towards the mirror and looked at herself in the glass with her head twisted over one shoulder. 'What a waste' she said to herself again. 'No *décolleté*, no *grande toilette* this season.'

She dropped into the chair and the charming softness

which, up till then, had dwelled in her eyes, gave way to a cold, matter of-fact expression. 'And no big balls for Cissy either. It's very bad, her losing a whole season like this. And yet, what with this business, it's just as well that she is in mourning. It makes it look so natural. Nobody will be able now to cut her at the balls because she won't be there to be cut. Strange, I never thought I would be grateful for mourning etiquette, but there it is.'

Lost in thought, she seized a comb and began to draw it in a zig-zag across the glass top of the table. 'It's the balls that matter and they are lost in any case. I could take her to theatres and concerts, of course, after the first six weeks are over; that would be quite in order. But that's no good to her, she won't meet anybody eligible in the theatre. And what if people start cutting me too, because she is with me? I don't think they would. But they might.'

The maid entered, put a peignoir round Mrs. Kelny's shoulders and began to brush her hair.

'It's a dreadful business, this to-do about the poem,' wailed Mrs. Kalny. Now that she had made up her mind, she could afford again to be the vague, moody woman, adorably scatterbrained.

'Very bad, Madam,' assented Louise.

'And the whole thing is so unnecessary. What makes it so bad is that it will all fall back on me. People will think I encouraged her to write it. They'll think we are a house full of – of revolutionaries.' And Mrs. Kalny fluttered her eye-lids, while she pronounced the word 'revolutionary' as though it were the name of a disease with which she was unacquainted but knew to be dreadful. 'And I cannot do anything about it, can I, Louise? If I stand up for her, they'll only accuse me too. Besides, why should I? There is no sense in it, is there, Louise?'

'No sense in it at all, Madam,' replied Louise gravely.

At the beginning, when Franciska had told her about the calamity, the maid had considered the business not only as an outrage to the whole Kalny family, but she had also been full of pity towards the young girl. Now, as Mrs. Kalny wriggled under the brush and twisted her fingers as though to make it quite clear to any observer how maternal feelings and social considerations wriggled and twisted in her brain, Louise had no qualms whatsoever in changing her attitude. Loyal she was and loyal she remained. The main thing was to be loyal, it did not matter very much to whom. So, without even knowing that she had become a turncoat, Louise repeated: 'No sense at all, Madam,' abandoned Franciska and stepped, loyal that she was, into Mrs. Kalny's camp.

'I think I'll send her to Vienna for the winter,' began Mrs. Kalny with a pretty look of resignation. 'Or Paris? Paris is more expensive. But then she could live with my aunt and that would be cheap. In Vienna, she could stay with my cousins but they are hard up and I'd have to pay them. It's all so difficult. I really don't know what to do.'

'It's very hard on you, Madam,' said Louise. She felt gratified that she was the first person to be told of Mrs. Kalny's decision.

'Yes, isn't it? I shall miss her, of course. But then, what can I do? I can't keep her here any more than I can keep a mad dog in the place. What if she starts talking at one of my parties? The sort of thing she picked up from Ling. No, no, Louise. I know all about it. Workers of the world unite but not in my flat.'

Mrs. Kalny, while bearing in mind Vienna and Paris, was not really worried about expenses. Being worried about money matters was merely a gesture assumed with her new widowhood, an indication that new responsibilities had been placed upon her shoulders. She had genuinely worried about money matters before her husband's death. But now, being reassured about her financial position, she had taken on the rôle of the helpless and charming woman who cannot cope with life. It was a rôle which she had begun to assume for the benefit of the junior partner in her lawyer's office, and being too experienced to trust to improvizations she rehearsed it already in front of the maid. This was good sense. Her cook too, always tried out a new dish before a dinner party.

'It's very difficult. I don't want her to miss anything,' said Mrs. Kalny. She mused. 'If I send her to Paris, she'll have a gayer time, Louise, than in Vienna. Do you think I should send her to Paris?'

'Not that she deserves it, Madam. But then, you are only young once.'

Mrs. Kalny nodded.

'You are almost too kind, Madam.'

Mrs. Kalny sighed. Her eyes, softened a few moments ago by the part she had acted, became cold again. 'Yes, she'll have a gayer time in Paris,' she repeated with a frown. 'And she should have a gay time, Louise. She will be missing all the important balls as it is.'

The maid assented gravely, filled with her own importance of being taken into her mistress's confidence. A gay time was a serious thing indeed and no trifling matter. Being a lady's maid, she knew better than most people how little gaiety and how much hard work went into what is called 'having a gay time'; before, during and after it.

Mrs. Kalny, on the other hand, who had used the expression 'gay time' so repeatedly, was not thinking of gaiety either. To her, it meant the marriage market. She had lived long enough to know that social pleasures, especially for young people, can be a source of humiliation and anxiety. If her daughter enjoyed them, all the better, because animation would increase her good looks and with it, her attraction. Apart from this, Mrs. Kalny did not care whether Franciska enjoyed balls and other gatherings or not, just as she did not care whether her daughter enjoyed having her hair dressed and her nails manicured. It was part of one's duties, that was all.

Yet, if one listened to Mrs. Kalny, she was not a marriage fanatic. Just as, in the Bible, one can find quotations for and against any human activity, so Mrs. Kalny's talk contained at different times good arguments for and against marriage. She would have been exceedingly angry if, as she had imagined for one moment, Franciska had wanted to become engaged to Ling. On an occasion like this, when the man in question was undesirable, she could be very convincing in reasoning against marriage. On the other hand, had there been a chance of an exceptionally good match, Mrs. Kalny would not have hesitated to push her daughter into marriage at the age of, say, sixteen. She would have said something like: 'The sooner you marry, the better. If you marry young, it's much easier to get used to it.' Whereas in the case of Ling she would have said: 'Why this tearing hurry? Do you think you are missing something? Do you think it's pleasant seeing the same man day in day out? You'll get there soon enough, believe me.'

CHAPTER 15

A WEEK AFTER her return from Merano, Mrs. Kalny
received a letter from Franciska's school, together with a
communication from the Ministry of Education.

The mail always arrived at eight in the morning. But as
this was a registered letter, it was delivered at eleven o'clock,
just as Mrs. Kalny was getting ready to go out. She had an
appointment at her dressmaker's and was already late.

She read the two documents quickly, put them on her
lap and, placing one hand lightly over them, began to file
a chipped nail on her ring finger.

'There you are,' she said to Franciska, who stood by the
window. 'You are out of it, altogether. No, don't take the
letters, leave them where they are, or I'll get my dress
dusty. Really, Cissy, you are terribly thoughtless. I hope
you will learn one day.'

She put on her hat and said: 'They are thorough at the
Ministry, I must say. Imagine writing out this endless list
of schools and colleges where you can't be accepted. Not
that it cost them anything, of course. But they had to put it
in with the headmaster's letter to save stamp duty, I suppose.
I did not know they were as bankrupt as this. No wonder
death duties are as enormous as they are.' And while she
buttoned her coat and surveyed herself in the mirror,
fluffing out the veil and smoothing a curl, she added:

'Perhaps, I should have gone and seen them personally. It might have done some good,' and she left, after having thus paid herself an oblique compliment on her looks.

Neither she nor Franciska realized that the letter itself constituted an act of mercy on the part of the authorities and was entirely due to Feldman's talk with the Minister. Originally, it had been intended to expel the young girl ceremoniously, in front of the assembled pupils and staff of the school. This had been planned not out of cruelty but in order to lend the weight of pomp to the decision.

Franciska, once alone, took the papers, returned to the window and began to read. She did not get very far. The letters fell from her trembling fingers, all the blood left her face and she had to bend down to pick them up again.

Louise, who had seen her mistress moved to tears over a singed petticoat and raised to fury over a lukewarm bath, greatly admired Mrs. Kalny's behaviour on this occasion; she took it for restraint. And when the maid praised Mrs. Kalny's kindness and composure, and the young girl cut her short, she was shocked at this display of ingratitude.

To bar a young person from all further education is, on its own plane, as irrevocable an action as to cut off someone's head. Franciska was never to forgive her mother for the utter flippancy she had shown when dealing with a major crisis in her daughter's life, dealing with it, as she had, between buttoning her coat and putting on her hat.

Although Franciska was not to receive compassion from any quarter, she was, at least, on one occasion, treated with the respect accorded to guilt and not with the disregard accorded to a nuisance. Two days before she was due to leave, Uncle Victor rang up and invited Franciska to dinner.

'Your daughter has become a celebrity,' he said to Mrs. Kalny who had answered the telephone. 'But I suppose

that's no consolation to you. It's not the right kind of celebrity, is it?'

'Not exactly,' replied Mrs. Kalny.

'Still, it's something. It's quite an achievement. It's not
everyone's daughter who can provoke a Government crisis.
She will go far if she does that sort of thing at eighteen.'

Mrs. Kalny, who did not think for one moment that he
was speaking the truth, regarded this remark as a joke in
the worst possible taste, and cut him short with: 'At what
time do you want her to come?'

'About eight o'clock, if that will suit your daughter. We
must consider her now. She is not just anybody, she is
somebody. It is really a pity that you are banishing her from
our midst, but I daresay you have no choice. Celebrities
are never comfortable to have in one's home.'

'Will you see her home or shall I send a maid to fetch
her?' asked Mrs. Kalny. 'I have given up the car.'

'I shall see her home. I shall look upon it as a privilege.
I never thought I'd be the member of a distinguished
family.'

He rang off.

There is always tension between maternal and paternal
relatives and Mrs. Kalny, who already despised Victor and
Hilda for their lack of sophistication, resented Victor's last
remark to her on the telephone. Victor was related to her
late husband's family and had, in Mrs. Kalny's opinion,
never paid due homage to her own people. That he should
now seize upon a schoolgirl scandal as a claim to distinction,
in order to make it clear that there had been none before,
cut her to the quick.

'Victor and Hilda have asked you to dinner for to-morrow
night,' she said to her daughter.

'At what time are we going, Mama?'

127

'I am not going. They didn't ask me. I am not distinguished enough for them. They have only invited you. They think you are very clever. I am glad that you have impressed somebody at last.'

'I am not going, Mama. Why should I? They are frightful. Last time I was there, they put my napkin in a ring to keep it for me till I should come again.'

Mrs. Kalny laughed. She seemed to be delighted. 'That's your father's family. You should be proud of it. No, you'd better go. I've accepted for you.'

'Mama.'

'You go by all means. And enjoy it. You deserve nothing better. That's the worst of an indiscretion. The right people cut you and the wrong people are all over you. Perhaps you will ask me next time, before you make friends with impossible creatures like Ling. Now you see what it leads to.'

The following night Franciska went to the dinner party. She was shown into the small, dark and narrow room that served as sitting room. Apart from herself, there was another guest, a Dr. Rieger, a bald man of uncertain age. She was given a glass of bad sherry.

Aunt Hilda entered, rather flushed, and greeted her.

'When do we eat?' asked Uncle Victor.

'In a moment.'

'What, isn't it ready yet?' asked Uncle Victor. He was in great good humour, trying to look petulant like a domestic tyrant.

Aunt Hilda responded at once, by throwing her head back, planting her feet well apart and putting her hands on her hips, a posture assumed by the market women before they start to quarrel. She screeched in imitation of the popular way of speech: 'What is ready? Nothing is ready. When I say ready, then it's ready. Now it's ready. R-e-a-d-y. Ready.'

After this, she relaxed and both she and her husband broke into prolonged laughter. Franciska forced a smile. Dr. Rieger raised one corner of his mouth and looked into his glass.

'This is going to be delightful,' said the young girl to herself.

Like her mother, she loathed any kind of homely joke alluding to domestic labour such as getting a meal ready. In Mrs. Kalny's house and in the houses of her friends no lady ever appeared to be in any way responsible for any household duties. The very thought that Aunt Hilda was helping to prepare the dinner was as shocking to the young girl as it would have been to see a stage manager giving directions during a play in the theatre in full view of the audience.

They went into the dining room.

'Let's give the celebrity some soup,' said Uncle Victor. 'It's an excellent soup. We eat like this every day.' Again, husband and wife went into fits of laughter.

Franciska quailed. No one in her mother's set would have ever made a remark about the food, be it praising or denigrating.

Yet, although the napkin in the ring was laid by her plate, although the soup tasted of bottled beef extract and the pineapple was tinned and not fresh, she was, as it turned out, not sorry that her mother had accepted the invitation for her.

'No, but seriously, Cissy,' said Uncle Victor. 'Joking apart. We were quite shaken by the whole business.'

'Not more than Miss Kalny herself, no doubt,' said Dr. Rieger.

'We don't approve, of course,' continued Uncle Victor. 'But I must say, just the same, all due respect. I've got to be fair. Your opinions aren't my opinions and so we shan't discuss that side of the question, but I've got to take my hat off to you for your courage. I said to you at first, on that Sunday, you remember, I said you were stupid. But, of course, I did not then know anything of the facts. And you yourself never said a word.'

'Perhaps Miss Kalny did not know the facts either,' remarked Dr. Rieger.

Franciska blushed, while her aunt and uncle behaved as though he had made a brilliant joke. She raised her eyes and looked at Dr. Rieger, who was seated opposite her. It was impossible to tell from his countenance whether he had intended to make a joke or whether he had spoken seriously. Their eyes met; his frosty and ironical, hers more uneasy than she realized.

She thought: 'In a way his eyes are as unpleasant as Feldman's. But with Feldman one feels that he penetrates and sees all. With him, it's as though he could, but does not want to. I wonder what he is.'

'Of course I could not help thinking that you were stupid, could I,' continued Uncle Victor. 'For instance that bit about the central heating. I said to Hilda afterwards, Why on earth does Ling publish that sort of thing? Is he a plumber or what? But then you see, I had my head screwed on the right way after all, because I noticed it straight away. The other bits I did not even mention, did I, Hilda?'

Again, the hot blood rose in Franciska's cheeks.

Uncle Victor, who thought that he had offended her, said: 'You can't expect everybody to jump to the right conclusions at once. And the St. Stephen's business was not advertised either, you can rely on that. Because you knew it, it does not mean that everybody knew. And I still say that the poem as such wasn't any good. It's no good getting stuck up about it. You only cashed in because you saw from which side the wind was blowing.'

The young girl listened, avoiding her uncle's eyes. The conversation reminded her of the so-called 'blank' map of Bohemia, Moravia and Silesia, which used to be brought out in geography lessons and on which towns were marked as circles but without names and all other aids to identification, such as rivers, mountains and railway lines were omitted.

Dr. Rieger said: 'Perhaps Miss Kalny would prefer not to talk about it.'

'Why not?' asked Uncle Victor. 'If she doesn't mind creating a scandal and being thrown out from every school there is, why should she turn coy all of a sudden?'

'Dr. Rieger is quite right. I'd rather not talk about it, Uncle Victor.'

'You are a funny girl, I must say. You are becoming as slippery as your father. Whenever I asked him about investments, he told me something and then the next time I met him, he would say that he had never said anything and that if he had said anything, he had not said that particular thing, and if he had said that particular thing, he had not meant it.'

'Perhaps the market had changed in the meantime,' said Dr. Rieger.

Uncle Victor glanced at him resentfully. He had, like everybody else, always tried to pick Mr. Kalny's brain, had blamed him when the advice given had been wrong, and congratulated himself on his own astuteness when the advice had turned out to be profitable.

'Have you heard the explanation about the new Stock Exchange?' he asked Dr. Rieger. 'As you know there are four allegorical figures above the entrance. What do they represent? The five senses. But there are only four? Taste is lacking.'

They rose from the table. Over coffee, the talk continued about some of the recent buildings in the town. The new Union Bank was mentioned, with its lavish façade of pink marble and the new building of the Ministry of Railways by the river, which illustrated all the styles the architect had ever studied. After this, inevitably, the two men began to discuss the other ventures of the new Republic; while Franciska moved her chair nearer to that of her aunt and gave distracted answers to her questions about servants and dressmakers. From time to time she glanced across the room, where Dr. Rieger was listening to her uncle. It did not surprise her that Uncle Victor was talking to his guest without trying to include his wife and niece in the conversation. This, she told herself with contempt, was only a further proof of her uncle's 'impossibility' and fitted in with the napkin ring and the jokes about the food. The keeping apart of the sexes during parties was considered in the Kalny household to be a sign of provincialism and lack of *savoir faire* and the hostess who allowed it to happen was not worth her salt.

She began to wonder whether Dr. Rieger realized the 'frightfulness' of his hosts. She imagined that he did.

Her uncle and aunt were both tall and narrow, with long, mild faces. Looking at them they reminded her of the pictures of a modern Italian painter, just then very much in fashion, whose portraits had all elongated faces, out of proportion, empty, and unsatisfactory. Seen beside them, Dr. Rieger's features appeared mature and finished like the drawing of an old master. 'I wonder who he is' she thought again.

At ten o'clock Franciska rose and said that she had to go.

Dr. Rieger, as though he had been waiting for this move, broke off in the middle of a sentence and asked whether he could see her home.

It was a dark night, cold and calm. The gates of the Chotek Palace Gardens were already closed; on the other side of the river the windows of the theatre were only dimly lit.

'I wonder,' said Franciska, 'what they are playing to-night, and whether it is still going on. Or is it already lights out after the performance?'

'It is the *Bartered Bride*, no doubt. What else could they play? And in that case the bride is still being bartered and will continue to be so for another half hour. I should think that by now they have got to the sextet in the third act.'

'You seem to know it by heart.'

'Don't we all, Miss Kalny? But the unimaginable may yet happen and they may have to stop playing it for—who knows?—perhaps a whole month. *Horribile dictu* or should one say *mirabile dictu?*'

'Why?' asked Franciska. 'I thought they could never get enough of it.'

'It would not be from choice, of course. But they may have to close down, if the coal strike goes on.'

'Really,' said Franciska. 'I did not know there was one on. Is it as bad as all that?'

'Some people think so. Are you tired, Miss Kalny?'

'Not at all.'

'Then what do you say if we continue on this side, past the new bridge and cross over by the Karls bridge? There are always cabs on the other side.'

'I should like that.'

He said: 'You cannot be as bad as people think you are. Because you still seem to have kept your guardian angel.'

'I don't know what you mean.'

'Don't you? I meant that it was fortunate that we did not have this conversation in your uncle's house.'

'What have I said? Have I said anything wrong?'

'Not as far as I am concerned. You have rather pleased me by what you said. I am still vain enough to be pleased when my theories are confirmed. Now I can say that I knew it all along. Can't I? And as we have got as far as this already, will you admit that you did not know what happened at St. Stephen's?'

'I knew that something happened.'

'Because your uncle mentioned it to-night? That doesn't count. Don't be ashamed. Tell me.'

'The headmaster drivelled something when he told me off. But I did not know what he meant.'

'And you didn't wonder, Miss Kalny?'

'I did. But not very much. I could not see what it had to do with me. I thought he was just drivelling.'

He said: 'Drivelling. He did not drivel any more than the members of Parliament drivelled, when they discussed the case.'

'Oh!' said Franciska. She said this sullenly and without the curiosity and wonder he had expected her to show. Ever since that Monday, that last day at school, she had learnt to expect nothing but unpleasantness from all those who talked about the matter. And not only unpleasantness; but something worse, which was yet in its way, a blessing: complete lack of understanding.

The school beadle had talked to her about the sale of his sausages, Matzka about the temporary teacher and old Miss Rehak about ill breeding; she was certain that the members of Parliament had talked about something different and yet of equally little concern to her.

134

He fell silent for a while, expecting her to ask for an explanation. Franciska did not speak.

Dr. Rieger thought that she was overwhelmed by what he had mentioned. He began to tell her what had happened. The coal strike had caused such a shortage of coal that most schools had run out of fuel. The pupils of St. Stephen's had decided to force the issue and proclaimed that they would walk out of the school and not return to it until it was heated. On that day, the headmaster, together with fifteen of the teachers, placed himself at the bottom of the stairs forming a chain of linked arms, hoping vainly, that this would stop the exit of the children. In two minutes the five hundred pupils stormed the living barricade and were gone.

The inability of the staff at St. Stephen's to maintain discipline caused grave anxiety not only at the Ministry of Education, but in other high places as well. The children's gesture of defiance was interpreted as a sign of the spreading of the political unrest which had caused the coal strike.

This, in itself, would have been bad enough, all the more as it was impossible to make a scapegoat out of five hundred school children. Franciska's school was the only school in the town which was not State supported, but run by private subscriptions. Thus, having much more money at their disposal, they had laid up large stocks of fuel and were in no way affected by the coal strike. Franciska's poem, stressing the by now notorious central heating, had drawn attention to the fact that money buys privilege, just at the time when the Government was trying to impress the people that although the coal strike was unfortunate, it was equally unfortunate for everybody and that the whole community was suffering the same hardships.

They were walking on the quay which runs parallel to

the isle of Kampa. The street lamps were so few that most of the time they walked in darkness. Dr. Rieger, as he talked, could not see that the young girl's eyes filled with tears, but he could hear the tears trembling in her voice when she said, 'So that is why he was so keen on the central heating.'

'You mean the editor to whom you showed the poem?'

'Yes.'

He said: 'And all the time you were just sick of your school the way most young people are and you just wanted to be funny at the school's expense?'

He thought that his words had revealed to her the full extent of her guilt and he thought that her tears were the confession of it. They were, but not in the way that he imagined. His explanation had not taught Franciska anything new, it had only proved to her what she already knew: Ling had made ill use of her. Now she saw why.

'I guessed all along that it was something like this,' he said. 'Strange, isn't it?'

Had she wanted to please him, she would have replied something like: 'Not strange at all, since you have a better brain than most people.' Instead of this, she merely assented and because Dr. Rieger felt that she had not paid due homage to his lucidity, he turned spiteful.

He said: 'All the others in Parliament took it for granted that you knew the whole time what you were doing. They thought you were very clever. Funny, isn't it?'

She did not reply. She did not care what unknown men thought about a young girl, unknown to them. Had he said: 'They saw you and they thought you were very attractive. Funny, isn't it?' she would have been offended.

He fell silent and Franciska, still taken up with her own shame, did not dare to look at him.

He drew a deep breath. 'What a terrible business!' he

said after what seemed to her a long time. 'It's the old old story. I have seen it happening over and over again. And you are not even innocent. Only ignorant. And like this, you slipped into it. Call it what you will, sin, guilt, betrayal, it comes to the same thing.'

Franciska said: 'You talk as though I had gone and sold my school for thirty pieces of silver.'

'That is exactly what you did.'

She said: 'How can you say such a thing? Yes, I know, I've done something wrong. But I did not mean to do it. If I had known it would come to this, I wouldn't have done it. Do you think I am as stupid as all that?'

'Yes. That is what I think. You are as stupid as all that. Of course, you did not mean to do anything like it. One never does. Do you really imagine that people go out of their house one morning, rub their hands and say: A fine day to-day, now I'm going out to sin? Do you really think for instance that Judas went and sold his master for thirty pieces of silver, because he wanted to betray him? Nothing like it, my poor girl. Judas was what one might call the cashier of that group and he was annoyed because Jesus was running up too many expenses with new robes and ointments and what have you. So what does he do? He wants to air his grievances and he talks to some people he meets. And he says more than he should have said. And so it came to pass. It always does.'

'Really? That's very interesting,' said Franciska. She said it without irony, quite politely, in the tone of voice she had used when visiting Vorel's studio and listening to the sculptor's explanations about his work. The betrayal of Jesus did not touch her any more than her betrayal of the school. And even if the thought occurred to her that the Government might seize upon the scandal as an excuse for taking over the school and thus destroying its old traditions, it did not trouble her very much.

The only words in Dr. Rieger's speech which had touched her, and touched her unpleasantly, were: 'My poor girl.' They sounded familiar, but not flatteringly so.

She glanced at him sideways. Under the wide brim of the hat his profile seemed sharper, smaller and meaner than it had done before. Also, as he walked beside her, she saw that he was hardly taller than she was. 'He must have very short legs and a long body,' she said to herself. 'And I suppose his baldness is his blessing. He looked quite distinguished in the room, with that high forehead and it wasn't really the forehead at all.'

He felt her eyes on him and turned his head towards her. 'Have I offended you?' he asked.

'No.'

He discerned the harshness in her voice. 'I have gone too far,' he thought. 'What right have I to preach to her? First I rescue her from the teeth of her uncle and then I set about her myself, and much worse.'

He said: 'I have been too hard on you. You must not take everything I say literally, you know. I was only trying to give you an illustration—to make things clearer to you.'

'Oh, quite, Dr. Rieger,' her voice sounded arrogant and bored.

'Poor little thing,' he thought. 'She is hurt. She is trying to sound indifferent. Oh, for the arrogance of youth.'

Had Franciska been able to read his thoughts, she might have replied: 'Oh, for the arrogance of age.' It was true, her voice had sounded bored, but simply because she was bored; there was no question of her being hurt. He could only have hurt her had he been able to penetrate to the core of her humiliation.

Dr. Rieger was so taken up with his own cleverness that he could not imagine that other people might not be impressed by it. It did not occur to him, that when people are impressed, it is mostly for reasons much more subtle, much more erratic and much more mysterious.

The young girl had just discovered for the first time in her life that some persons have the power to fascinate in certain conditions only. Thus, if Dr. Rieger had made his speech in a room, sitting down, and not wearing a hat, the fascination would have worked and Franciska would have been impressed by what he had to say. She did not fully understand this. She only knew that he had impressed her earlier on in the evening and that now he had ceased to do so.

They climbed up the stairs leading to the Karls bridge. It was so quiet that they could hear the lapping of the waves. It was a sound which Franciska had never heard before, because she had never before walked along the river at night. And just as there are sounds in a city which one only hears when the noise of the day has died down, so there are feelings which one can only fathom when the heart is at rest and untroubled by the clamour of the usual, everyday emotions. But this time had not yet come for Franciska. She did not allow herself to stop and to listen to that which flowed through her heart.

'A pity they don't illuminate the bridge properly,' she said. 'The statues would look splendid lit up, against the darkness.'

He smiled. 'It would be a splendid waste of fuel. You should know by now that it is a dangerous thing to throw light on darkness. Need I say more?'

They crossed the square formed by the façades of the Church of the Cross and the Church of St. Saviour, and turned to the right.

'We ought to get a cab any minute now,' he said.

CHAPTER 16

MRS. KALNY did not see her daughter off at the train.
Franciska saw in this negligence a further proof of her
mother's flippancy and felt lonely and resentful, as she drove
with Louise to the station. The maid's presence, instead of
being consoling, sharpened the poignancy of her loneliness.
She had always seen in Louise a sort of extension of her
mother and an unpleasant extension at that. And just as an
object left behind by a long-lost friend increases our sense of
loss, so the presence of the maid was an eloquent reminder
of Mrs. Kalny's callousness.

When one despises people, nothing they can do pleases,
not even their kindness. Franciska should have been touched
when she was met by Uncle Victor and Aunt Hilda on the
platform; instead, she considered them as merely a nuisance.

Louise was in an exceptionally soft mood, partly due to
the fact that she had been put in charge of the young girl,
and partly because leave-taking and departure are the visible
signs of the drama of life, and as such, like weddings and
funerals, are beloved by simple natures. She could have
said: 'Now, come along with me, Miss Cissy. I can't spare
you. It isn't that I mind seeing to your luggage and the
rest, but what's the good of my doing it, if you don't know
where I'm putting everything? You can speak to the lady
and the gentleman afterwards, if there is time.' Instead

of which she said: 'You go and speak to them, Miss Cissy. I'll fetch you when it's time,' and she turned away from the young girl and followed the porter.

Franciska looked after her; for a little while she could still hear the click of Louise's heels mingling with the rumble of the luggage trolley, echoing across the empty platform. She listened. And an inexplicable sadness filled her, that melancholy which comes when a part of our life draws to its close without our knowing it.

Uncle Victor and Aunt Hilda had not only taken the trouble to come to the station, they had also brought with them a box of chocolates, as yet concealed, as a present for Franciska. And as they were both in great good spirits, they enacted a little scene, as was their habit on such occasions.

'How is our celebrity?' asked Uncle Victor with a happy smile, pleased in the knowledge that he had, by now, established a joke which would carry him safely for years to come through his relations with the Kalnys.

'Did you get home safely the other night?' asked Aunt Hilda.

'Yes, thank you.'

'Did you like Dr. Rieger?' asked Uncle Victor.

'Mama says she doesn't know him.'

'No, I don't think she does,' replied Aunt Hilda, quite ignorant in her 'frightfulness' that there was nothing anybody could reply when confronted with the statement: 'Mama does not know him.'

'No, I don't think she has ever met him,' said Uncle Victor, a remark which showed that his ignorance matched that of his wife. Franciska looked with irritation at their long, smiling, well-meaning faces. There is nothing more annoying than to administer a snub which is not recognized as such by the intended victim.

'They are hopelessly impossible,' she said to herself. The fact that 'Mama did not know him,' did not, of course, necessarily mean that Mama did really not know Dr. Rieger or whoever else she professed 'not to know.' Mrs. Kalny was quite capable of knowing certain people, of having met them and spoken to them and of being familiar with their family background, their place of birth and their private and professional circumstances, while still professing not to know them. It was merely her way of saying that she did not think it worth her while to strike up acquaintance with them and that they did not deserve the honour of being known by Mrs. Kalny.

If, on the other hand, as sometimes happened, Mrs. Kalny said: 'I don't know the man. I've never heard of him,' it could also mean that she really did not know him and that, just because the name was unfamiliar to her, this was a proof of his lack of distinction, on the assumption that she was bound to know all people of consequence.

'The train is terribly empty, isn't it?' said Aunt Hilda. 'It just shows you. People have not got the money these days for travelling.'

'Oh, really,' said Franciska in her politely interested voice. She could not see what the one had to do with the other. When one had to travel, one travelled; it was quite simple. It did not enter her mind that it was expensive and therefore a luxury. To her, as a result of her upbringing, the objects of life were not divided into necessities and luxuries, because the question of money never entered into them at all.

'Celebrities still travel, even nowadays,' said Uncle Victor. He put a hand into the pocket of his coat and pulled out a box. Franciska observed him. 'He must have a bad tailor,' she thought. 'Bartok never allowed father to carry anything in his pockets.' With one glance she recognized the hallmark of Berger: the fat whirls of embossed gilt scrolls and the brown silk ribbon. 'I must tell Mama,' she thought. 'Amazing that just for once they've done the right thing. Wonders never cease.'

Berger was a confectioner of great renown, and the fact that her uncle and aunt had bought the chocolates at Berger's only enhanced their 'frightfulness' in her eyes.

It was at this moment that Aunt Hilda felt impelled to give one of her cheerful little performances. 'What's this?' she cried as though in great astonishment and looked at the box. Then, she tried to snatch it out of her husband's hand, saying several times over: 'Thank you very much for the chocolates, how kind of you to get them for me.' He avoided her, turning on his heels, while she pretended to chase after him.

At last he said: 'They are not for you, you know.'

'Aren't they? I like that, I must say. He buys chocolates for other people and not for me. Do you think, Cissy, he'd ever buy me any? How would you like it if you were married to a man——'

After this, Franciska ceased to listen, until a loud burst of laughter proclaimed that the joke had come to an end. A trickle of people appeared on the platform and the blue-clad porters filled the place with their shouting. Franciska took a deep breath of the cold, sooty air.

'I think you'd better get in,' said Uncle Victor.

'I'll be all right. Louise said she would fetch me.'

'You are a lucky girl, having Louise,' said Aunt Hilda.

'I have not got her, Aunt Hilda, she belongs to Mama. I shan't get my own maid until I get married. Mama always says that she won't spoil me.'

'Not spoil you?' repeated Aunt Hilda, turning away from

the young girl and trying to catch her husband's eye. 'Incredible,' she added.

'What if you marry a man who can't afford to keep a lady's maid?' asked Uncle Victor.

Franciska did not answer. When, about three weeks ago, Susy had said to her: 'What if you get married and have to live in two rooms?' it had been meant as a very witty remark and they had both been greatly amused by it. But this very similar remark of Uncle Victor's was meant, as Franciska realized, in earnest, and she considered it to be too stupid to deserve an answer.

Clouds of white steam mounted to the dome of dirty glass which formed a roof above the train. Louise came and said: 'Excuse us a moment,' and drew the young girl aside. 'I've put out the eau-de-Cologne and I've given him a tip, as Madam told me. And don't forget now. Before you go to bed, give him your ticket and your passport and your keys and you won't be bothered at the frontier.'

'Yes, yes, of course, I know,' said Franciska and added after a pause: 'Thank you, Louise.'

'Well, the time has come,' said Uncle Victor.

After Franciska had taken off her coat in her compartment, she stepped out into the corridor and asked the attendant to lower a window.

She shook hands with Aunt Hilda and Uncle Victor.

'It's no use our hanging about, we might just as well be on our way.'

Only Louise remained. As the train drew out, Franciska, to her own surprise, began to wave to Louise and Louise waved back. After a few moments, the maid's figure was lost from sight, but, leaning out of the window, Franciska could still see her hand, in the brown glove, fluttering like a dry leaf in the air.

144

PART TWO

CHAPTER 1

'WHEN DID you get home last night?' asked Franciska.

'About three in the morning,' said Mrs. Kalny.

'And was it nice?'

'Very nice. We did not stay there after you had left. We went on to the *Monocle* and then to *Chez Susy Solidor* and then somewhere near the *Halles* and had onion soup.'

'It sounds lovely, Mama. What a pity I could not stay.'

'It's no good looking at me like this, Cissy, and making sad eyes like a dead calf. We all asked you to stay, if you remember. And in any case, I arranged the whole thing, and when I see Johnny, I will tell him that it is boorish, to say the least of it, to break up a family party.'

'Oh, don't, Mama. He hates night clubs. And he only went to please you.'

'Then he might have seen it through. Or he could have left you with us. If you are not safe with your own mother, you never will be with anybody. Not that you want to be safe, needless to say. But that is what I would have told him, in your place. You must learn to manage your own husband, I can't do it for you. And the Merry Widower would have been only too pleased to see you home.'

'Was he very merry after we had gone?'

'Very much so. And Roland and his wife continued bickering about her marriage settlement and Marcel brought

147

out his watch with the indecent clockwork to distract them, but it didn't help, and the bartender came to our table and told us his life story—he comes from Prague, you know—he made a bee-line for your Aunt Clotilde. I was a bit surprised, I did not know she liked that sort of thing.'

'And what happened afterwards, Mama?'

'Oh, I don't know. I suppose she gave him her address. Or perhaps he went home with her. I was not there to hold the candle, as they say, so how can I tell?'

Franciska got up from the hard little settee and went to the window. 'He should be back any minute now, Mama. He only went round the corner to the garage. He wants to see if the car is all right, for to-morrow.'

'You are going on the ferry from Dunkerque? You will be dead by the time you arrive. I should put on a jersey dress for the journey, and then you won't look so crushed. I don't envy you your trip, I must say. Although, I suppose, it will be interesting.'

'To tell the truth, Mama, I am a bit scared.'

'Oh, nonsense. Johnny is a very good driver. After all, he was in the Armoured Corps and they are all glorified drivers in these engineering regiments. Do you remember what Feldman said about him? He is a modern man; modern man is a chauffeur.'

'Oh, Feldman,' said Franciska and, giving a sidelong look at Mrs. Kalny's elegant figure, she thought: 'Anybody who pays her court is infallible, in her opinion.' She repressed her irritation and said: 'I did not mean that, Mama. I was thinking about going over there and meeting them.'

'Well, what of it? You've got to meet them sooner or later. And you are lucky as it is to be living here in Paris. What if you were in Coventry and had them on your doorstep the whole time?'

'That's true. But even so . . . they sound so very, oh, I don't know. Johnny always says: If mother saw this, she would have forty fits and: Do you think mother would put up with a thing like that? And they have a whole house entirely to themselves, Mama. They would not dream of living in a flat. And they have a garden, and yet it is a town house. They must be frightfully rich. And they have fitted carpets in the whole house. Johnny says in England only poor people and cranks have rugs. He thinks our parquets and rugs are shocking. In their place in Coventry they have not an inch of bare floor showing.'

'But how is that possible?' asked Mrs. Kalny. 'Persian rugs never fit a room exactly. Do you mean to say they have their carpets specially woven for them?'

'I don't know, Mama.'

'Well, you will see. Don't let it worry you. He did not pick you up from the gutter.'

'No, Mama.'

Mrs. Kalny rose and joined her daughter by the window. 'Another thing I wanted to tell you, Cissy. I daresay your mother-in-law will give you some of her jewellery. Mine did, when I got married. Take it as it is, it will be probably very grand and hideously old-fashioned. And when you get back here, take it to a jeweller and have it re-set. Unless, of course, it is antique. But whatever you do, don't criticize it to their faces, it would offend them. You know my dog-collar, as your father called it? When it was given me, it looked so huge and ugly, I could have screamed. I would have needed a bosom large enough to hang over the edge of the box at the opera, to have been able to wear it. But I thanked them and looked pleasant about it and took it to Jaeger's and he made a beauty of it. In those days Jaeger was still on the Graben. Remember this for life, Cissy.'

'Yes, Mama.'

'And if they have a butler–I think they will–don't make him run off his feet for you. A butler only stands about and pours out the wine at table; he does not work like a servant.'

'Yes, Mama. I think they must have a marvellous cook, because Johnny could not stand Elise's cooking. And I thought she was very good, you know. I had to get all the recipes from the other English wives on the staff here. Johnny would not eat the foreign filth, as he calls it.'

'I daresay his parents are a bit eccentric, Cissy. But then, lots of the English are. Anyway, look pleasant, it will be only for a short time. And perhaps you will like it very much. The English are very hospitable, they are bound to make you welcome. If Johnny's mother had not fallen ill just before your wedding, you would have had them over here and that would have been much worse for you.'

'Yes, Mama.'

They fell silent and looked down into the courtyard, where the light of the afternoon sun gleamed on the squares of white wall revealed between the leafy trellis. Two shrubs planted in blue tubs flanked the entrance to the passage that led through the front part of the house and into the Rue Perrault.

'It looks charming,' remarked Mrs. Kalny. 'Isn't that just like the French, to dress up everything, even a yard? In Prague they would think of nothing but dustbins and carpet racks.'

'I like it too,' said Franciska. 'But Johnny says it's the French all over, frills on top and filth beneath. He says they only do it to cover up the dirt.'

Mrs. Kalny did not reply.

'I wish he would come, Mama. As soon as he is back, we will have tea.'

'I don't want any, Cissy. I can't stay long, in any case. I only came to say good-bye. I have to be at Rumpelmeyers' in half an hour.'

'Which one, Mama? The one in the rue Faubourg St. Honoré or the other?'

'St. Honoré. One does not go to the other, that's for tourists. Your Uncle Victor and Aunt Hilda would go there. But then, that is where they belong. I am amazed, Cissy, at your naïveté. You must learn about things. Really, you are most irresponsible.'

'Are you meeting anybody there?'

'The Merry Widower and a friend of his. Why don't you come along with me? The Merry Widower would love to see you.'

Franciska would have liked to go, but: 'Why should I?' she said to herself. 'If she is so keen on my coming, it means that she wants to have a free hand with that friend, while I keep the Merry Widower off her.'

She said: 'Johnny does not get on with him, Mama. He was shocked at the story he told yesterday.'

'Which one? About the girl on her wedding night and the green paint?'

'No, about the champagne in the dancer's bath.'

'Good God, that was tame. I suppose Johnny did not understand the other. Anyway, are you coming?'

'I can't, Mama. There is still some packing to do. And I must pay Elise and put the flat in order.'

'What a bore. You should live in an hotel, as I told you in the beginning. You could have taken a little suite in the *Jena* or the *Wagram*.'

'It's too expensive, Mama.'

'He can well afford it. If he must have three cars, he can also live more comfortably.'

151

Franciska did not reply. Her mother had only voiced her own thoughts and those of her Parisian relations. She could have answered, as she had answered them on similar occasions: 'He likes home life,' which was, after all, a repetition of Johnny's own words; but she remembered the titter which had met her answer then, and she had no desire to see it repeated now. 'If he likes home life, why does he go shooting and fishing every week-end?' they had said and had added indulgently: 'Perhaps it all comes to the same. Here the men neglect their wives for their mistresses and the English neglect them for sport. And why not? It amuses him.'

Mrs. Kalny said: 'If you have to pack, so be it. A pity I have left Louise behind in Capri, she could have done it for you.'

'Yes, what a pity, Mama. Tell me, do you miss Sylva?'

'No, I don't. You know, it's funny, I thought I would, but I don't at all. And it's a blessing she stayed in Prague, because I dare not imagine what she would have been like there, with the Italians. I think she would have gone about with a revolver.'

'She was really very silly, Mama,' replied Franciska and, looking out of the window, she added: 'Here he comes.'

Franciska opened the window and they leaned out. They saw Mr. Parker emerge from the shadowy passage and make his way across the cracked uneven flags. He was walking with his hands in his pockets. His head was thrown back, his eyes half closed against the westering sun. His lips were twisted as though he were whistling; but they could hear no sound, except that of his footsteps.

CHAPTER 2

MR. PARKER entered and greeted Mrs. Kalny with that sternness which he always assumed in her presence; this he did to cover up his feeling of being ill at ease because he sensed that she found him ridiculous.

Mrs. Kalny responded with ill-concealed boredom. She fell to asking him a few questions about his proposed trip and the conference he was to attend in Coventry, making it only too clear that she was hardly listening to his answers. She even asked him the same question twice over and made no apologies when she became conscious of her lapse.

Franciska left them to order the tea and then came back again. It pained her to observe her mother's behaviour with her husband. On the one hand, she was thankful that Mrs. Kalny did not go to any trouble to please him. On the other hand, that very fact hurt her, because it showed that her mother did not find him interesting in any way. 'If Ling had married me, it would have been a different story. I wonder how she would have behaved then?'

The tea was brought in.

'But you will have just a cup, Mama, won't you?' said Franciska.

'No, really, Cissy. I told you before, I wouldn't.'

'You have plenty of time, please do, it will refresh you.'

Mrs. Kalny looked at her daughter, slightly astonished at

her insistence. She guessed that it was not solicitude for her well-being that had brought this insistence into Franciska's voice.

'Mother would never go without her tea,' said Mr. Parker.

'I am sure she would not. Very well, pour me one cup, Cissy.'

And, leaning back in her seat, Mrs. Kalny added in that bright, innocent voice which she used to deliver her careful insults: 'I have been told that the English soldiers refused to go into combat during the war unless they had been served with their tea in the trenches.'

Mr. Parker said: 'The English Tommy is the finest soldier in the world.'

'I am sure he is,' and Mrs. Kalny, receiving her cup from Franciska, gave her daughter a long glance which seemed to say: 'Aren't you pleased with me? I am now having tea, just like mother. What more do you want?'

Mr. Parker moved to the window. 'I shall be damn glad to get out of this damn place for a while. The French don't mind, they are used to it, they don't know any better and it's all right for a visit, I suppose. Gay Paree. Ha! Mother had embroidered a firescreen for us, to take back here. I did not dare to tell her we had not got a fireplace. In Coventry we have a large brick fireplace in the lounge. You should see it.'

'It sounds lovely,' said Mrs. Kalny. 'I wish I could see it all. Well, perhaps one day I will come over. But now, I must really say good-bye.'

'It's a shame you won't be here when we get back,' said Mr. Parker. 'We are going to bring the dog back with us, Blackie's puppy, you know. Dad wrote he'll be just old enough for the trip.'

'It sounds lovely,' said Mrs. Kalny. 'Well, perhaps another time.' She gave the impression that she had not listened. As though to make up for the enthusiasm which was lacking in her mother, Franciska said eagerly: 'I will have him photographed and send you a picture to Capri.' She followed her mother into the hall.

When she returned to the room, she found her husband pacing up and down, frowning, with his hands in his pockets. As usual, his lips were twisted in that defiant way which, when seen at a distance, gave the impression that he was whistling. However, when one was face to face with him it was obvious that it was a grimace as though he had bitten into a sour apple. It was not the grimace of a man who was bitten into a sour apple and has put it down with quiet disgust. It held the implication that he had dashed his apple to the ground and crushed it underfoot, with that unreasonable fury of children who will hit the table against which they have knocked and hurt themselves.

When Franciska had first met him in Paris, this tall, well-made, handsome young man had been referred to by her relatives as *beau garçon*. However, the more discerning ones, like the Merry Widower, after contemplating the softly waved brown hair, the long black eyelashes, and the graceful carriage, said with a titter: '*Oui, il est beau garçon, mais presque trop beau garçon, si tu sais ce que je veux dire.*' When, a year later, the Merry Widower had returned from a cruise round the world, he had declared: 'He looks like a husband now; he has become a man.' The family had agreed approvingly; by then, the grimace had already coarsened and hardened the handsome face and they had, as so often happens, mistaken its brutality for strength.

Mr. Parker stopped in front of the window and jingled the coins and keys in his pocket.

Franciska said: 'Mama thinks we are very lucky to be living here.'

'She does, does she? And I suppose she thinks it lucky to have that filthy spying concierge, always cooking a stinking stew, to greet you, when you come home, and this flat full of dust traps and all the people gibbering away in that lingo and saying they don't understand you, when they have understood very well, and cheating you right and left?'

'But Johnny,' said Franciska, 'I always thought you were glad to give it up. The Army, I mean. Would you rather be back at Camberley?

'Of course I wouldn't.'

'So you are not sorry that you left the Service, after all?' asked Franciska, avoiding his eye as people do when they have asked an important question and wish to hide the importance they attach to it.

Once, when Franciska's mother had shown Feldman a letter from her future son-in-law, Feldman had said: 'This boy suddenly throws up everything and leaves the Service and nobody ever knows why. If you could get it out of him, you'd get to know a lot. But you never will. Eh.'

'Because of a woman?'

'Rubbish. What's a woman? He doesn't know what's a woman.'

'Don't be ridiculous, Feldman, he is twenty-five.'

'When is Feldman ridiculous? Feldman is never ridiculous, Feldman is right. The boy is ridiculous, the truth is ridiculous, what has Feldman to do with it? Nonsense, eh.'

For a moment Franciska closed her eyes, as though blinded by the flash of the diamond which she saw again as inevitably as she heard the creaking voice.

'Well, aren't you sorry?' she said and began to place the

cups and saucers on a tray. She avoided her husband's eyes.

The jingling ceased for a while.

'You women are all the same. I suppose you have been caught by the uniform. You think if I had stuck it, you'd be a Captain's wife by now. What are you carrying on about? I get three times a Captain's pay now. All the rest is tripe.'

'But you could not have known then, that you would do so well. Why did you really leave?'

'Oh, stop nagging. I've told you before. It wasn't much of a life all day long in barracks, with chipped cups and bare floors. I want a decent life.'

The jingling recommenced. 'Anyway, once you see the old home, you'll see what a decent place looks like. And you'll love mother. And dad. He's one of the best. I'd do anything for him. I'd cut off my little finger for him, I would.'

Franciska gave him a sidelong glance. She knew this intense low voice. It was the same voice in which he had told her, shortly after their wedding, how, after they had become engaged, he used to walk to the Sacré Coeur on a fine Sunday and facing the direction in which Prague lay had used to say to himself: 'There she is—over there—a thousand miles away,' and had felt a dagger slowly twisting in his heart.

A pronouncement like this, or like the one about the little finger, has to be accepted or rejected out of hand. It is impossible to cavil or quibble. One cannot say: 'Well, in that case, go and cut off your little finger,' or: 'It did not feel at all like a dagger twisting in your heart.' Such pronouncements stand or fall by the sincerity with which they are spoken. Franciska never questioned her husband's sincerity on such occasions and the strength of his feelings frightened her. She thought that the vehemence of these feelings was the vehemence of his love for her; she did not know that it was his effort to love her which was so strong, not the love itself.

At the same time, it filled her with contempt, because he had never succeeded in making her feel strongly for him. 'And all these *façons de parler*, what does it all come to?' she asked herself.

Mrs. Kalny, if she had been consulted, would have asked: 'And where should it come from?' which would have been much more to the point. Once, when alone with her son-in-law, she had questioned him about his experiences with women. She knew very well that this was distasteful to the young man, whose own mother used to say: 'To Johnny, these things are sacred.' On the occasions when these things were not considered sacred, Johnny's mother referred to them as 'monkey business.' 'He goes out with girls, you know, in a healthy sort of way. There is nothing nasty in it, you know, no monkey business.'

Mrs. Kalny had first approached the young man in her habitual pose of a woman of the world. When she perceived that he was shocked by her frivolity, she had changed to the woman who is not familiar with the under-currents of life but who has heard that they exist, and who is willing to listen to the exploits of those who have, at one time or other, plunged into them.

At last she had got it. It appeared that Mr. Parker was one of those, more often to be found in England than in other European countries, who boast that they have never had any dealings with whores. When pressed further, he admitted that he had gone to a brothel in Paris once, but 'just for the fun of it.' What he meant by 'fun' was, charac-teristically, to sit about in the downstairs part of the establishment, partake of a drink of sour champagne and watch the comings and goings of the customers. 'I was quite young then,' he had concluded, 'but, as you see, I already had my head screwed on the right way.'

Afterwards, Mrs. Kalny had a talk with Franciska, between making a list of the trousseau linen. 'Do you think he is the right man for you, Cissy?'

'Why not, Mama?'

To Franciska, as to all her previous girl friends, anybody was the right man, who had money, a position, and was sufficiently appetizing in looks. After her departure from Prague, a fourth qualification had been added; he had to be someone outside her own society, preferably a foreigner. It was true that Mr. Parker was not a man of private means, as Mrs. Kalny and Franciska would have wished him to be, though the money he earned was sufficient, if not abundant. But the young girl felt that this was a reasonable punishment for her crime, and Mrs. Kalny was glad to marry off her daughter as quickly as possible; she was, at that time, giving up her household in Prague and contemplating buying a house in Capri. A pretty daughter, grown up and unmarried, is never welcome to a lady of fashion and the sooner she is disposed of, the better.

'I have nothing against him, Cissy, except that he is your own choice. If an arranged marriage goes wrong, you can always come running home and blame your parents. But in your case, you will have nobody to blame.'

Franciska did not reply.

Then her mother said something which seemed to the young girl quite irrelevant at the time: 'Do you know why men are always so keen that the girl they marry must be a virgin? So that she cannot compare them with other men and cannot know what rotten lovers they are.'

Since her marriage, Franciska had often thought of these

words. As with so many other young girls, her reaction after getting married had been: 'Oh, my God, is that all?' thoughts which, although hidden, could never be really silenced.

She had seen in Paris Watteau's famous picture '*L'embarquement pour l'isle de Cythère*'. The isle of Cythera is the island on which Venus first set foot when emerging from the foam of the sea. It is the island of love. Franciska had seen the wreaths on the statue and the garland on the prow and the cheerfully determined postures of the couples under the bright sky. She had not wondered why the shore only is shown, with a narrow tongue of water; she had not wondered why the island itself is not to be seen. She had not felt the melancholy which flows beneath the surface gaiety of the painting and which makes it one of the saddest pictures in the world. And she had been naïve enough to believe that the island of Cythera existed. How could it not exist, since these people were setting out to conquer it?

As the first weeks of her marriage passed, as the months passed and the first year, she had come to the conclusion that there existed a secret league, a kind of freemasonry on a gigantic scale among all those who have embarked for the island of Cythera and that all those within this league pretend to have reached the blissful island, for fear of being judged cold and insensitive. It was, she felt, a case similar to the tale about the Emperor's new clothes: nobody has ever seen them because they do not exist, yet everyone goes through the motions of feeling their texture and admiring their cut, for fear of being thought stupid. Why was it like this? She did not know. It just was. In the society in which she had grown up, it was held that there was a time and place for everything. In her husband's society, 'these things were sacred', and when a thing is sacred it means that there is hardly ever a time and place for it and that it is beyond criticism and explanations. She had accepted this attitude, just as she had accepted the way of roasting beef and boiling puddings in her husband's country. Why did the English roast the beef in that fashion? She did not know. They just did.

And so, when Mr. Parker asked her, as he so frequently did: 'Do you love me?' and 'Are you glad you married me?' she always said 'Yes,' simply and unthinkingly, just as she prepared the roast beef, without wondering any further about it.

'Have you finished packing?' asked Mr. Parker.

'Yes, Johnny, nearly.'

'It looks like rain, I hope it rains, I'll get much better fishing and shooting in that sort of weather. They bite like mad when it rains.'

'I hope it won't. It would be so dull.'

'You don't have to come out with us in the rain. What are you complaining about, for crying out loud? First you'll be with mother and dad, and then, when we go in the country and stay in the hotel, you'll have your books and your knitting.'

He stepped to the wall between the two windows and tapped on the barometer.

'What does it say?' asked Franciska. She added: 'Do you think the hotel will be full?'

'Bound to be. And there will be other wives, so you can natter, natter, natter, to your heart's content. That's all you women care for.' And he laughed in that knowing way which he always adopted when he said something about 'all you women.'

She did not speak.

'And remind me to send a wire to mother to-night,' he

said, 'so that she can get things ready. She'll give us such a spread – you see.'

'Yes, Johnny.'

'And we'd better eat early to-night. We start at seven o'clock sharp tomorrow.'

The sound of footsteps in the yard drew him to the window. He leaned out, his twisted lips pushed forward, as his grimace sharpened. 'Would you believe it, here they come again, just like that, in broad daylight. And she is old enough to be his mother.' He raised his fist and brought it down on the window-sill. 'My God, if this were my own house, I'd soon clean it up. I would not stand for that sort of thing under my own roof.'

He took out his handkerchief and wiped the streak of soot off his hand. 'Nothing but filth in this damn place. Get me a clean handkerchief, will you?'

'Yes, Johnny.'

'Well go, for crying out loud, and get it. What are you waiting for?' His face had gone red and his eyes grown small and shining.

'I'll have to get it out of the suitcase,' said Franciska. Before she closed the door, she could hear her husband's voice: 'Women, women, I don't know,' and his laugh.

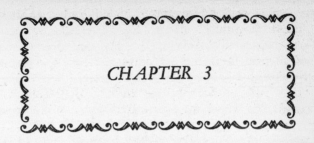

CHAPTER 3

THE WAY from Coventry to Lechworth goes past Bluecroft Motors and the new hospital, down the London road and up Cleve hill, until the aqueduct has been passed on the left. Mr. Parker had taken the road which branches off to the right behind the aqueduct and was nearing the entrance to the Roman villa, when he was overtaken by another car; an event which invariably was to him a source of much bitterness and had to be expatiated upon at great length. He could never bring himself to admit that the other car had overtaken his because it was more powerful; there were always other reasons.

Franciska, who was sitting in the back of the car with the spaniel at her feet and the suitcases beside her, was glad that on this occasion at least, she could listen to her husband's bad-tempered comments without paying any attention; she could pretend to be occupied with the dog.

'The crafty beggar with his flaming sodding car. Comes up right behind me in the bend, before I can see him, the basket. Pardon my French.'

As always when her husband used swear words, Franciska felt frightened and contemptuous. Frightened, because his temper was not the kind which is born suddenly and must equally suddenly be spent in order to die down. On the contrary, when he swore, he betrayed that there ran inside him a constant stream of ill will and resentment, gushing forth in these outbursts for a brief time, yet never stilled. She also felt contempt for his way of expressing himself. During her short stay in England she had learned of the existence of certain words by seeing them chalked up on the walls in the streets and cut into felled tree trunks in those fields where she had walked with her mother-in-law, exercising the dogs. She had heard them muttered by furniture removers and shouted by the men who repaired the road. And when Mr. Parker used expressions like 'beggar' and 'flaming' and 'basket' she knew them to be emasculated renderings of the genuine swear words. Thus, even when he lost his temper, Mr. Parker did not lose his respectability. 'If at least he would swear properly,' she said to herself, divining that in this, in this second-rate form of abuse, her husband was nearer to the standards of Sylva the hairdresser than to those of herself and her mother.

Franciska turned her eyes away from her husband's back and looked at the hedges, partly in leaf and partly in flower, bordering the road which now began to stream past her at an increased speed.

'I'll catch up with him yet, the sodding swine.'

Franciska was unable to understand her husband's preoccupation with the cars he owned, a preoccupation he shared with many men of his generation. He possessed three cars though he only used one, the one which was least costly to run. On the week-ends when he did not go shooting or fishing, and at other leisure hours, he spent all his time in the garage, probing into the entrails of their engines, taking them apart and putting them together again, with a grim serious devotion which was a mystery to his wife. She could not see how a mass-produced machine-made object could, as he asserted, have an individual and glorious personality of its own.

He spoke about his cars with an amorous intentness. This, and the fact that he referred to them as 'she', made her think that in her husband's emotions the cars took the place of women. In this she was wrong. She did not understand that in his cars he saw an extension of his own self, just as others might see it in their work or in their children. When he thought that his cars possessed outstanding and unusual qualities and were capable of extraordinary speeds, it was merely his way of raising himself in his own esteem. Mr. Parker wanted his cars to be big and powerful because he wanted to be big and powerful himself. Therefore, every slight that was cast upon his cars, such as being over-taken by another car, was to him a personal insult.

Had Franciska realized all this, she might have asked herself why her husband had this desire to be big and powerful. Or, in other words, why he in reality felt small and weak. She might have discerned a path which led, through his blustering bad temper and his bullying, to something in her own attitude towards him. But even if she had been able to perceive all this she would have stopped short with a protest and said: 'But this is absurd. It does not make any sense. And besides how can he know?' She would have been unable to follow the link between her feelings of: 'Oh, my God, is that all?' and her husband's passion for cars. The heart is a maze of crooked paths in which one must walk crookedly, never knowing what one will find at the turning of the way, never knowing whether the way itself may not branch off into another or cease altogether.

As soon as they had left the main road and the Roman villa behind them, and entered the narrow lane, the pursued car came in view.

'It's all right. Any minute now,' said Mr. Parker between his teeth.

Soon after they had passed the offending vehicle, he said over his shoulder: 'Did you see who it was, Cissy?'

'The American, wasn't it?'

'Yes. The swine. And his bit of fluff. Disgusting. He's got a wife and child at home.' His grimace sharpened. The sour apple seemed to be very sour at this moment. Mr. Parker had restrained himself by saying: 'He's got a wife and child at home.' He could have added richness to his statement by saying: 'He's got a beautiful wife and child at home.'

The American, only a few days before, had, during the conference, shown some photographs of his family to a group of the engineers at Bluecroft Motors, the company which owned the branch factory in Paris where Franciska's husband worked. Mr. Parker was one of those who were shown the pictures; and the sincere admiration provoked at their sight, made him feel safe enough in his wonted indignation against the American, to exclaim: 'Really, with a wife as lovely as yours, I can't understand how you can even look at another woman.' The American had replied: 'I don't look. So what the hell are you talking about?' The reply had spread among the members of the staff and with it, the ridicule of him who had provoked it.

Mr. Parker had met the American on several occasions before, both in Coventry and in Paris, and had always expressed his disgust at the other's conduct. When Franciska had seen him for a few moments in a tea-shop in Coventry, she had been somewhat disappointed at his appearance; he seemed to possess the good-naturedness of large people and large animals and she could not reconcile what she saw with what her husband had told her. She said: 'He cannot always be alone. He is bound to get lonely.'

'Yes. Lonely. He calls it lonesome. I'd give him lonesome.'

Mr. Parker returned his attention to the wheel and added: 'And she is a brazen hussy if ever there was one. Wears a wedding ring and thinks she can get away with it. Last Friday, with mother, we saw them together at the Cadoma, do you remember? Mother saw the wedding ring at once and remarked on it. Do you remember, Cissy?'

'I don't. I never looked.'

'Mother did. She always does look for that sort of thing.'

'A pity Roland was not with us, he likes blondes,' said Franciska.

'Thank God, he was not with us,' replied Mr. Parker grimly.

Franciska, who had started to laugh, fell silent. She knew that her husband disapproved of all her Parisian relations and that his remark was meant to remind her of it. Yet, for once, she did not feel put out but repeated to herself silently: 'Yes, thank God, he wasn't. If Roland knew, I should never hear the end of it And Mama! She must never come to England.' She was never to forget the feeling of disbelief and horror that had invaded her when Mr. Parker had driven down the street in which the house of his parents was situated. She was never to forget those two rows of small brick houses each built exactly like the other, each identical with all the rest, down to the diamonded panes in the windows and the knocker on the front door. Up and down the street they stood, as far as the eye could see, with that horrible regular prettiness of a row of false teeth. And yet all that her husband had said was true: a whole house to themselves, the brick fireplace, the fitted carpets. But it had not been necessary for Fran-

ciska to see them; before she had stepped inside the Parkers'
house she already knew that it was 'impossible' and with it,
its inhabitants. The only thing which had surprised her was
the extent of this 'impossibility.'

They drove into Lechworth. The first large house
appeared, with stone pineapples on the gate piers and a
garden descending in terraces to the bank of the water.

'Isn't it lovely?' said Franciska. And she thought: 'In
such a house they might even have a butler and wear
family jewellery.'

'Looks all right,' replied Mr. Parker.

On the other side of the trout stream, the buttresses of
the old mill stood like an outdated menace, useless and
still awful.

'I wonder if he will make a scene because I said that
about Roland. He can't stand Roland since that night at
the *Boeuf*,' she thought.

They drove up in front of the Pelican.

'This is what I call a nice joint, eh, Cissy?'

'It looks very old.'

'The Pelican, the Pelican,' Franciska said to herself. 'I
wish it were the *Boeuf sur le Toit*. That is what I call a nice
joint. But he won't make a scene.' And although the
thought of a scene scared her, the thought of the *Boeuf sur
le Toit* brought an ironical smile to her lips, so that, as she
stepped out of the car, Mr. Parker remarked: 'You seem to
be in a very good mood.'

Franciska had been to the *Boeuf* many times before and
after the incident. Yet, she remembered the night club only
as it had been on that particular evening; all the other
evenings she had spent there had fused together in her
memory into one indistinguishable whole. This was natural,
as one remembers a landscape revealed by a sudden and

single flash of lightning much more clearly than when one has seen it often under an ordinary sky.

Although they were already engaged, she had not been allowed to go out alone at night with Mr. Parker. On that particular evening, her cousin Roland had gone with them.

The downstairs part of the *Boeuf* had been stifling on that night at the end of May. For a while they had remained by the balustrade that encloses the dance floor and had looked at the celebrities whom Roland pointed out to them. There was one of the Rothschilds and there was a very famous music-hall star. 'And over there, you see, is her gigolo, the Neapolitan. And the man with him, is also a gigolo.'

'Also hers?' she asked.

'No, you don't understand. The first gigolo is for her and the second gigolo is for the first gigolo.'

'How wonderful,' said Franciska.

'Isn't it?' said Roland.

'Isn't it wonderful, Johnny?'

'What's that? I didn't hear.'

'It is of no importance,' said Roland. 'Let's go upstairs. It will not be so full.'

Upstairs was a room which, because it was small, was what managers of night clubs call 'intimate.' They waited till the *diseuse* had finished her song. Franciska remembered it very well. It was, as Mrs. Kalny would have said with a smirk, 'highly unsuitable': '*Le prince m'a voulu dans son lit, mesdames, il m'a voulu dans son lit, messieurs,*' and, in the end: '*Je me fiche pas mal du prince, mesdames, je me fiche pas mal de lui, messieurs.*'

'Isn't it wonderful? asked Franciska.

'Isn't it?' said Roland. 'And when you are a married woman, you can go and listen all by yourself.'

'What's that? What was it about? I only understood

madame and *monsieur*. I wish I knew the lingo, the way Cissy does.'

They sat down, all three in a row, on a bench underneath a window, ordered drinks and began to talk, as the *diseuse* retired. Franciska did not know how long they had remained like this, but she knew that there had been two more songs and it was shortly afterwards that the tall blond man had come into the room with a small slight youth close behind him.

Roland nudged her: '*Les voilà, les tapettes*,' he whispered. He laughed delightedly and Franciska joined in his laughter. Roland was delighted because, at the time, that particular form of love was considered in Paris to be highly amusing and the appearance of a couple like the one which had just entered, was regarded as a huge joke, better than any that the *diseuse* could provide, and more cheering, because gratuitous. Franciska did not really see why it should be so amusing, but she at once responded to her cousin's laughter. She felt flattered to share in the joke, all the more so, as the existence of such things had only recently been explained to her.

The two men leaned against the bar and began to take their drinks, posed in elaborately languid attitudes.

A fat man rose from his table, moved to the bar and placed himself behind them, aping their postures behind their backs. The youth looked round nervously, as soon as he realized that the cheering and laughter of all the people was directed against him, and he changed his attitude at once. His companion, however, did not seem to pay any attention to the general uproar and he only looked up, and then very calmly, when the fat man had gone so far as to pluck at his coat and touch his elbow in the parody of a caress.

Because he did not show any signs of surprise or shame, the people in the room grew bored and did not look at the couple any more. And the tall blond man, after glancing haughtily round the room, made as though to resume his posture and had already placed an elbow on the bar counter, when his eye came to rest on Mr. Parker. He abruptly left the bar without a word to his companion.

'Look, he's dropped him,' whispered Roland and nudged Franciska. 'I wonder what's up now.'

The young girl nodded. They resumed their talk.

It was a few minutes later that Mr. Parker began to edge more closely to Cissy, saying: 'I wonder if you could move up a bit, there isn't much room.'

After a while he made the same request again, looking rather uncomfortable. Roland, who sat on the other side of Franciska, nudged her and whispered into her ear: '*Regarde, il lui fait le genou, a ton petit Anglais.*'

Franciska looked up and there, next to Mr. Parker, stood the tall blond man. His body was pressed against Mr. Parker's thigh and he had placed one arm on the window-sill above the bench, so that it touched the whole width of Mr. Parker's shoulders. It seemed to Franciska that the man's arm hardly rested on the sill, but lay on Mr. Parker's body in a heavy embrace.

Roland began to titter and so did Franciska. Mr. Parker looked at them, ill at ease. He seemed to be too preoccupied to notice their merriment.

'This place is getting awfully hot and stuffy,' he said. 'And terribly overcrowded. I say, Cissy, can't you make room for me? I seem hardly to be able to move.'

'I have not got any room either, Johnny. Nor has Roland.'

'No, I have not, Johnee,' said Roland, spreading out his

hands as though in despair. 'Already I am hanging in the air with one half of my bottom.'

Whether he was stung by the jeering way in which Roland had drawled his name, or by the fact that the renewed laughter of his two companions was coloured by a malice which had been lacking before; or whether it was because the stranger's arm did not rest any more on his shoulders as though by accident, but had come to life, Mr. Parker blanched, his lips twisted wryly as though he were trying to swallow a morsel that choked him with its bitterness, while his eyes, those handsome eyes, shadowy beneath the long lashes, stared into space, focused at an object at a great distance, much farther removed than the walls of the room.

Thus he stayed for a few seconds, facing Franciska and her cousin. The young girl, embarrassed by his countenance, turned her eyes away from him and, lowering her glance, she saw how his trembling hand tried to come to a rest on an ashtray.

Then the trembling ceased and Mr. Parker spoke to the stranger. He said: 'Look here, why don't you go and stand somewhere else? There's plenty of room elsewhere.'

The tall blond man bent down to him with a loving-kindness that startled the young girl.

'I thank you, sir,' he replied, 'but I am perfectly comfortable where I am,' and he remained bent above Mr. Parker, remained smiling and dignified.

'Oh, my God, what is this?' said Franciska to herself. It seemed to her that the stranger did not smile with impertinence, nor did he smile from glee at having been the cause of an upset. It was the melting smile of: 'Why don't you surrender? Why don't you? You know you want it as much as I do,' and the loving insistence of it flowed and ebbed as the sun-warmed water that tempts the bather's foot.

Mr. Parker did not see it, because he was looking straight ahead, his face still pitifully white; he clasped the bottle of whisky on the table. He said, to no one in particular: 'If the fellow doesn't go away, I'll break the bottle on his head.'

Roland got up with an admonishing glance at the young girl and pointed to Mr. Parker. And while Franciska, obediently, laid her fingers over Mr. Parker's hand, which was still clasping the neck of the bottle, her cousin went up to the tall blond man and addressed him with gestures which were cynical and apologetic at the same time. Franciska could not hear what was said. She could not even tell whether the stranger was listening to Roland's words or not, because Roland was much shorter than he and the stranger was looking above his head with the languid and unconcerned expression he had shown all the time.

And glancing beyond the two men, Franciska could see a black-clad gentleman standing in the doorway; he had appeared there suddenly, drawn no doubt by that mysterious power of scenting trouble brewing that calls forth hotel managers from their habitual resting places.

The tall blond man stepped away from Roland, gave one look in the direction of the bar, and made towards the door. The slight youth followed him. And by the time they had reached the door, the manager had already vanished.

Franciska's cousin returned joyfully: 'You see, he's gone, he's gone, just like that,' and he blew on his outstretched hand and kissed the tips of his fingers in the direction of the door, as though wishing the stranger an ironical farewell. '*Vraiment, ces types là, ils sont incroyables,*' he whispered to Franciska as he regained his seat by her side. He was

173

delighted. He repeated: 'T . . . *t* . . . *t* . . . *ils sont incroyables.*'
He behaved like the mother of a naughty boy who feels
compelled for the sake of the company to say: 'Isn't he a
little devil?' while in reality she is very proud of him.

Franciska suppressed her laughter. 'It is all right, Johnny,'
she said.

'Is it? I should jolly well hope so. By jove, if he had
stayed another moment——.' His complexion was fresh and
pink again, but his eyes still avoided hers, as though still
beholding a far-away object that filled them with horror.

Franciska said: 'Wasn't Johnny lucky? I mean, wasn't it
lucky that the man understood English? And he spoke such
good English, too.' She blushed and added: 'Really wonderful English, wasn't it?'

She was quite sincere when she said: 'Wasn't Johnny
lucky?' although the stranger's English had not astonished
her at the time. It was the smile that had astonished her and
touched her to the quick. And when she said: 'Wasn't
Johnny lucky?' she meant it enviously. 'Why does nobody
ever smile at me like this?' she thought. One cannot recognize a thing unless one has seen it before and if Franciska
recognized this smile for what it was, she only did so,
because desire had always existed in her imagination. And
now that she had beheld it for the first time in her life, it
stayed in her mind for ever after, the first signpost to the
way she was to follow.

Mr. Parker said between his teeth: 'That's Paris for you.
Gay Paree. For crying out loud.'

'Yes, gay Paree,' said Roland, delightedly. He was very
pleased with himself.

'What did you say to him, Roland?' asked Franciska.

'I said, Look here, there is nothing to be got. He has a
young girl with him, do you understand?'

174

'He was very good-looking, wasn't he? Don't you think he was very good-looking, Johnny?'

'Who? The fellow? I didn't look. I wouldn't know what he looked like,' and Mr. Parker swallowed some whisky with an injured air.

Franciska tittered. 'Anyway, it's something to write home about. It was terribly funny.'

'At home they would not even understand. Thank God.'

'Oh, come, come, Johnee,' said Roland. He winked at Franciska.

Mr. Parker turned, and, for the first time since the incident, he looked them full in the face. 'They wouldn't, I tell you.' His face was red and his eyes grew smaller, as though the lids had become swollen from the uprush of blood. His fist crashed on the table. 'In my country such a thing does not exist. I am telling you. It—does—not—exist,' and with each word he hammered on the table.

Franciska shrugged her shoulders in bewilderment and turned to her cousin who shook his head and motioned her with his hand not to say anything further.

When they left, Mr. Parker refused to be taken home by car. He wanted air and exercise, he said. And it needed some persuasion on Roland's part before he allowed himself to be driven to the rue du quatre Septembre.

'I did not dare to let him walk,' said Roland to Franciska, after having seen Mr. Parker to his home. 'It only needs one *poule* to accost him on his way and he will explode. These English are eccentric, but eccentric. In the beginning, when I first knew him, I thought, such a nice young man, and all alone in Paris, and does not know a soul. I thought, I'd let him in on my mistress, go half and half, expenses and everything. It's much cheaper that way and it's safe. I nearly said it to him, you know. But then, I didn't. I am glad.'

'And you would have done it? Really?' asked Franciska.

'Yes, of course. He is a nice young man and a good connexion for business. It is always good to be friendly with the people you meet in business.'

Mr. Parker could never afterwards forgive Franciska for behaving as she did that evening. 'To think that a wife of mine could have laughed.'

'What should I have done, Johnny?'

'You should have been shocked, of course.'

This failure of Franciska's to behave as she should have behaved, was brought up by Mr. Parker again and again, every time she had done something which displeased him, irrespective of what it was, as though to prove Mr. Parker's superiority over her. Thus, she began to be afraid to show her amusement at anything which her husband might consider disgusting; and as their marriage went on, he found more and more grounds for his disgust. She did not wonder at the source of this disgust, but she sometimes doubted his sincerity. It was true, he had been deeply upset on that evening at the *Boeuf sur le Toit*. One can pound one's fist on the table, but one cannot go white and red in the face intentionally. Yet she knew that on one point at least he had pretended. Because, when two days later, they had been sitting in one of the open-air cafés on the Champs Elysées, the tall blond man had passed by, stopped for an instant and moved on.

And before Franciska had had time to exclaim, she had observed Mr. Parker's white and twisted face.

CHAPTER 4

FRANCISKA put the dog on the leash. The porter came out and picked up the suitcases and he would have taken the fishing tackle as well, if Mr. Parker had not stopped him. He carried it himself into the lobby of the Pelican and placed it carefully in a corner.

The American drove up and halted behind Mr. Parker's car.

Mr. Parker returned. 'Go inside, Cissy, while I park her.' He resumed his seat behind the wheel, while the porter stepped on the running board to direct him to the garage. 'See you anon.'

Franciska went inside and sat on the hard wicker chair by the table with the stack of old magazines. The manageress came out from behind the reception desk. 'We've given you a nice room, Mrs. Parker. And this is your little dog? I am afraid you will have to get his meat from the butcher, yourself. The butcher is very good, however, he is used to doggy visitors. The weather is not so good; is it? I hope you have brought better weather with you.'

The American came in with the fair, fresh-looking young woman and Franciska drew the dog close to her chair so that he would not get between their feet in the dark and narrow space between the wall and the desk.

The couple talked loudly and laughed a great deal, the

manageress laughed with them and Franciska thought: 'He has not brought any fishing rods with him. They will just be together all the time.'

Mr. Parker entered and she rose. They went up the dark stairs, preceded by the porter. At the turn of the landing, as the light from the window fell on her husband's face, she saw that it was suffused with blood. She thought: 'He is going to make a row. Oh, God, I wish I had not laughed in the car.'

As soon as they were alone in their room, Mr. Parker began to beat with his fist against the doorpost.

'You sit there,' he shouted, 'you just sit there, until I come in. Do you think anyone else's wife would behave like you do?'

Although he was hitting hard against the post, he did not seem to feel any pain. 'You should have asked to see the room and gone up with the manageress and made some remarks about it. Mother always does. She always wants to see what they give her.'

'But the room was reserved for us already,' said Franciska. 'And it is very nice, in any case. I cannot see what difference it would have made.'

'Can't you? You wouldn't.' His arms dropped and he stepped over to the window. 'A wife is sure of herself when she comes to an hotel. It's only hussies who keep quiet and hang about till the man comes.'

At the corners of his mouth bubbles of saliva stood out in white patches. In utter exasperation he beat both arms up and down in such a way that it seemed to Franciska that he was not human but moved like a marionette whose arms are jerked about on wires. She had often noticed it before, and it frightened her, when in moments of great fury her husband's movements became those of an automaton.

'Don't you see?' he shouted. 'You stupid bitch. You don't behave like a wife. They'll all think we aren't married and have just come down for a week-end. And the American saw you too. He'll think I am as bad as he is.'

'Johnny, I don't——'

'Oh, shut up or I'll swipe you one. I want to be respectable. I won't have people thinking that I am not.'

They had not heard any footsteps but now the laughter of the American came muffled, yet unmistakable, to their ears. And as it moved away, they heard a woman's shriek, one of those half-stifled faint shrieks, which are uttered in delight although they are intended as a protest.

Mr. Parker sat down on the luggage rack and buried his face in his hands.

CHAPTER 5

A TABLE had been reserved for the Parkers at the far end of the dining room, by a window. And as the American's table was situated in the centre of the room, they had to pass by it.

The American and the young woman were already having their after-dinner coffee and the dessert plates, stained red from the strawberries they had eaten, had not yet been cleared away.

Mr. Parker passed the table with a slight nod of his head. The American, like so many heavily built men, did not turn his head in the other's direction, but instead, swung round his whole body on his chair. This, although it was probably due to physical reasons, gave an impression of great cordiality. He said with a guffaw: 'Good evening, Parker,' and, growing serious: 'Good evening, Ma'am,' and half rose from the table, while the young woman, fresh and smiling in her white dress, played with her gold bracelets and tried to catch Franciska's eye.

Mr. Parker moved on, laying a hand on Franciska's bare arm; and under the disguise of this seemingly affectionate gesture, he pinched her arm violently. 'Trust you to stop, you would stop,' he said into her ear without moving his lips. He pinched her again and as she caught her breath sharply, so that it sounded like a sob, Mr. Parker, with his hand still grasping her elbow, pushed her forward and dragged her back again, so that it looked as though she had stumbled and been steadied by her husband.

If anyone had reproached Mr. Parker for his loss of self-control, he would have said, 'Why? What's wrong with it? Nobody saw it,' and he might have added in his low intense voice: 'Besides, what does it matter as long as I love my wife? And my wife knows that I love her. I think she is the most marvellous little woman in the world.'

Franciska was on the verge of tears when they sat down to dinner.

Her husband said: 'Oh, for God's sake, what's all this in aid of.' And, turning to her with a bitter laugh: 'And all this because I tell you not to stop at that American's table. Don't you think I get enough of him as it is in the factory? You've dropped your napkin. Women's tantrums. Can you beat it? I don't know.'

Franciska did not reply.

'For crying out loud, don't look so upset. People are looking at us. And what am I to do? Shout with joy? I won't be henpecked, no fear,' and he gave his knowing laugh.

Mr. Parker frequently asserted that he was not willing to be a henpecked husband; and nobody could have said that he was. On the contrary, he went to the other extreme. Yet the reason for his bullying sprang from the same source as that which makes henpecked husbands, the only difference being in outward appearance. Thus, the Saint and the gargoyle stand side by side beneath the cathedral spires and are carved from the same stone.

The soup was served and eaten in silence. By the time the boiled chicken arrived, Mr. Parker had passed from indignation to high spirits which were increased as he surveyed the plates: 'That's as it should be, I get a leg and you get a wing. That's how I like it. Women can't have the

same as men, they must be kept in order. Dad gave me that
tip when I got married, and by God, the old man was right.'

Franciska thought: 'Why do the English get married at
all? They hate women. But they would never admit it,'
and she recalled several occasions during her stay in
Coventry, when her husband and his father had raised their
glasses to their lips and had said with emotion: 'The ladies,
God bless them.'

After they had finished the chicken, Mr. Parker said to
the waiter: 'Just the pudding for us. Nothing wrong with
the pudding, is there?'

'We've got some very nice strawberries, sir. They are
not on the menu, of course. Bit early in the season.'

Mr. Parker looked grimly in the direction where the
American was sitting. 'No fear. You can keep them for
your other guests. I'm a plain man. Pudding is good enough
for me.'

'And madam, sir?'

'The same for my wife, thank you.' And after the waiter
had gone, he said: 'It's chaps like the American who make
a place like this go to the dogs, chucking their money about
all over the place. Why can't the swine go to Torquay or
somewhere smart? I didn't tell him about this place. I
suppose the others told him, trust them to suck up to him.'

Franciska looked towards the middle of the room. The
Americans' table was empty.

'I did not know you knew him well.'

'Of course I do. He comes to the works in Viancourt
more often than he is wanted. He is the chief's little blue-
eyed boy. Does not feed with us from the senior staff, that's
not good enough for him. He has to eat in the directors'
dining room. It makes me sick.'

'How long has he been over here?'

'Six months. Six months too long, if you ask me. I'm sick of these experts from the States. If you tell him to sit down on his arse—pardon my French—he'll sit down on the carburettor. Mr. Miles, Mr. ruddy Miles. Throws parties at the Ritz when he comes to Paris, while we have to do his work for him. But I don't care. I tell you, I wouldn't go to one of his ruddy parties, not if you paid me a million dollars, I wouldn't.'

The grimace sharpened. The morsel seemed to be more bitter than ever.

'But I would,' thought Franciska, observing her husband. 'And without being paid anything at all.'

'One day, I'll go out to the States myself,' said Mr. Parker, 'as the English representative of our crew. We're tied up with Detroit.'

'Yes, I know,' said Franciska.

'The big white chief always comes up to me and says: "If you'll look after me, boy, I'll look after you." Well, he'd better. He's had two of my inventions already.'

Franciska thought: 'Johnny is really very clever. Roland said so too.'

After dinner they went into the bar. Mr. Parker took a whisky and Franciska had a liqueur.

She fetched the dog and they went outside and walked along the water, past the row of cottages and back again. The daylight was fading but the water was so clear that they could still see the dark shapes of the trout in the stream, each fish by itself, standing as though in a little pool of its own, motionless, facing the current.

Mr. Parker said: 'I say, Cissy. I'll go off to the garage for a while, she didn't sound so good the last twenty miles. Why don't you go inside and read?'

There was a garden belonging to the Pelican, for the use

of the guests. It did not lie behind the inn, which would have been usual, but in front of it, stretching between the façade and the drive, the stream and the small bridge. There were no trees, only shrubs and a meander of low-cut box; so that, sitting there, one could watch the life on the road and in the inn.

It was there that Franciska wanted to go. She dreaded the gloom of the panelled lounge with the faded cretonne and the brass ashtrays; and her heart sank at the thought of those middle-aged women who would be grouped around the empty grate, sunk into their habitual coma induced by the twin drugs of aspirin and knitting. She wanted to go and sit in the dark garden, but she did not go. It was not an angel with a flaming sword who barred the entrance to this paradise; it was the shimmer of a woman's white dress, the sparkle of her eyes and teeth, and the glitter of the gold bracelets. And beside her, the ruby glow of a cigar. And in the water below the bridge the white and the gold and the ruby mingled with the reflected starlight. Franciska's heart beat very fast. The smell of sun-warmed green and sun-warmed water was still in the air. Behind her, the dog barked and she said: 'Be quiet, Teddy.'

She felt again the envy and the desolation which she had first known as a child when her mother *en grande toilette* used to come to her bed to say good-night, before departing to a ball or the opera. Later too when at parties at home, the men had paid court to her mother and had barely talked to her. And still later, at the *Boeuf sur le Toit*, when the stranger had given his smile to her husband and not to her. 'Why can't I go to the ball too? Why don't they pay me court too? Why does nobody ever smile at me like that?' and now: 'Why am I not there, standing by the bridge with him?'

She said: 'Come away, Teddy,' but it was really to herself that she said it, and she returned to the inn, taking deep breaths to steady the irregular beating of her heart. She received her key from the porter and went upstairs.

'The American,' she thought, 'why do I mind so much? She has the American and I have Johnny. I suppose all men are the same. It is always the same. I am a married woman. I know what it is like.'

She was a married woman. She did not wonder any more, as she had done with Susy Graber, where and how a bride undressed on the wedding night. She did not speculate any more, upon meeting a single woman, whether she was a virgin or not. Nor did she belong to those, mainly found among elderly widows, who cannot see a carrot or a sausage without giggling.

She began to undress. 'And Johnny is very brilliant. Roland thinks so too. He will go far. After all, that is the main thing.'

She was seized by the desire to lean out of the window and to breathe the fresh air. And when she did so, she saw the white dress by the bridge and her heart beat painfully.

Those who have pledged themselves to Venus can only be paid in the coin of that goddess. The gifts that other gods might bestow are as valueless to them as foreign currency is to him who stays at home. Happy those, who, at least, recognize the useless currency and do not try to seize it and purchase with it the necessities of life. But Franciska was not among them.

'Johnny is really brilliant,' she repeated to herself. 'If only he were more possible. If he were better bred, everything would be all right.'

In a way, it was a relief to Franciska to have seen her husband's home and parents; everything that she disliked about him could now be explained. She was not so naïve as to think that well-bred men never lose their temper; but she was convinced that they do so in a manner different from the common people and it was in this difference that she saw the source of her bitterness. She believed that each social class has its own sort of suffering, just as it has its own sports, its own way of speech and code of honour.

Sylva's adventures with men had delighted Franciska as a young girl, yet she would have been indignant if men had ever accosted her as they did the hairdresser. If Sylva had been married to Mr. Parker and been subjected to his brutality and ill temper, Franciska would not have pitied her. Nor would Mrs. Kalny. She would have said: 'These people, they are used to that sort of thing.'

If someone who has never seen a giraffe before in his life beholds one for the first time, it is impossible for him to know whether the animal is a fine or poor specimen of its kind. Only a person well acquainted with other sorts of animals might, by applying general rules, arrive at some judgment. For the same reasons it had been impossible for Franciska, who had never before met any English people, to know what distinguishes an Englishman who is a gentleman from one who is not. And she had not a sufficient knowledge of people in general to discern certain traits which are common to those of gentle birth in all countries.

Thus, she said quite truthfully: 'It really isn't my fault. If I had known he was impossible, I would not have married him.' She said this to herself, just as, three years ago, on a November night she had said to Dr. Rieger: 'If I had known it would turn out like this, I would not have done it.'

If Franciska had seen the similarity between then and now, she would only have called it superficial. She would have merely admitted that in both instances she had made a mistake. During her connexion with Ling, she had denied to herself that thoughts of 'cuddling' had led her to the disaster which was to sever her from her roots and subsequently drive her into marriage in a foreign country. And she continued in her sin against herself, deceiving herself, and finding an explanation for her unhappiness where it did not lie.

This was a night in May, in a village in Warwickshire far removed from the November day in the dining room in the Esplanade. There was no Feldman this time, to say: 'Rubbish. Feldman says it's all rubbish. Go out and get yourself a nice young man instead. Or better still, get two or three.' There was only the sight of a white dress by the bridge and the beating of her own heart.

When, about an hour later, Mr. Parker entered the room he found Franciska in her dressing gown and slippers sitting in a chair facing the window. She was filing her nails.

'What's all this in aid of? Why haven't you gone to bed?'

'I did not feel like it.'

'Why don't you at least sit by the dressing table where you have the light?'

'Oh, I don't know. I wanted to be near the fresh air, by the window.'

He moved near her and indulged in some tired and well-meant caresses to which she did not respond, and from which she freed herself at last by getting up and putting the file and nail scissors into a drawer.

A few minutes later he said: 'Well, come to bed, for crying out loud. I've got to be up at six to-morrow morning.'

'Will they give you breakfast?'

'They'll give me something. I've spoken to them downstairs. You can sleep till lunch. Aren't you a lucky girl?'

CHAPTER 6

THE FOLLOWING day, Franciska slept till ten. Mr. Parker's
wish had come true: it was raining. She threw off the bed-
clothes and got up. On the bed next to hers, she saw Mr.
Parker's striped pyjamas, lying neatly folded on the pillow.
She turned away shrugging her shoulders. At home, her
husband never folded his pyjamas, but left them crumpled
up, as he discarded them. Yet, in hotels, the thought of
strangers invading his privacy made him overcome his
natural laziness, and he always put on a dressing gown and
combed his hair carefully before calling the waiter to his
room. To Franciska, who had been brought up to think of
servants as 'canaille', necessary but not human, this was
incomprehensible. The sight of her husband's pyjamas
recalled to her mind one of Mrs. Kalny's sayings: 'Remember
this for life, Cissy. There are four professions where the
men are not men: the tailor, the doctor, the waiter and the
hairdresser.' Franciska had never questioned this rule and
she had not been sympathetic when her mother-in-law made
remarks like: 'So I said, no thank you, doctor, another
time. I couldn't let him examine me all alone, without even a
nurse in the room. It would not have been quite nice.'

She rang for the chambermaid who, when at last she
came, told her that it was too late for breakfast.

'But couldn't you get me a biscuit or a sandwich or something?'

'I'm afraid not, madam. That's the lounge service, for after-dinner coffee.'

'That's Lechworth for you. Gay Lechworth,' said Franciska to herself.

She gathered her towel and soap and went into the dark passage.

In front of the bathroom door she came face to face with the smiling young woman. 'What lovely teeth she has,' she thought.

'It's no good' said the young woman. 'Unless you like it cold. But I'm not a stiff upper-lipper. Are you?'

To belittle oneself in front of another person is a form of flattery which is disarming. Franciska was disarmed.

'No,' she said. 'But I wish I were.'

'Oh, don't say that, it's much more fun if you aren't.'

They laughed. They remained standing in front of each other.

'I say,' said the young woman, 'I was admiring your dinner blouse last night.'

'Did you really? It's quite old.'

'It's lovely, though. And you've got such a pretty neck and shoulders. Aren't you lucky?'

Franciska felt herself blushing under the scrutiny of the other. It was not the first time that women had paid her compliments about her looks. Dressmakers appraised her pretty body in a professional way, just as Sylva had praised her hair, less for its beauty than because it was 'easy to do'. The English women she had met till now, the wives of her husband's colleagues, often told her that she had a lovely skin; this was as far as they went. But whereas dressmakers spoke of her 'figure' which is less fleshly than 'body', this young woman had praised her neck and shoulders, and although this flattery pleased her, it held an implication which she sensed, without comprehending it and which had brought the blood to her face.

Franciska thought she knew 'everything'; yet she had never witnessed the spectacle of a husband who, in a night club, approaches a stranger and invites him to join him and his wife at their table. Nor did she know that the custom of the eldest wife's choosing and approving younger wives or concubines is not confined to Oriental countries.

'Oh, that blouse,' she said. 'My mother sent it to me from abroad.'

The blouse which she had worn the evening before had been sent to her a few months ago by Mrs. Kalny from Capri. It was one of those pieces of fine needlework which are noticed and admired by all women alike, even by those who have no feeling for beauty, because the intricate working of lace and embroidery commands their respect.

Mr. Parker's mother had admired it too. But her perception was so vitiated that she could notice every detail of a new pattern of embroidery and not see the pretty neck above it. '*Quelle différence*,' thought Franciska. She could not have explained why she thought this in French, instead of in her mother tongue or in English. Yet, by pronouncing these words in her mind, it was clear that she had already placed this encounter in the no-man's-land of adventure, the land whose capital lies in Paris and whose royalty resides in the *Boeuf sur le Toit*.

She said: 'I suppose the bath water is cold because it's too late. I couldn't get any breakfast either.'

'Oh, you poor thing. Really, aren't they beastly in this beastly hotel?'

'Yes, aren't they?'

'But you can't exist like this. You must come with me. We'll give you something.'

'No, really.'

'Yes, really. A poor little thing like you. Didn't your husband make a row?'

'No. He's gone fishing. He got up at six.'

'Aren't husbands incredible?'

'Yes, aren't they?'

The young woman took her arm and they walked down the passage.

'Miles will be so pleased when he sees you. He said already to me last night that he doesn't know how a man like yours could have got a girl like you. It's always the same, isn't it?'

'Do you think so?'

'Yes, of course. Mine was such a bore, too. He's a Major in India. I haven't seen him for years. I hope the weather keeps fine for him, down there.'

She opened the door of the room.

'And here is Miles. Miles and miles and miles of him.'

The American was sitting up in the large bed, laughing, when they entered.

'He's got such nice teeth, too,' thought Franciska.

'Mrs. Parker. Where did Jo pick you up?'

'The bath water was cold,' said Franciska.

'Yes, wasn't it lucky, Miles?'

'I'll say it was lucky. Make yourself at home, ma'am.'

'And she hasn't had any breakfast either, Miles.'

'That's lucky, too.'

'And her husband has gone fishing.'

'That's grand. Aren't we all lucky?' He got out of bed. 'Sit her down, Jo. I'll see that she gets her breakfast. I'll raise the roof in this place and I'll go through them like a dose of salts.'

As he bent down to get into his slippers, Franciska thought that he was even taller and broader than he had seemed the night before.

'He should not really go to all this trouble,' she said to the young woman, after he had gone. She was filled with uneasiness.

'But of course,' replied the other and, as though guessing Franciska's thoughts, she added: 'Don't worry. He knows how to do things.'

She took two newspapers from an easy chair and made Franciska sit down. Franciska noticed that the newspapers were still folded up and had not been opened yet. 'He hasn't even looked at the papers and he and she must have been awake for some time,' she thought. On the occasions when Mr. Parker did not rise early, he always used to read the newspapers in bed. And the same feeling of envy seized her as when, the day before, she had noticed that the American had brought no fishing tackle with him.

'I am called Jo, it's really Josephine. Will you call me Jo?'

'I'd love to. My name is Cissy. It's really Franciska.'

'I am so glad you've got an old-fashioned name too. I like being old-fashioned sometimes. Don't you? But not all the time.'

'No, not all the time.'

It was not the chambermaid who made an appearance this time, but a waiter. He brought a tray with an egg on toast and a pot of marmalade and a dish of butter, but no tea.

The American got into bed again. He said: 'We'll get a second breakfast too, for ourselves. Because we are all so lucky.'

And the waiter came again, accompanied by that clinking sound which Franciska knew so well but which she had not expected to hear during this fishing week-end.

'Good God,' she said, and the young woman exclaimed: 'Isn't Miles a darling?'

After the waiter had arranged the champagne glasses on the dressing chest and put the ice pail beside it, he asked if he should open the bottle.

'No, thanks a lot. We'll wait till the lady has eaten her breakfast. Come here, George.' And the American, laughing, gave the waiter a pound note, saying: 'This is for your bad eyesight,' and a second pound note: 'and this is for your bad memory. Go and see the doctor, will you, George?'

'I will, sir. Straight away. Thank you very much, sir,' and the man left the room with a grave countenance.

Franciska said: 'I did the same thing once, too. But it was no good.'

'Why?' asked the American. 'Didn't you give him enough?'

'No, it was not that. It's just that it was useless because my mother knew in any case that I'd come home late.'

'Mothers can be very awkward,' said Josephine.

'Not really, Jo. I never had much trouble with them. With a mother, it's generally pretence. What I don't like, is husbands. I like to keep my dignity. I hate saying, stand back, sir, give me room, let me get on my trousers first. You know, ma'am, your husband despises me. He thinks I'm weak. Whereas I have the greatest admiration for him. And now, let me organize things a bit. That's why they sent me to this backward country.' He got up, carried the silver pail to the bed and put the glasses on the bedside table. The American did not like the popping of corks; he opened the bottle quickly and silently. And without looking up, as he filled the glasses, he said: 'And you girls had better come to bed. I like to have everything at hand.'

Josephine said: 'Come on, Cissy. Miles is quite right. You'll only get cold, hanging about. And Miles is getting cold, too. Aren't you, Miles?'

The American laughed and said: 'That's quite true. I am shivering. I am an extinguished volcano, this morning, anyway. I am as safe as an extinguished volcano. Come on, girls,' and, still laughing, he added with great cordiality: 'Give your daddy a kiss.'

So it happened that at half past ten in the morning Franciska found herself in bed, in the arms of a stranger drinking champagne; both things which had never happened to her before, which she had never envisaged and which, in spite of that, she accepted with full composure. She knew that while her mother-in-law would have considered the American to be 'bad company,' to Mrs. Kalny he would have been perfectly acceptable. It was true, that, living as he did, his reputation would have acquired a social *haut goût* anywhere. Yes, this was quite different from being 'impossible.' Nothing in the situation went against her grain, as it did not clash with anything in her upbringing. It seemed to her a much more natural way of life than, for instance, looking after Mr. Parker's creature comforts.

Her feeling of being at home was increased by Josephine, who continued the sort of small talk which brings the extraordinary down to the level of the ordinary. She said: 'Don't you think Miles is awfully comfortable to lean on? and 'Are you sure you've got enough blankets?' and 'Wouldn't you like another pillow?' It all reminded Franciska of Mrs. Kalny taking friends out in her car for a pleasure drive and asking: 'Are you quite comfortable? Have you got enough room? Would you like another rug over your knees. There is one, you know.' And just as a person who has never before in his life been in a car, would reply as though he were comparing it with many other cars, so Franciska, who had before this day only been in bed with her husband, replied: 'Yes thank you. He is lovely and comfortable.'

The American did not speak. From time to time he detached his arm from Franciska, in order to fill the glasses. Every time after he had done so, and his arm returned to her, she awaited it with longing and let herself sink more deeply into the embrace.

Josephine, at the other side, leaned across him, saying: 'I hope he behaves. Don't let him bother you, Cissy. He's got wandering hands, it's an American disease.'

And Franciska replied: 'Oh no, he is quite all right, really, Jo,' just as, at a tea party, she would have told the hostess that she did not mind being pawed by the dog.

The American said: 'This drink is doing me good. I feel quite warm now. If only I were in bed with a nice woman. Oh, what couldn't I do to a nice woman.'

'Isn't he silly,' exclaimed Josephine. 'I don't know what Cissy will think of you,' and while she broke into laughter, she leaned back and shook her head at him, with a warning look. And he responded with a look as though to say: 'Don't worry. I shan't.'

Josephine's admonition had been unnecessary. Most men in this position would have believed that they were irresistible to Franciska, but the American knew that it was the piquancy of the chance encounter which up till now had worked in his favour. He believed in letting events take their course. He could foresee her friendliness change into cold reserve, he could foresee her withdrawal, and he was altogether too experienced to be convinced of his final

195

success. To him, women were not a mystery and because of it, he expected them to behave as unpredictably as other human beings.

He also realized that Franciska relaxed much more on this particular occasion than she would have done had she been alone with him; and that she was ignorant enough to believe that 'nothing could happen' while the other woman was present.

It is said that when Pavlova danced, she never moved her arms to produce an æsthetic effect; when she raised an arm, she did so because it was necessary to keep her balance when raising a leg. It is the same sense for economy that guides the real seducer of women. The American kept quiet during the hour that passed and did not flatter or court Franciska in any way; he knew that his time was yet to come.

When Franciska went downstairs shortly before one o'clock, she met her husband in the hall with the spaniel, both sodden with rain.

He said: 'I would have skipped lunch if the weather had been better.'

'You are not a stiff upper-lipper, I see. I am disappointed in you,' replied Franciska. She seemed absent-minded. Then, as though remembering her husband's presence with a start, she asked: 'Did you catch anything?'

'Nothing really.'

'How sad. But I have a great admiration for you just the same.' She stretched her arms. 'I stayed in bed all morning. There is nothing else to do, in this beastly place, in this beastly weather, is there?'

'Well, I'll be seeing you in five minutes,' he said.

When Mr. Parker came downstairs again, he found Franciska in the hall, talking to the manageress.

They went into the dining room. The American and the young woman were already seated at their table, but this time Mr. Parker had no reason to fear that his wife might be tempted to return the American's greeting in such a fashion that they might feel compelled to stop and talk for a few moments. This time Franciska did not even look in his direction but turned her back on their table, and, pointing to the plates ranged on shelves against the wall, she said with great animation: 'This blue-and-white china always looks very pretty, doesn't it? Do you think it's old, Johnny?'

'I can't tell. I suppose it is. The whole place is very old.'

'Yes, it is supposed to be very old,' said Franciska eagerly.

But as soon as they started their lunch her animation vanished and she went through the meal in silence.

CHAPTER 7

AS FRANCISKA climbed through the coppice behind the vicarage she could see the American and Josephine standing on the path above her, laughing and talking.

Josephine ran to meet her. 'You are late, Cissy. Where have you been? We were wondering what had happened to you. Miles said your husband was short of flies and had put you on the hook as bait for the trout. Isn't Miles silly?'

'I am sorry I have been so long,' replied Franciska. They joined the American and began to descend the other side of the hill where he had left his car.

'I had to see the butcher,' explained Franciska.

'What, again?' asked the American. 'Is the butcher handsome? Is he better looking than I am?'

'I don't know. I never look at him.'

'Perhaps he has a beautiful voice?'

'Leave the poor little thing alone, Miles,' said Josephine. 'She looks quite worried.'

'I am getting worried too, Jo,' and he unlocked the door of the car. 'I thought I was making an impression on her and now it has been the butcher all the time. Get in, girls. We are going to Burford for tea and we'll be back in time to wash our hands before dinner and eat our meal at our respective tables, as decently as anybody could wish for.'

'Let's stay there for dinner,' said Franciska.

He shook his head. 'I will not listen to your improper suggestions.'

'It is all right,' said Franciska, 'Johnny has gone to Coventry and he won't be back till late to-night.'

'So you went to the butcher and arranged a rendezvous?'

'I did not. He was absolutely beastly.'

The interview with the butcher had indeed been very unpleasant. Mr. Parker had caught eleven trout during the morning and had asked Franciska to take them to the butcher, to be put in his cold-storage room. At first, the man had been impressed by the sight of the trout.

'Ah, what it is to be a gentleman of leisure,' he had said. 'I'd like to take off a week myself, sometime.'

'But my husband caught them to-day, you know, this morning. And he is not really having a proper holiday, he has to go back to Coventry, to the factory. And in two days' time we shall be leaving, altogether.'

'What? Eleven blooming trout in half a day? Not on your life, madam.'

'Well, he did.'

The butcher's countenance had changed. 'I thought I was a butcher but it looks as if your husband is putting me out of business.' He smacked the fish on a platter in the disdainful way with which he used to handle the strips of inferior meat he sold Franciska for the dog. 'All right. I'll put them by. For the first and last time. I don't know nothing about them. But you can tell your husband from me that he'll get himself in trouble one of these days and I shan't feed him buns in prison.'

The American and Josephine listened attentively while Franciska was telling them about the butcher.

Then Josephine said: 'And how many did he catch

before? He has been fishing for days now, don't we all know it?'

'Nothing, I think,' said Franciska.

'It is quite obvious,' said Josephine. 'Of course, you can't know these things, you have not been in this country long enough.'

'What is it?' asked Franciska. She felt that Josephine was going to tell her something shameful, because the American had begun to whistle, as though to indicate that he was not listening to their talk.

'It's just that your husband isn't–you know. Never mind. Be glad you've got the day clear and enjoy it. I suppose he'll bring you a present when he gets back from Coventry.'

'He never does bring me anything,' replied Franciska. 'Except to-day, the eleven trout.'

'Well, mine always did, he was very quaint that way. I could count his affairs not on the fingers on my hands, but on the rings on my fingers. Husbands always think that you will not ask any questions when they give you something. Quite touching, you know.'

As on several occasions before, Franciska felt disappointment at Josephine's words. Always, an explanation was hinted at and never given. It reminded her of the shop windows of the great dressmakers in Paris, where a dress is exhibited, coiled up in such a way that it is impossible to tell what it looks like.

The American turned his head and said as though sensing her thoughts: 'You'd better tell her, Jo. She knows already, she's seen his home.'

Josephine said: 'But it is so difficult to explain. You see, Cissy, trout are caught with dry fly, it isn't really a fly, you know, it only looks like one, and it doesn't really look like one, either. Anyway, that's how it is.'

'Oh, yes, I have seen them,' said Franciska.

'There you are. And it is very difficult to catch trout with them. That's why it's done.'

'Oh yes?'

'It is sport, you know. It gives the trout a fair chance. And your husband, it is quite evident to me, must have used live bait. They go madly for live bait, they adore it. That's why it isn't done. And the butcher was quite right, he knows as well as anybody.'

'And the buns in prison?'

'There he was quite right too. Fishing trout with live bait is strictly forbidden, you can get heavily fined. They even frown at wet fly. You ask your husband when he gets back and you will see.'

'There will be a row if I do.'

'What? A row? First fishing with live bait and then a row? He should hang his head in shame,' said Josephine.

'But he does not hang his head in shame,' said the American, 'that is the trouble. It is Cissy who hangs her head in shame, don't you, Cissy?'

'Poor little thing,' said Josephine. 'By the way, where did your husband go to school? Do you know?'

'He went to a–grammar school I think. Is that right?'

'In his case it seems to have been all wrong,' replied Josephine with a disgust she had never shown before. 'I think it was very brave of you to marry him.'

'Johnny says it was a very old school,' said Franciska. 'It was founded in the fifteenth century.'

Josephine did not reply. The American said with a laugh: 'I am getting old too, and it does not improve me. An old man is not a good man.'

Now that the knowledge that Mr. Parker was 'impossible,' was shared by her companions, Franciska, to her own surprise, experienced a sense of relief. Yet it was not surprising. It is always gratifying to have one's suspicions confirmed by others, no matter how shameful they may be. She thought: 'No wonder I have been so miserable ever since I got married. And nobody can blame me either. Josephine would be miserable too, in my place.'

'But why did you marry him in the first place?' asked Josephine.

The American said: 'Enough of this girlish talk and chatter. We are getting into Burford, girls. Compose yourselves.' He thought: 'Yes, why did she? Who shall ever know?'

He listened absent-mindedly while Josephine was talking about her marriage in India. He heard Franciska say: 'How dreadful for you, Jo.'

'Dreadful? No,' said Josephine. 'Certainly not. Dreadful is too much, dreadful is simply too much. One doesn't make a tragedy of that sort of thing. It was unpleasant. But then, one has one's way of hitting back.'

'How do you mean, Jo?'

He said: 'Where do you want to have tea, girls?' and he thought: 'I wish Jo didn't go on. It's no good. She does not know what's tragic any more than a squirrel does. She just jumps from tree to tree and one tree is as good as the other as long as there are plenty of nuts on it. And Cissy listens as though waiting for a revelation any moment.'

He slowed down as they approached an inn.

'How's that, girls, do you like the look of it? The river goes past there, on the other side and we could sit out, under the trees.'

'How lovely, Miles,' exclaimed Josephine and she added, turning to Franciska: 'Whenever Miles picks a place, you can be sure it is the best in the whole town. You never have to worry when you are with Miles. He knows how to do things.'

The American helped them out of the car.

'How nice he is,' thought Franciska. 'Johnny never helps me to get out. And he is so nice all together. The way he talks to waiters, for instance. He knows how to do things. Johnny is hopeless when he orders a meal.'

She did not allow herself to think any further on these lines. Just as people, on the occasion of a fashionable wedding, show great interest in all the arrangements of the ceremony and discuss with eagerness the details of the clothes because this serves as a cloak to the quite different thoughts which are aroused at the idea of a wedding, so Franciska cloaked her conviction that Miles 'knew how to do things' in remembering his way with waiters.

They chose a table in the garden and the American went inside to see if he could get any deck chairs. When he came back, the sight of Franciska, sitting next to Josephine, gripped his heart.

'I should not go on,' he thought. 'Yet it will come to that, in the end. To Jo, it would never happen. And Cissy will never understand.'

He sat down. 'Stop reminiscing, Jo. Cissy is too innocent.'

Josephine shrieked with laughter. 'If she is, she won't be much longer.' She added: I'm trying to explain to Cissy why her husband is the way he is. It isn't really his fault, is it, Miles? It's the way he was born and bred. If you fall into a sausage machine you come out the other end as a sausage.'

But Miles did not answer.

CHAPTER 8

'NASTY THINGS, these migraines,' said Dr. Craig.
'Nasty pain.'

Franciska, propped up in bed, looked at the red-cheeked,
soldierly man, thinking: '*Quelle différence*,' a phrase which
had become habitual with her since her return from Lechworth.

It was true of course, that Dr. Craig's manner was quite
different from that of the Kalnys' family doctor in Prague.
Whereas the family doctor had been conciliatory and
soothing, the Englishman's attitude was belligerent. He
felt aggressive towards disease and attacked it, while the
other had approached it with resignation and respect,
always keeping in mind that he who cures completely,
cures to death.

'Nuisance, isn't it,' said Dr. Craig. This was his strongest
form of commiseration. To him, disease was a nuisance because it kept the patient from playing golf, and if the disease
was grave, it kept him, the doctor, from playing golf, too.

'I suppose he is quite sound,' thought Franciska. 'After
all, he is from the Embassy.'

'Nasty business,' said Dr. Craig. 'Have to get rid of it.'

'My mother suffers from it, too,' replied Franciska, feeling
nettled. As migraines were in her family, she did not see
how they could be called 'nasty'.

'Ah, there you are. These things are always hereditary. How long have you had them?'

'It is funny,' said Franciska. 'Only since I got married. At first every three or four months, that was nothing, much, but now it is getting very bad, once or twice a week. It is becoming unbearable. Do you think it is the climate? Yet Paris has really a very pleasant climate, hasn't it?'

'Difficult to say, could be anything. Have you been upset recently? Under any emotional strain?'

Doctor Craig felt impelled to ask these questions, they were part of his routine, and he was a conscientious man. At the same time such questions were loathsome to him for he dreaded the confidences they might bring forth. So in order to satisfy his conscience and at the same time to forestall further awkwardness, he pronounced his words in the same tone of voice which he had used when dealing with subordinates during the war. When he said: 'Been upset recently?' it was as though he had said: 'Any complaints?' with that undertone which implies: 'Don't you dare.'

'Strain?' asked Franciska. 'Upset? No, why should I be? There is no reason for me to be upset, is there?'

'Well, I don't know. Sorry. I was only asking.' This, with a face as though to say: 'Good girl. Knew you would play fair.'

'Do you sleep well at night?' he continued.

'Yes, I do. But I cannot go to sleep for a very long time. I generally lie awake for two hours before I fall asleep.'

'But once you sleep, you sleep well?'

'Oh, yes.'

'I see.' The doctor ran his fingers down his cheeks. Then he said: 'What brings it on? Any idea?'

'It is strange, you know, but I nearly always get a migraine when I go out in the car with Johnny. And I get terribly sick in the car. I cannot really understand it. At home, I used to love going for a drive. I could never get enough of it. But then we had a chauffeur. Do you think it makes a difference?'

'It shouldn't. Your husband should be an excellent driver.'

'Yes, he is. I am sure he is. I cannot really understand it.'

'I see,' said the doctor. He stroked his face. Franciska noticed that he suddenly looked very tired.

'These complaints are very difficult to get at, Mrs. Parker. I'll give you one lot of tablets and if that doesn't work, I'll try out another and so on, till I hit on the right thing. Of course, you know, you may grow out of it yourself.'

'Do you think so?' asked Franciska.

'Yes, I do. I have seen it happen.' He looked at her. He thought: 'It is always the same old story.' He said aloud: 'Yes, I have seen it happen, Mrs. Parker. It may be sooner than you think,' and he thought: 'I give her two more months. But I won't say anything to him, why should I? Lord, if only all my patients were as easy to cure as she is.'

'Here is the medicine,' he said.

Franciska noticed that his voice sounded quizzical. She thought: 'He doesn't believe in the stuff himself. He knows it's no good.' In this she was right. But in thinking that Doctor Craig didn't know the right remedy she was mistaken.

'Take two straight away,' said the doctor, 'and next time, when you feel an attack coming on, nip it in the bud, do you see? And another thing of great importance: you should be lying in the dark.'

'Yes, I know,' said Franciska. 'My mother always used to lie down with the blinds drawn. But what am I to do? We have not got any blinds in this flat. There were some, I think, but they fell to pieces.'

'Get new ones, or shutters.'

'Yes, that is an idea,' said Franciska. She knew that there could be no question of getting new blinds. Mr. Parker, who spent freely on guns and fishing tackle was spartan when it came to his domestic surroundings. In winter, when it was bitterly cold, he preferred to cover himself with an overcoat rather than to allow his wife to buy more blankets. Franciska saw in this a sign of his stinginess. She did not understand that it was merely one way of expressing his fear and hatred of the feminine sphere. It was true of course, that by depriving her of sufficient housekeeping money he deprived himself of many comforts as well but this was natural in the man whose grimace of brutality did not only denote that he was brutal to others, but that he was also brutalizing himself.

'Well, give it a try, there's a good girl. See how you get on. If it gets worse, let me know. If I don't hear from you, I'll know that you are better. No news, good news.'

He was at the door when Franciska recalled him. She said: 'I wonder, Doctor Craig, if you could not give me a sleeping drug after all. Just something very harmless, please.'

'Of course I will. I would have given you something sooner, but you said you slept well.'

'I do, doctor. That is to say, I did. But now, that my husband is away such a great deal, I get so frightened at night that it keeps me awake. I know it's very silly. I have the dog, but he is very young, you know, and I don't think he is much of a watchdog.'

The doctor fetched the black bag which he had left in the hall and gave her a handful of pills in a screwed-up piece of paper. 'It's a nuisance for you, being so much on your own. Why don't you have someone to stay with you?'

'I don't know anybody who would.'

'Doesn't your mother ever come over?' he asked.

'She is living in Italy now,' said Franciska. 'She was here last month. She won't come again till next year, I think.'

'Pity,' said Doctor Craig. 'Never mind. Cheer up.' Once more, at the door, he turned round and raised his hand, saying: 'Cheer up.'

'Idiot,' thought Franciska. She closed her eyes. The pain in her left temple had increased. 'It is just as with Mama,' she said to herself. 'She too, always had it on her left side.'

This thought filled her with some satisfaction. Then, the memory of the comfort and attendance which had surrounded Mrs. Kalny's migraines aroused in her an envy which turned into self-pity at the thought of her own circumstances. She knew that her mother would not return to Paris till the autumn of the next year, when the famous dressmakers would be showing their new collections. She knew that if she asked her to come now Mrs. Kalny's attitude would be the same as it had been when she had accepted Uncle Victor's invitation to dinner on Franciska's behalf: 'Since you are married and living the way you do, I wish you joy of it. This comes from making friends with impossible people.' The thought that her mother still lived in comfort, while she herself had only one maid-of-all-work, filled her with a feeling which she mistook for homesickness. 'I'd give anything to see somebody from home. Even Louise.'

Her eyes filled with the easy tears of those whose nerves are weakened by pain and lack of sleep. 'I used to be beastly to Louise.' Her tears began to flow and she did not restrain them. It was the first time that Franciska had shed any tears on the maid's behalf. She thought them to be tears of remorse and pity; they were tears of pity, but not for the maid.

Elise entered and at once Franciska stopped weeping.

It had been inbred in her that one did not let oneself go in front of the '*canaille*,' and her upbringing was stronger than her desire to be comforted. She asked the maid to replenish the water in the jug by her side and while Elise left the room, the dog came in and ran up to Franciska's bed. And although she lowered her hand to stroke his head, she turned her face away from him. 'I shan't save you another time, Teddy,' and then, as he licked her hand: 'It is no good, Teddy, I can't.'

The maid returned. Franciska said: 'I am sorry about it, Elise, just on your free afternoon. You must really go now, I shan't want anything any more. If you could just take the dog down for a minute or so.'

'Is monsieur coming back to-night, madame?'

'I don't think so.'

Immediately after their return from England Mr. Parker had been assigned to a different job by the man he always spoke of as the 'big white chief'. The new work entailed frequent journeys to other motor-car factories and lengthy absences from home. Mr. Parker attributed this change to the fact that the American had, once more, taken up residence in Paris, and: 'always finds somebody to do his ruddy work for him. If they had a posh hotel in the provinces, he'd soon go, himself, doing his own flaming inspection tours. Liaison he calls it. He thinks of nothing but liaison, but not this kind.'

Franciska never found out whether this change had been imposed on Mr. Parker in his capacity as an engineer or in his capacity as her husband. But she remembered her clandestine good-bye in the garden of the Pelican.

'We'll say *au revoir*, shall we?'

'I am afraid not. I don't suppose I shall ever see you again.'

And Josephine's laughter: 'Don't worry, Cissy. Miles knows how to do things.'

She listened to the maid's footsteps and she heard the slam of the door. She lay still, without shutting her eyes. Despite of it, the pictures which had come to her in the darkness of the night, came again now, in full daylight.

She saw again the bedroom in the Pelican, as it had been on their last evening in Lechworth. Mr. Parker was sitting on his bed in his pyjamas. Franciska, in her dressing gown, was busying herself with combs and brushes on the dressing table. This was one of her ways of dawdling and she hoped, as she always did, that if she pretended to some sort of activity last thing at night, her husband would go to bed before she did and thus, once settled, would go to sleep straight away.

He said: 'What's all this in aid of? Fiddling about, eh?'

'I only want to tidy up, Johnny.'

'Well, stop it, for crying out loud. I want to get some sleep.'

'Sorry,' she said.

'Well, come on. Show me how sorry you are.'

He got up and took her by the shoulder. His body, pressed to hers, felt hard and bony.

She freed herself from his arms. 'You are not comfortable,' she said. 'I—leave me alone.'

'What's the matter with you?'

'Nothing. I just want to be left alone.'

She had often wished to act in this way but it was the first time that she had thus defied him. She did not know what had suddenly, on this occasion, given her the courage. She did not even realize what had made her choose the very words she used.

'Women are funny,' he said. 'I don't know. What do you want? Do you want a new hat?'

She looked at him in silence.

It was only then, when he felt that there was something beyond his comprehension, which somehow raised his wife on to a plane beyond his grasp, that Mr. Parker's face took on that flushed and swollen look that Franciska dreaded.

Penelope, while waiting for her husband to return, kept off the clamours of her ten wooers by unravelling at night the work on the tapestry which she had done during the day. Many marriages are like this; what has been done during the day, is unravelled at night. But there are many marriages where what has been destroyed by day is built up again at night. This was Mr. Parker's way. He forgot how he treated his wife during the day, he forgot his rages, and he therefore took it for granted that she did the same. Since he had never yet met with any opposition on her part at night, there was no outward sign that anything might be amiss.

'Come on to bed,' he said. 'I tell you for the last time.'

'No, I won't,' Franciska said and she thought: 'Thank God, we are in an hotel.' She added: 'If you touch me, I'll scream.'

His eyes were still small and shiny with rage, but to her surprise he did not shout. He said: 'I won't touch you. I'll go and talk to Teddy instead. Here, Teddy, my lad.' And walking to the chair on which the dog was lying, he repeated: 'Eh, Teddy, my lad.'

It was only when Franciska recalled the scene afterwards, that she remembered that the dog had not wagged his tail at his master's approach but had made a movement as though trying to get away.

Mr. Parker said: 'If you don't do as I want, I'll hurt him.'

'Don't be silly,' said Franciska and as she turned her back, she heard the dog's yelp.

It is possible to find courage for the horror which can be known or imagined. But when the unexpected occurs, it is apt to shatter one's composure.

'Stop it,' she cried.

Franciska did not possess that inordinate love for 'our dumb friends' in which the English glory and in which they glorify their own dumbness. But she had a fear of bodily violence; not so much on moral grounds but because it turned her stomach. It was her nerves not her heart, which set her trembling when she heard this high squeal, long drawn out, and wavering, such as she had only heard once before, when someone had trodden by accident on the dog's paw.

'Stop it,' she cried.

She reached her husband and had to sit down on the chair beside the dog, as her knees gave way under her.

After they had returned to Paris there had been no repetition of that scene. Mr. Parker did not stay at home very long before he had to go on his first inspection tour. And when Franciska pleaded tiredness and headaches, he had contented himself with saying: 'Have your headaches while I'm away, will you?'

Franciska heard the slam of the front door and after a few moments, the spaniel was by her bed. She gave him a biscuit and while he crunched it, she took another one and began to eat it herself. The door bell rang. 'Oh, Elise. Now she has forgotten something. Why can't you open the door for me, Teddy?'

She slipped out of bed and ran into the hall barefooted. She opened the door. The American entered.

'Why, Mrs. Parker, what sort of a house is this? It

seems to be full of beautiful women. I just saw one leaving.'

'Oh, that was the maid, Elise.'

'I thought so. I am a connoisseur. I know a maid when I see one. And you are very beautiful too. In a different way. What's the matter?'

'I am in bed. I have a migraine.'

'It suits you awfully well.'

'I did not expect you,' said Franciska.

'Yes, I know. This is so sudden. But what am I to do? You don't have a phone, so I had to come and look you up. I had a letter from Jo. She sends her love.'

'Oh, how is she? I hope she is very well. I'd love to see her again,' said Franciska gravely and emphatically. She was naïve enough to believe that by showing her friendliness towards the American's mistress she would make it clear that she did not consider him as a man on his own merit but merely as Josephine's property. She added: 'You should not have come here at all. There is nothing wrong in it of course, as it is——'

'Of course not. *Honi soit qui mal y pense.*'

'As I was saying, there is nothing wrong in it, but my husband might have been in and he would not have liked it.' And forgetting the coldness she had tried to assume at first, she said with a laugh: 'And you don't like husbands, I know.'

'What a wonderful memory you have got. I must have made some impression on you, after all, or you would not have remembered.'

She did not reply.

He said: 'Anyway, God's in His Heaven and all's right with the world and Parker is in Nancy as far as I know. That's quite far away.'

She said coldly: 'Not as far as India.'

'Just as far. They are both in the same latitude.'

Franciska pretended to ignore this. She said: 'I am really ill, you know. I should be in bed–I mean, I should not be on my feet at all. The doctor gave me something to take and I must rest.' He looked at her with an amusement which she resented. She moved away from him, towards the door to the drawingroom, and doing so, she tripped over the spaniel who had come up behind her. The American caught her with one arm.

'Steady, ma'am,' he said. He released her and took a step away from her.

'Thank you,' said Franciska. A feeling of disappointment took hold of her which she could not explain. She looked at him.

The American was not a wencher, he was a seducer. He knew that forbidden fruit, like all other kinds, must be allowed to ripen before it becomes palatable; he had not the schoolboy's appetite for green fruit. Josephine, who held that gentlemen give their prey a 'fair chance,' would have approved of that.

'He is very decent, really,' said Franciska to herself and although this thought should have filled her with satisfaction, it increased her sudden hostility towards him. She did not know that it was not decency, but calculation, that made him stand as he did, at a respectful distance from her, with a harmless, cordial expression in his eyes. He laughed.

'As a matter of fact,' he said, 'I was going to ask you if you would care to come out with me to-night. I have asked two or three other people and I thought we'd drive out of this renowned and cosmopolitan capital and have dinner in the country. How is your head? It looks lovely to me from the outside. But then, I will not pretend to know what goes on inside the heads of beautiful young women. I don't think even your doctor knows.'

'Of course he does. Don't be so silly. My mother has these attacks too, sometimes.'

'I quite believe it. Daughters never do what their mothers did not do themselves.'

Franciska said: 'Of course. These things are hereditary,' and it was only after she had said it that she began to wonder as to the meaning of his remark.

'Well, will you come?'

'I really don't know if I should.'

'I shall be very disappointed if you don't, you know. After all, you should look after me, now that I am deserted by Josephine.' He glanced at her so ironically that she thought: 'Oh, my God, have I said something dreadful again?' He continued with his ironical expression: 'Will you come, for– Jo's sake?'

'If I am well enough by then.'

'Splendid. I'll pick you up in front of the café at the corner at half past six. And before I forget. I brought some blue-prints and a message for your husband. It's all in this envelope. If he returns to-night ask him to let me know what he thinks about it. He knows my number at the Ritz and if I am not in he can leave a message. But if he does not come back until next week, don't bother about it. It cannot wait and if he is not back by Monday we shall have to go on without him.'

'Thank you,' said Franciska. And while she went with him to the door, she thought: 'Jo was quite right. He knows how to do things.'

She returned to the bedroom and, getting into her bed, she saw the tablets on the table.

'Oh, God, I should have taken these a long time ago. I'll take them now.'

She swallowed two and drank some water. She lay back and closed her eyes. Only then did it occur to her that the pain in her head had completely gone.

She had been resting for a very short time – barely a few minutes, it seemed to her, when the door bell rang once more Her heart jumped. 'It is the American again, he will cancel the dinner.' This time, she put on slippers and a gown and arranged her hair before she went to the door. Opening, she saw a boy in livery; he had a small parcel in his hand. 'It is the *chasseur* from the Ritz,' she thought, while her heart beat painfully.

'Madame Parker?'

'Yes. What is it?'

She took the parcel from him.

'There is a letter inside.'

'Are you from the Ritz?' she asked.

'No, the Crillon, madame.'

'The Crillon?'

'The Crillon.'

'But I don't know anybody staying at the Crillon,' Franciska thought. She closed the door abruptly with a sense of relief. It was only while she tore through the wrapping that it occurred to her that she should have tipped the page.

The letter was placed on top of a jeweller's case and as she opened the case, the letter slipped to the floor. She saw a bracelet worked in the shape of a snake, the eyes made of rubies, the scales of red, white and yellow gold. At the first glance she said: 'Feldman. Oh God.'

The bracelet had no clasp but as she placed it on her wrist, she felt the grip of a concealed spring. 'How hideous. If mama saw it she would faint.'

She picked up the letter and read it: 'I am staying at the Crillon for three days. Have dinner with me to-night, I hope you are free. Raphael Feldman.'

She took off the bracelet and put it in its case and before shutting it, saw the name of a famous jeweller on the lining. 'He must have turned the whole shop upside down before he found this horror,' she thought. 'Thank God, Mama did not marry him.'

She did not go back to bed and began to wander from room to room, driven by a sudden restlessness. 'I will ring him up and tell him I can't come,' she repeated to herself. 'I'll just tell him that I am not free. I may be having dinner with Roland and his wife, or anybody, for all he knows.' She began to dress.

At six o'clock she left the house and walked to the café at the corner of the street. She order a Dubonnet and asked if she could make a telephone call.

The telephone was on a landing, half way between the ground floor and the basement. It was so dark that she had to pick up the directory and ascend a few steps in order to be able to see. She thought of her lunch at the Esplanade, her walk through the snowstorm, her meeting with the beautiful Mrs. Reiser, and her mood of defiance changed into fury.

At last she made the call. There was the usual delay before she was connected with Feldman and while she waited, she thought angrily: 'He always turns up when I am in trouble and gives idiotic advice.' And then: 'But I am not in trouble, this time. There is nothing to worry about. I am upset because of Doctor Craig, the idiot, with his questions about emotional strain. Oh, God, why can't they all leave me alone.'

Then she heard the rasping voice, and although she had been prepared for it, it gave her a start.

'This is Feldman speaking. Feldman asks you to have dinner with him to-night.'

'I want to thank you, Mr. Feldman, for the lovely——

'Eh, it's rubbish. How is your mother?'

'She is very well, Mr. Feldman. She was here last month on a visit. I wanted to tell you that I am very sorry but I cannot see you to-night.'

'Why say you are sorry? You are not sorry when you've got somebody better to go out with than an old Jew. Where is your husband? Has he gone away?'

'Yes, on a business trip. I should have loved you to meet him. What a pity.'

'Nonsense. If I don't see him, I don't see him. I don't have to have everything in life. Be careful to-night. You think you will go somewhere where nobody will see you, but somebody always does. Eh.'

'You don't understand, Mr. Feldman. My cousin Roland and his wife have——'

'I know. Ring me up to-morrow, when you are free. And enjoy yourself. Everything in life passes, even the most beautiful Jew gets shabby. Have a good time. Feldman says you should have a good time. And come and see me to-morrow. Good-bye.'

Franciska went upstairs and sat down. She had not finished her drink when the American arrived. They went out to the car.

'We'll go straight on to Versailles,' he said, 'to the Chapeau Gris. The others will meet us there. Are you better?'

'Oh yes, I am quite well.'

'You are looking very thoughtful. Would you rather not come out with me? I'll take you back to the rue Perrault if you'd rather.'

'No, I want to come.'

'Would you? I wonder. You are worried. Has another butcher come into your life?'

'Not a butcher. But I am annoyed. A friend of my mother's has come to Paris and he wanted to see me to-night and I told him I couldn't and he knew straight away that—you know.'

'I don't know. I wish I knew.'

'He guessed that Johnny had gone away.'

'Well?'

'And I told him that I was having dinner with my relations and he didn't believe me.'

'Apparently he knows you.'

'Of course he does. He is a very old friend of ours.'

'And now you are worried that he will tell your mother?'

'Oh no,' said Franciska. 'I never thought of it. And even if she knew she would not care. And I would not care either.'

'What else did he have to say?'

'Nothing much. He told me to have a good time.'

'He sounds very reasonable to me. Why are you so put out?'

'Oh, he just annoys me. He is not really reasonable, you know. He is—oh, I don't know.' While she spoke, Franciska realized that she felt irritated with Feldman in the same way as she felt irritated with the charwoman who came twice a week to the flat to help Elise.

'He is just like a bad servant,' she said. 'He picks up everything and then moves it to a wrong place. Nothing is ever put back where it belongs.'

'You mean he misunderstands you?' asked the American. He laughed. He added: 'But perhaps it is you who are like a bad servant and perhaps it is he who puts your emotions in the right place.'

'Oh no, he is terribly crude.'

'Some emotions are terribly crude. All the emotions that matter are terribly crude. Have you never thought of it?'

'You are silly,' said Franciska. 'And he is idiotic. He always was, he was just like that in Prague, too.'

'So he misunderstood you in Prague too? What was there to misunderstand? A love affair?'

'Not at all. He thought so. But I wasn't in love—of course.'

'Of course,' repeated the American. 'And you are not in love with me either, of course?' He began to laugh.

'Don't be ridiculous. I believe that you are expecting me to make you a declaration of love,' said Franciska.

To her surprise the American stopped laughing and said in a serious tone of voice: 'No, that is not quite true. I do not expect it, although I was hoping that you would.'

'You were—?'

'Yes, I was.'

'My mother always said,' said Franciska, 'that lieutenants of the Imperial Guard were the vainest creatures in the world. But I should say the vainest creatures are American motor-car experts of thirty-five.'

'And I have to say thank you for this because you were kind enough to spare me four years of my age.'

'Oh, really?' asked Franciska. 'I did not know.'

They were silent.

He lit a cigar. 'Jo might have made the same replies,' he thought, 'but she would have done it deliberately, out of coquetry, *on recule pour mieux sauter*. But this one doesn't. She really believes what she is saying, she is still like a child, she takes the play seriously.'

He said: 'We are getting into Versailles. Can you see the

rue St. Roche, it's a turning on our right, I think that's it, yes, there it is. I hope you will like the dinner. '

He thought: 'This dinner. And one more dinner. And then——. Young men always think that innocent women are difficult to make but they fall more easily than the most hard-boiled demi-mondaines, that's the tragedy of it.' He smiled to himself. 'Parker's idea of innocence would probably be a girl who took as long to surrender as Troy did. The fool.'

IT WAS late at night when Franciska returned from Versailles and she was tired out. Yet she slept fitfully despite the sleeping drug which Doctor Craig had given her. It was only at dawn that sleep came to her and then it brought a succession of dreams which, although forgotten upon waking, left her with an uneasy feeling for the next few hours.

When she lay in bed, she was forced against her will to relive in her mind the various unpleasant incidents of her married life. They filled her with a bitterness which grew with each repeated vision, but they did not frighten her. Yet when she had told the doctor that she was frightened during the night, she had spoken the truth.

'What am I afraid of?' she asked herself without being able to find an answer. Her relations took it for granted that she was afraid of burglars and she left them in this belief. She despised those who believe in ghosts; in her home country, ghosts were regarded as the fiction of uncouth minds, peculiar to servants only. And yet, without knowing it, it was both ghosts and burglars that she dreaded.

Burglars break into a domicile stealthily and unasked, and rob their victim of his dearest possessions. Ghosts rise from the past, the French call them '*revenants*', that is, those who return. Once living, now dead, they rise again before him who has known them and their appearance s usually taken as a warning of things to come. She did not ask herself why her fear of the darkness had only arisen after her stay in Lechworth, and this fear which was the voice of her soul, remained unheard, just as she accepted her migraines without understanding that they were the language of her body.

It was not only pictures from her married life that she saw. On that night, after the dinner with the American, the episode with Ling had risen before her with a strength and insistence she had not known before. Ling had started their first conversation in the Boccaccio by telling her that he had been one of her mother's admirers in the past. Franciska did not love her mother, she disapproved of her flirtatiousness and of the way in which she attracted the attention of men. At the same time, she tried to copy her in every way because this disapproval did not spring from repulsion but from envy. And it was because Ling had been the first of her mother's admirers who had shown an interest in her, the daughter, that the young girl had felt drawn towards him. Thus, when Ling came into her mind, it was the ghost of her first desires that appeared before her, as a warning of things to come. And just as ghosts, though dead themselves, are signposts on the road of the living, so the thought of Ling was pointing towards the road which led away from Mr. Parker and seemed to lead into the arms of the American. It was impossible to ignore this road. As Franciska's disgust for her husband grew, so did her fondness for the American. Yes she refused to see this disgust and fondness for what they were.

She pretended to herself that she was revolted by her husband because of his ill-bred brutality and that she was attracted to the American because of his decency and kindness. 'Johnny would never have got me breakfast after ten. And he would not have ordered champagne,' she thought, among other things. Or: 'Johnny would never lie in bed with me and talk to me. All he wants to do is to read the papers.'

This pretence was her dearest possession. And it was therefore not astonishing that the welling up of those forces which threatened to break in and rob her of it, filled her with fright. Although she explained her migraines by the fact that she had inherited them from her mother, she would not admit to herself that in other ways as well, she was her mother's daughter.

On the following day, in the late afternoon she met Feldman in the Crillon bar. His first words were: 'You are looking more like your mother than ever.'

She forced herself to smile as they sat down. She avoided his eyes. As of old, she had the feeling that he knew her most secret thoughts. 'But he doesn't,' she said to herself, 'it's all nonsense.' Her uneasiness grew. She had expected him to question her about the night before, but he seemed to have forgotten their conversation on the telephone. Almost at once he began to tell her one of his fabulous tales:

'So she says to me, Feldman, it is not usual to show the handwriting of a six-year-old. But here it is. I am worried to death about my son. I look at it and I say: This is not your son, it is not your blood. That boy is a murderer. Put him out of your house at once, or he'll kill you. So she wept and fell on her knees and said, Feldman, how did you know? It is an adopted child and only yesterday he picked up a kitchen knife and said he would kill me.'

He talked without stopping for half an hour, until the appearance of his secretary. He signalled to the young man to wait and rose from his seat. They walked slowly to the door. He said: 'I leave the day after to-morrow, I shall not see you any more, till the next time. Are you going to stay in Paris?'

'I suppose so, Mr. Feldman. Unless Johnny is transferred to England.'

'Johnny. Eh. Rubbish. I ask about you, not about Johnny.'

She did not answer.

He said: 'Do you need any money?'

'No, of course not, Mr. Feldman.'

'How do you know? When you need it, you go to the manager of this hotel and say to him, Feldman says that you should give me money.'

'But really, Mr. Feldman. Johnny earns quite a lot.'

'Let him earn.'

'And besides,' said Franciska, 'I have got my relations.'

'What's the good of your relations? They ask you this and they ask you that, but the Crillon doesn't ask you anything. Eh.'

He walked out with her and said good-bye to her on the pavement. After thay had parted, Franciska thought: 'He just wants to ingratiate himself with mama.'

Feldman, returning to the hotel, said to himself: 'Talking to her is as much good as feeding a lion with cauliflower.'

CHAPTER 10

It is a well-known fact that gossip anticipates events before they have taken place; and just as it has been said that many things would never have happened, had they not been predicted, so one could believe that many things would not have happened, had they never been gossiped about.

Among the Viancourt staff of Bluecroft Motors the rumour went round that Mr. Parker's marriage was 'cracking up.' Mr. Parker was not a popular man, and it was therefore not from kindness that a complete silence was observed towards him, regarding his wife's movements during his absence. From the beginning, the marriage had been the cause of many speculations. On the few occasions when Mr. Parker spoke about his wife, he did so with a bragging pride that was found revolting. Once, when two engineers from the factory had been asked to dinner, Mr. Parker raised the soup ladle and said: 'This is my wife's silver. Just feel how heavy it is.' 'He's made a good catch' was what most of them said.

They did not understand that Franciska's husband like so many men carried within them a craving for the romantic. To any Englishman, Franciska was exotic and by marrying her, Mr. Parker had committed the only romantic act he was ever to commit in his life. This was not all. Mr. Parker had left the Tank Corps in order to, in his own words, 'lead a decent life'. And this craving for respectability led, quite naturally, to his desire to live the life of a married man. With this in mind, it might have seemed strange that he should have chosen Franciska. He had been disgusted by Mrs. Kalny's frivolity and had been equally disgusted by Franciska's own attitude and that of her Parisian relatives, culminating in the scene at the *Boeuf sur le Toit*.

His colleagues were ignorant of all this, yet they had only to look at Franciska, to see that she did not fit into that society from which her husband sprang. 'They go as well together,' someone had once remarked, 'as the hedgehog goes with the lavatory paper.'

They none of them realized that Mr. Parker's choice had been inevitable. Just as the naturally jealous man will marry a flirtatious woman in order to be able to exercise his jealousy, so Mr. Parker, with his obsession for respectability, had married a woman who would keep this obsession evergreen.

Nobody wondered what had given rise to this obsession. Franciska herself did not wonder either, although she had been intrigued by Feldman's remark: 'If you could find out why he left the Service, you'd know a lot.' She did not connect the two things. Nor was it clear to her whether Feldman, on that occasion, had seen more than he chose to say, or had been as ignorant on the matter as everybody else.

But although the staff at Bluecroft Motors had every intention of enjoying the spectacle of the breaking marriage to the full, and to drag it out as long as was in their power, they could not resist the temptation to bait Mr. Parker with seemingly harmless remarks and to watch his reactions to them. There is great satisfaction derived from knowing more than the other person, and they were not willing to forgo it.

So, on the Thursday morning when Mr. Parker returned to the factory, they said to him things like: 'It's hard luck on you, being away so much from home. I'll suppose you are missing it. You'll get sick of hotel life very soon.' And: 'Your wife must be very lonely, now that you are away so much. I suppose she goes to the Ritz to console herself. There are always plenty of nasty old men to step in your shoes. Aren't you worried at all?' And: 'I bet she treated you like the returning hero. All your favourite dishes, eh?'

To which he replied: 'Oh, I don't mind.' And: 'Oh, she doesn't mind.' And: 'I brought her some trout home. You should have seen them. It would make your eyes pop out of your head.' At tea-time in the canteen, one of them started a long-winded story about 'a friend of mine. Very sad, you know. He had to divorce his wife in the end. Rotten luck some fellows have.' But Mr. Parker did not seem to pay much heed to the story. Finally, they asked his opinion on the matter. With this face twisted into his habitual grimace, Mr. Parker said:

'I would never divorce my wife in such a case.'

'Wouldn't you?'

'Of course not. Do you think I would stand having all that filth dragged through the divorce courts, and the papers, and everybody talking about it? Not on your life.'

'But in my friend's case everybody knew about the goings on. Long before it came into the courts.'

'Well, that's different. In that case he couldn't do anything else, he had to keep his self-respect. It was the only respectable thing to do.'

'It's very sad though, don't you think?'

'I don't know. He just couldn't keep his wife in order, if you ask me. I've no patience with henpecked husbands. Pooh!'

And with this, Mr. Parker pushed his cup away so violently, that the dregs of the tea spilled over the table.

They exchanged glances behind his back. Yet what had just been said was not astonishing, considering that he who had said it, used to refer to female dogs as 'lady dogs', and called his wife a 'bitch' when no one else was present.

Like all those who are anxious to be regarded as respectable, Mr. Parker took himself very seriously. He could not view lightly anything that went contrary to his comforts.

On that Thursday evening, when he returned from work, there was grilled ham for dinner. After the first mouthful he laid down his knife and fork and said: 'Elise grilled it just half a minute too long.'

He covered his face with his hands and remained like this for a while. He than said with a groan: 'And you know how I love grilled ham. I'd been looking forward to it so much.'

Franciska said: 'It's very good. Won't you eat it?'

'Why should I? It's completely spoilt for me.'

Franciska thought his complaint was too ludicrous to be answered. She did not realize that what had revealed itself as pettiness in this case was that sense for precision and perfection which made him the excellent engineer that he was.

He rose from the table and walked to the window, turning his back to her, as self-important people do, when they are annoyed, intending by this gesture to punish those who have offended them, by half-withdrawing their presence.

'You should have cooked it yourself. Mother would never spoil ham like this.'

'Your mother is used to cooking,' replied Franciska.

'Thank God she is. Not useless like your family.'

'Would you like something else?'

'No, thanks,' he returned to the table and sat down. He stared into space.

After a while he said: 'All right, I'll have something else.'

Presently he said: 'A fine sort of home life for a fellow. Travelling about all the week and then coming back to this.'

Franciska was reading a book and she did not reply. 'What an idiotic fuss about nothing,' she thought, contemptuously. The situation struck her as ridiculous and deserving contempt because she felt, quite rightly, that Mr. Parker's injured attitude was quite out of proportion to the injury he had received. Yet she had never felt that it was equally ridiculous when she herself, for instance, had refused to listen to Feldman seriously because of his bad table manners. She had never thought it ridiculous when Mrs. Kalny had refused to engage the services of an eminent lawyer, because he had, upon greeting her, extended his hand instead of waiting until she should give him hers.

Franciska never queried the particular brand of sophistication to which she had been accustomed at home and which Mr. Parker called frivolity. Yet frivolity was only a part of this sophistication. Frivolity consists in trifling with serious matters. Sophistication does not only trifle with serious matters, it also takes seriously things which are normally considered trifling. It is really this attitude of turning upside down all the values of life that forms the essence of sophistication. And it is not for nothing that the book which was and still is, regarded as the bible of the sophisticated, is called *A Rebours*, that is '*Against the Grain*' and that in it, day is turned into night, natural flowers are made to look like artificial ones, and finally the eating of food is replaced by nourishment with the enema. Franciska could never understand her husband's serious attitude over trifling matters, because what was trifling to her, was not trifling to him.

Mr. Parker sat down in his chair, looking at a paper. After a while he rose and started to pace up and down between the two windows, with his hands thrust into his pockets.

'A fine sort of home life for a fellow,' he said.

Again Franciska did not reply.

She thought that she was being very wise in ignoring her husband's bad temper and she could not understand why this attitude of hers, which to her, seemed so soothing, never pacified him at all. In reality, her lack of response did not spring from any desire for peace and quiet, but was simply an expression of the contempt she felt for her husband. It was therefore the worst possible thing she could do on such occasions.

It is said that it takes two to play a game and equally, it takes two to make a quarrel, and if one person thirsts for a quarrel and the other does not respond, a mortification arises similar to that when amorous advances are ignored.

It is well known that the most violent clashes between husband and wife always arise from trifling incidents. These incidents are not the real causes, but they serve as pretext for the clash, while the real causes are never mentioned. Thus, when Mr. Parker said: 'A fine sort of home life,' alluding to the badly grilled ham, he really referred to a quite different part of his home life, which to him was unsatisfactory.

He approached her chair and said: 'You are absolutely useless. Why don't you do something, instead of sitting here and reading? For crying out loud.'

Franciska looked up: 'What should I do?'

'Well, just do something. Knit or mend or something. Like other wives.'

Franciska looked at him in silence, just as she had looked at him in silence in the room in the Pelican.

'Can't you answer?' and he kicked the book out of her hand.

During that scene in the Pelican, Mr. Parker had used bodily violence, but not on his wife. He had not done so because he sensed his lack of mastery over her and he who is not a conqueror cannot indulge in the gestures of conquest. It was in this part of their relationship that the core of his bitterness was buried, that bitterness which had inscribed its hieroglyph on his face and which drove him to seek for power in his cars.

But now they were not in the bedroom, which had been the place of his humiliation; they were in the sitting room, where he was the master of his house. As Franciska bent down to pick up the book, he kicked it further away from the chair, shouting: 'Why don't you answer? Do you think I am going to stand for this?' and as she still remained silent: 'Stop staring at me for Christ's sake. I have to work all the week, I suppose, so that you can just sit and stare. You are no good as a wife. Other wives give their husbands a proper welcome when they come home after a week. And what do I get? Bad ham. And then this. I'm browned off.'

He remained standing in front of her, balancing on the tips and heels of his feet, so that it was impossible for her to move away.

'Let me get up, Johnny.'

'Oh no. I've got you now.' His mood changed to archness. 'I've got you now properly,' and, bending down, he attempted to put his cheek close to hers and to embrace her.

'Let me go.'

'No. Why should I?'

She felt frightened. To hide her fright, she said: 'It's a pity you did not come back before, Johnny. A friend of ours was here for a few days only, and he would have liked to meet you.'

'Oh, who was that?'

'A Mr. Feldman. He is very famous and very rich.'

'And you saw him?'

'Yes, of course,' replied Franciska.

'Where? Did he come here?'

'No, I had drinks with him at the Crillion.'

'You stupid bitch. For crying out loud. No wonder the blokes at work are talking their heads off. I won't have that sort of thing going on, do you hear?' He began to shake her.

At first she tried to slip out of his arms and then she began to struggle.

'Leave me alone.'

He repeated jeeringly: 'Leave me alone,' and then, with a renewed spurt of fury: 'All right, I'll leave you alone.' He put his hands round her throat. She screamed as long as she could, but it was not very long, before her breath was stopped. She was still conscious, when he released his stranglehold, dragged her out of the chair and kicked her on the floor. She fell, too dazed to stop herself from falling.

Without giving her another look, Mr. Parker sat down in his chair and took up the newspaper 'Can't you shut your mouth, you stupid bitch? Suppose the neighbours heard you?'

It was only then that she realized that he had not released her out of pity, but because he was afraid for his respectability. She picked herself up, breathless and trembling. Her only thought was: 'I must get out of this. Before he kills me.' Then, the contempt which she felt for him returned. 'He wouldn't kill me. It would not be respectable. I am not getting out because I am afraid. I am getting out because he is impossible.' It was this feeling which restored her strength; contempt knows no love. But it also knows no fear. She had been kicked and assaulted. But because she despised her husband, she could not take him seriously and could not credit him with any feelings. It did not occur to her that he might have been hurt by her refusal to share his bed, any more than Mrs. Kalny would have credited her servants with the capacity for emotion. And because it had been inbred in Franciska not to give way in front of the *canaille*, she now forced herself to be calm, arranged her dress and sat down in a chair.

She looked with distaste at her husband as he sat hunched over his newspaper. His face was still flushed and the eyes, small, dark and shining, seemed to look out from it as though they belonged to another face, hidden beneath that red mask of fury.

She rose, picked up the book from the floor and put it back on one of those shelves, from which, at her husband's request, she had been made to remove the works of Oscar Wilde when they first married.

Franciska had been taught that it was fatal to run away from an animal of whom one is afraid. It was with this in mind, that she now walked out of the room slowly and casually. She did not think of anything in particular. And just as she had, years ago, on her way through the school corridor, noticed cracks on the wall she had never seen before, so now, closing the door behind her, her eyes caught on a stain on the keyplate. 'Elise is shockingly bad,' she said to herself. 'I must tell her to-morrow.'

She had to move slowly; it was a black night and the

stairs were dark. She did not dare to put the light on, for fear of attracting her husband's attention.

Outside, it was drizzling. She stood for a while in the yard, too dazed to take shelter. Only now did she notice that she was still trembling. Her throat ached from the bruises she had received. At the far end of the passage she could hear the voice of the concierge. On the second floor of the house where, up till now, only two windows had been lit, two more windows sprang into light, then one more.

'That was the salon. Now he is looking into the bedroom. I must go.'

She began to run.

It was only when she had passed the round lamps which shed their white light on the low columns of the Palais Royal that she realized where she was going.

'It's an hotel. It's always open. He will tell me what to do. And I cannot go anywhere else, in the middle of the night. All my relatives will be asleep by now.'

The porter, to her relief, did not ask her to wait in the lobby but took her straightaway upstairs. On the first floor landing there were three glass cases containing a collection of dolls, dressed in the national costumes of various European countries. It was there that she stood, trying to pick out a doll dressed in the Bohemian national dress, when the American came upon her, followed by a chasseur.

'Admiring our collection, Ma'am?'

'Yes.'

'Have you found anything interesting?'

'I thought I saw something from home. But then it wasn't.'

'It never is.'

He did not talk much, nor did she. Lying between the sheets, thin and soft as all hotel sheets are from too frequent laundering, peace came at last, but nothing more. And later on in the night, as though sensing it he said something which she was to remember all her life: 'Never mind the past. And never mind the future. It is dark, it is warm, and you are safe.'

CHAPTER 11

THOSE MEN who are the darlings of women are generally disliked by other men. Standing in Mr. Parker's garage, with one foot resting on the mudguard of the Bentley, the American took it for granted that Mr. Parker would look at him with hatred. He had been prepared for rages and insults. But he had not been prepared for this wordless despair, this hopeless resignation.

'There is nothing to worry about, Parker. Take it easy.' And then, cynically counting on the other's lack of imagination, 'She made friends in Lechworth with Jo, my girl friend, you know. And she thought, naturally, that Jo was over here, with me. Surely you don't think—there is nothing to worry about.'

'I know that. Naturally. I quite—I quite understand.'

Mr. Parker gave him a look which, the American thought, was envy. 'He can't know,' he said to himself. 'What the hell. And even if he does. What the hell again.'

He was right. Mr. Parker did not know, did not suspect what the other tried to hide. If he had glanced at the American with envy, it had been the envy of the outcast, who has, once upon a time, achieved an entry into normal life and who has been cast out once more. Mr. Parker's marriage had been his victory. With this act he had locked the door of that room from which he had fled upon leaving the army. That door had refused to stay shut; it had once stood ajar for a few moments on an evening in the *Boeuf sur le Toit*.

'He doesn't really care for her,' thought the American. 'He did not even inquire about her. He only thinks about himself.'

He was not moved by pity. There was no one at this moment who was moved by pity for Mr. Parker, because no one knew the reason for his despair.

Embarrassed by this brooding silence which he could not explain, the American said what one usually says on such occasions:

'Take it easy, Parker. Perhaps you can patch it up. And if you feel you can't, well; perhaps it is a good thing in the long run. There are plenty more fish in the sea. You just weren't suited, that's all. Nobody's fault.'

It was impossible to tell whether Mr. Parker was listening for he had sunk down in the driving seat of the car and, leaning against the wheel, hid his face in his hands.

At last he said with a groan: 'It's the end. I just could not make a go of it. And everybody will know. They know already. They knew from the beginning, Roland and everybody.'

'Nonsense, Parker. Your wife made friends with Jo—that's my girl friend, you know—out there in Lechworth. And we took her out once or twice. No bones broken.'

'I know that. That's not what I meant.'

Returning to the Ritz, the American found Franciska in the small bar behind the Grill Room.

'He is shattered,' he said. 'Make room for me, Cissy. We must have a drink to restore Parker's shattered nerves. We'll do it by telepathy. I have always believed in telepathy. Haven't you?'

'What did he say?'

'Nothing.'

She fell silent.

He ordered drinks in quick succession. 'Parker is feeling much better now, already,' he declared. 'The things I have to do for Parker.'

'And for me, Miles. I am sorry you had all this trouble. It must have been ghastly for you.'

He laughed. 'I am used to being the white knight,' he said. 'I am, you know, although people never believe it. It is because, when I go out, I leave my white horse round the corner.'

'Aren't you silly,' said Franciska, smiling. Then her mood changed.

The American lit a cigar. 'Roland is your cousin, isn't he?' he asked.

'Yes.'

'Why is Parker afraid of him?'

'Johnny? He is not afraid of Roland. Why should he be?'

'He mentioned him just now, when I saw him. Somehow, I thought it was peculiar.'

'It is, isn't it?' replied Franciska. 'I can't understand it. But he hates Roland, you know, because he is so frivolous. And he hates me too, because I am so frivolous. It's because we both laughed that night at the *Boeuf sur le Toit*. But it seems so silly, really.'

'Let's hear it, Cissy. The sillier the better. I must relax after doing my white knight act.'

He listened attentively while Franciska told him. 'He never forgave me for laughing, you know. It is idiotic. But still, I feel now quite guilty. I should not have married him.'

'Why did you?' he asked quickly.

But again, as once before, she was evasive. 'Oh, I just

wanted to get away from home. And I suppose, I made use of him.'

'And he made use of you.'

'What makes you think so?'

He drew at his cigar, then looked at her: 'How innocent you are.'

She began to laugh but he did not join her. He finished his drink in silence. Then he said: 'I am sorry for Parker. The poor devil.'

PART THREE

ONCE MORE it was Louise who had seen her off at the station. Mrs. Kalny had said good-bye across the table at Quadris and the Colonel had walked with Franciska through the Merceria, as far as the landing stage by the Rialto.

It was a hot, grey morning in September and Franciska had already woken up with a headache.

Now, as the train had left Venice and was rolling through the desolate plain behind Mestre, she opened her dressing case to search for the phial. She still had the pills which Dr. Craig had prescribed for her and although in the beginning of her stay in Italy she had not needed them, she had been forced to take them more and more often, as time went by.

'Curse Louise, where has she put them?' thought Franciska as she explored the small leather pockets lining the inside of the case. She was not really cursing Louise. Unless one has a lady's maid, one cannot curse her, and Franciska's pretended annoyance was her way of savouring to the last drop the luxury she had enjoyed which, on this morning, had come to an end.

She opened the phial and rang for the attendant. He came at once. After he had brought her a bottle of mineral water and a glass, she asked him, while she looked for her purse, what time lunch was served.

'The first service at noon, the second at one o'clock, madame.'

'I'll eat at one. Will it be full?'

'Not at all. There are two more people in the whole *wagon-lit* apart from madame. But I'll reserve a seat.'

'Will you call me before one? I am going to lie down.'

He nodded, lowered the window and pulled down the blind. 'I hope madame will be comfortable,' and then, with a smirk: 'All alone. Venice is very tiring, madame. The most tiring place in Italy.'

As he went out, she caught a glimpse of a man's figure standing by the window in the passage. As soon as she was alone, she bolted the door and locked it. 'I need not have done this. The sleeping car is quite empty. Still, just as well.'

She lay down.

A shut door forbids entry, but a door which has been shut, locked and bolted is an invitation to enter to the man outside. Franciska swallowed the pill and drank two glasses of water. She felt indignant. 'These Italians are all the same. What did he mean by being comfortable all alone? They think everybody who goes to Venice goes there for a honeymoon. That's all they ever think about.' With rising indignation she thought of the conversation with the night porter at the Bauer Grunwald which had been repeated night after night. While Mrs. Kalny and the Colonel stayed at the Gritti, Franciska had had to stay at another hotel. Mrs. Kalny had made this arrangement, so she said, on the ground of economy, but if this had been the real reason, she would hardly have chosen for her daughter an hotel that was scarcely less expensive than her own. Night after night when Franciska had entered the Bauer Grunwald, alone, and, as she told herself, unprotected, the night porter had feigned surprise at her presence.

'My key, please.'

'Madame wishes to go to bed?'

'Yes, I do.'

He handed her the key with a bow.

'Madame is going upstairs?'

'Yes, of course.'

'To sleep?'

'Naturally.'

'And all alone? It breaks my heart to see madame like this. It is not good to sleep alone.'

And every night, as the lift carried her upstairs, Franciska, flushed with anger, had said to herself: 'It is not fair the way she treats me. She is all right. She has got the Colonel with her. The *canaille* would not dare to be impertinent in front of the Colonel.'

Indeed, it was impossible to imagine anyone taking a liberty in front of the Colonel. But this was the least of it. The Colonel had not only authority and distinction, he also had charm. Franciska envied her mother the company of the Colonel, only, because, as she thought, the Colonel acted as her protection. If Mrs. Kalny had been in the company of another, less charming man, for instance with Feldman, it would have been possible for Franciska to be amused at the nightly exchange in the lobby of the Bauer Grunwald and she would have stepped into the lift without any indignation whatsoever.

The Colonel's behaviour towards Franciska had been as reserved, as correct and as respectful as any daughter could have wished it from her mother's lover. In spite of this, his presence had been a constant thorn in her flesh. In fact, it was because of it. And something Mrs. Kalny had said had not improved the matter either.

It had been in Verona, shortly after the Colonel's arrival. Mrs. Kalny, alone with her daughter on a shopping expedition in the Via Mazzini had sighed over the price of a blouse. As the garment was being wrapped up, Franciska said: 'Aren't you sorry, Mama, after all, that you did not marry Feldman? He is terribly rich, you know.'

Mrs. Kalny replied: 'Every day I am sorry. Every night I am glad.'

'The Italians are all horrible,' thought Franciska. 'Even the Colonel. He is horrible too, but he hides it.' Her thoughts returned to her mother. 'Now she is going back to Capri, because he has got to go to Rome. I wonder who she has got in Capri. She has not changed at all.'

If Mrs. Kalny had not changed, neither had Franciska. Just as of old, she pretended to despise her mother's attraction for men, whereas in fact, she envied her for it. And as of old, she did not admit to herself the reason for her hostility.

'No wonder, I've got these migraines again. She just gets on my nerves, that's all.'

Sin is that which corrupts the soul and all sin consists in sinning against oneself. This is especially apparent in the fourth commandment. If we find it impossible to understand and honour our parents, it is impossible to undertsand and honour ourselves, as our parents are part of ourselves. Franciska would not see that she was her mother's daughter and that the same forces which reigned over her mother's life also reigned over hers. The voluptuous air of Italy and the presence of the Colonel had made these forces more overwhelming than ever before and had thus poured a poison into the heart that was already overflowing with it. When Franciska said: 'That's all the Italians ever think about' and 'The Italians are horrible' and 'She hasn't changed at all, I wonder who she will have now?' she really meant to say: 'That's all the Italians ever think about. But I don't. I am better than they are. All the Italians are horrible. But I am not. She hasn't changed at all. She still has lovers. But I am not like my mother. I don't.' If anyone,

246

guessing these thoughts had asked: 'Don't you? What about the American?' she would have answered: 'That was different. I only did it to get away from Johnny.'

'And didn't you enjoy it?'

'That's beside the point.'

The lunch in the restaurant car had been opulent. Franciska's headache was much better and she experienced thar feeling of splendid isolation and superiority over the rest of the world which is induced by taking good food and good wine in a speeding train.

She spent the day reading in her compartment and looking out of the window. The train arrived in Milan at eight and was to stop there for an hour.

Franciska decided to get out and stretch her legs and buy some newspapers. The sleeping car attendant helped her down the steps on to the platform with an exaggerated air of solicitude. 'Is madame quite rested? There will be dinner after nine o'clock, as soon as we leave Milan. Will madame be careful when she goes back to the train? We shall be at another platform. *Binario* number nine it will be.'

'Why is that? Do you always do it?'

'Always, madame. We get joined to another part of the Orient Express. From Bucharest. That's not so nice. Venice is nicer. *Venezia bella*. But very tiring.'

As Franciska walked down the platform, she had the feeling that he was looking after her with a jeer and as though to ward it off, she jerked her shoulders in a movement of irritation.

After the train had left the station, Franciska washed her hands and refreshed her face. She could hear the clanging of the bell, more insistent as it approached, announcing that dinner would soon be served. She went out into the passage and the white-coated boy gave her a reservation ticket. A man with an attaché case came out of one of the doors, as the waiter swept past.

'Isn't the boy silly,' she thought. 'I suppose the man wanted to reserve a seat as well.' Then she returned to her compartment and sat down.

There was a tap at the door and the man with the attaché case entered.

'*La douane,*' he said. '*Le passeport, s'il vous plait. Customs inspection. The passport please. Gepaeckskontrolle. Den Pass bitte.*'

Franciska thought: 'Make your mind up,' and then, while opening her handbag: 'But this is idiotic. We are still miles away from the frontier.'

She held out her passport to him. He glanced at the dark blue gilt embossed cover and made a gesture of refusal. He said in English: 'That's quite all right, madam. I don't want to see it. Where are you going?'

'To Paris.'

'You are going straight through? You will not stop anywhere in Italy?'

'No.'

'May I see your ticket, please?'

She gave him her ticket and turned away from him, looking out of the window. Although she could not observe him, she had the feeling that he was not looking at the ticket but at her.

'*Voilà,*' he said. 'Your ticket to Paris.' And then, after a pause: 'Can I see your luggage, please?'

'It's up there.'

'Is that all the luggage you have got or have you registered anything?'

'No, I haven't. It's all up there.'

'Will you get it down, please?'

She said: 'I am not a porter.'

'Neither am I.'

She looked at him fully for the first time. He was taller than most Italians are and he was not dressed with that neatness and swagger which she had observed so often in Italian men. As he bent down, looking at her, a silk scarf swung loosely from his neck and a strand of straight black hair fell across his forehead. Then he opened the door and stepped out, tossing the hair from his forehead.

'He got tired of me. Thank God for that.'

But almost at once he came back again with the attendant. The attendant lifted Franciska's suitcases down from the rack and, saluting, withdrew.

'Here are my keys,' said Franciska.

'Have you got anything to declare?'

'No, nothing.'

'But what have you got in the suitcases?'

'What one usually has. My dresses and things.'

'How long did you stay in Italy?'

'Three months.'

He sat down on the edge of the seat: 'That's a long time, isn't it?'

'I suppose so.'

He said: 'You are not an art student.' He did not say it in a questioning way, but as a statement. She shrugged her shoulders.

'Did you go to visit friends or relatives?'

Franciska thought: 'It's because the train is so empty. He's got too much time on his hands.' She said: 'I went to stay with my mother.'

'But you are not an Italian. And you are not English.'

'You can look me up in my passport,' replied Franciska.

'What is a passport?' and he added: 'Didn't your mother buy you anything?'

Franciska had several pieces in her luggage which were new and which she should have declared. But she was too annoyed by now to be conciliatory in order to gain favours from the official. Since that time, when, at four o'clock in the morning, Franciska had tried to bribe the porter with two crowns, she had come to the conclusion that it did not pay to placate the *canaille*. She said: 'Yes, my mother did buy me a few things. You can have a look.'

'I don't want to.'

He rose. The dark dignity of his face, unsmiling and un-moved, filled her with exasperation. He said: 'Shall I put your luggage back?'

'No, thank you. You are not a porter.'

'I am all sorts of things. It depends how I feel.'

Franciska thought again: 'Make your mind up,' and she watched him, as he lifted the suitcases on the rack. 'He is very tall and very strong,' she thought, and, with a shudder: 'I should not like to meet him on a dark night.' She did not thank him. He took his attaché case and went out.

She turned to the mirror and powdered her face, although she had done so ten minutes ago. Then she rang for the attendant and said: 'Here are my keys, my passport and my ticket. I don't want to be disturbed in the night. When do we get to the frontier?'

'We shall be at Domodossola at one o'clock in the morning, madame. Madame shall not be disturbed.'

'But there will be a revision?'

'Oh, yes, naturally, madame. At the frontier always.'

'But what did he do? And he wasn't in uniform either? He said he was the Customs.'

'Special police, madame. It's a new *chicanerie* and it's very efficient.'

'Oh, I see. I think it is an efficient nuisance. Still.'

'We've got order now in Italy, madame. Before that, no order, no police.'

There were a few people in the passage, as she made her way to the restaurant car, but the man with the attaché case was not among them. 'I suppose he has gone to the second class,' thought Franciska.

'He'll have a wonderful time there. Lots and lots of lovely passports and gorgeous suitcases. He speaks English very well. I wonder how many languages he knows.'

When she entered the restaurant she saw him sitting at a table at the far end, drinking that heavy-blooded dark wine which the Italians in some parts of the country call *vino nero* and which is of that same crimsoned black as black roses and black cherries.

'I suppose he gets his meals free,' she thought.

The dinner started with those small tightly rolled, dust-green artichokes that resemble buds of waterlilies, and their leaves, silvered with oil, made her think of moonlight on water. With it were slices of raw ham, cut so thin that she could see the light shining through as she raised them on her fork. 'The Italians are horrible but they do cook well, I must say that for them. *Quelle différence* from dinner in Coventry,' and, smiling to herself. 'Johnny would call it foreign filth.' Already she was able to recall her husband with complete calm. The only tragedies she was ever to know were to be tragedies of love, and as Mr. Parker had never touched her heart she could not feel any bitterness towards him.

She looked at the man with the attaché case. He was pouring out another glass of wine. 'He should really eat with the waiters in the kitchen. That's where he belongs. Anyway, the food is much too good for him.'

She watched him as he drank. 'They drink like fish,' she thought and took a sip from her own glass. It was a pale yellow wine from Conegliano. She always drank red wine when she had the choice, but this evening, as soon as she had taken her seat at the table, she had decided to drink white wine. 'I must get to know something new, while I still have the chance. In a few hours' time, it will be the end of Italy.' Her face felt suddenly very hot and she asked the waiter to drop a cube of ice in her glass.

The man at the far end of the restaurant continued to drink quietly and slowly, not raising his eyes. She sipped the iced wine but it increased the burning in her cheeks.

He was still drinking when she paid her bill. Without knowing why, she tried to linger on, asking the waiter idle questions.

'When do we get to Paris?'

'Half past ten in the morning, madame.'

'And when is breakfast?'

'Any time from seven o'clock onwards. No fixed hour, madame.'

In her compartment the seat had been transformed into that narrow bed on which so many travellers before her had shared their rest with their imaginary sleeping companion.

'I won't lock my door in case they want to get at my luggage at the frontier.'

She took her dress off and went into the adjoining *cabinet de toilette*. She returned and looked at herself in the mirror. Her powder and rouge were washed away, but still her face had that same rosy glow that it had shown during dinner.

'I must have had too much to drink.'

252

She sat down on the bed and began to look at a paper. The slit between the lowered blind and the window frame continually flashed with light and sank into darkness as though unrolling a string of burning beads, while the small gusts of night air ran through her hair and over her bare shoulders. It was the sudden draught that swept the hair across her eyes and blinded her for a second and made her heart jump.

The draught ceased and there was the click of the bolt. 'What do you want?' she said and she put her hands to her throat as though gathering a garment round her. It was only a moment later that she realized that her shoulders were bare.

He remained standing by the door. 'Oh, nothing. I just wanted to talk.'

'Haven't you got anything to do?'

He shrugged his shoulders. 'Nothing. Nothing till Domodossola. There I get out. Are you afraid of me?'

'Of course not. Why should I be? Will you go now?'

'Yes, I will go,' he did not stir. She turned her eyes away from him. She heard no movement but suddenly she was buried under him. Her lips seemed to be melting under his mouth, her body dissolving under his limbs. It was the cracking of buttons, the rending of silk, the snapping of elastic that made her emerge from those dark waters whose tides are those of the juices of the body and whose currents are governed by the pulse of the blood.

He released his hold on her and sat up.

She said: 'I will ring for the conductor.'

'What has he to do with you?'

'You beastly Italians.'

'I am not an Italian. I am from Catania.'

'Will you go at once now. I will ring for him.'

'Why are you so afraid of me? I shan't touch you any more '

He took her hand and turned it upside down. As he touched the palm, her hand felt as though it was melting away under his kisses. She tore it away and slapped his face.

When a woman slaps a man's face, it is not a signal for him to stop, but an invitation to go on. It is a gesture which pays homage to the conventions which govern the outside of our lives, but it is nothing more than a hollow gesture.

'I'll ring for him and I'll complain,' said Franciska, but already she knew that she had entered a country where the men wear no livery and do not answer a bell.

She lay awake for many hours after the stop at the frontier. She did not reflect how it had been 'possible' for her to surrender to a man who had not been introduced to her and whose very name she did not know. She did not feel mortified at the thought that he had approached her with less ceremony than those men who made up the adventures of Sylva, the hairdresser. She did not feel any more the contempt of: 'That is all they ever think about,' and 'She has not changed at all,' because she now realized that this was all she ever had thought about herself and all she ever wanted and that she would not change any more than her mother would.

The Island of Cythera is to be found in many unexpected places. At last the goddess had shown her the island and ironical as always, had led her there by a messenger who was not a gentleman, who was brutal and who had not even pretended to any feelings for her.

In the years to come there were more men who entered Franciska's life and after they had passed out of it, she thought of them often. But the only man who ever appeared in her dreams was he who had to get out at Domodossola.

254

THE HOGARTH PRESS

A New Life For A Great Name

This is a paperback list for today's readers – but it holds to a tradition of adventurous and original publishing set by Leonard and Virginia Woolf when they founded The Hogarth Press in 1917 and started their first paperback series in 1924.

Now, after many years of partnership, Chatto & Windus · The Hogarth Press are proud to launch this new series. Our choice of books does not echo that of the Woolfs in every way – times have changed – but our aims are the same. Some sections of the list are light-hearted, some serious: all are rigorously chosen, excellently produced and energetically published, in the best Hogarth Press tradition. We hope that the new Hogarth Press paperback list will be as prized – and as avidly collected – as its illustrious forebear.

A list of our books already published, together with some of our forthcoming titles, follows. If you would like more information about Hogarth Press books, write to us for a catalogue:

40 William IV Street, London WC2N 4DF

Please send a large stamped addressed envelope

HOGARTH FICTION

Behind A Mask: The Unknown Thrillers of Louisa May Alcott
Edited and Introduced by Madeleine Stern

Death of a Hero by Richard Aldington
New Introduction by Christopher Ridgway

The Amazing Test Match Crime by Adrian Alington
New Introduction by Brian Johnston

Epitaph of a Small Winner by Machado de Assis
Translated and Introduced by William L. Grossman

Mrs Ames by E.F. Benson
Paying Guests by E.F. Benson
Secret Lives by E.F. Benson
New Introductions by Stephen Pile

Ballantyne's Folly by Claud Cockburn
New Introduction by Andrew Cockburn
Beat the Devil by Claud Cockburn
New Introduction by Alexander Cockburn

Chance by Joseph Conrad
New Introduction by Jane Miller

Lady Into Fox & *A Man in the Zoo* by David Garnett
New Introduction by Neil Jordan

The Whirlpool by George Gissing
New Introduction by Gillian Tindall

Morte D'Urban by J.F. Powers
Prince of Darkness and other stories by J.F. Powers
New Introductions by Mary Gordon

Mr Weston's Good Wine by T.F. Powys
New Introduction by Ronald Blythe

The Revolution in Tanner's Lane by Mark Rutherford
New Introduction by Claire Tomalin
Catharine Furze by Mark Rutherford
Clara Hopgood by Mark Rutherford
New Afterwords by Claire Tomalin

The Last Man by Mary Shelley
New Introduction by Brian Aldiss

The Island of Desire by Edith Templeton
Summer in the Country by Edith Templeton
New Introductions by Anita Brookner

Christina Alberta's Father by H.G. Wells
Mr Britling Sees It Through by H.G. Wells
New Introductions by Christopher Priest

Frank Burnet by Dorothy Vernon White
New Afterword by Irvin Stock

J. F. Powers
Morte D'Urban

New Introduction by Mary Gordon

'This is the book for which his many admirers have long been waiting' – *Evelyn Waugh*

Father Urban Roche is a formidable golfer, raconteur and star of the preaching circuit – no ordinary priest he. Hardly surprising that he harbours less-than-meek ambitions of inheriting the highest of posts, Father Provincial to his Order. Then, banished to a deserted retreat in the wastes of Minnesota, this man for all seasons is forced to confront the realities of life on earth which, through a sequence of events at once uproarious and moving, he triumphantly does. A novel about a priest, a special priest, *Morte D'Urban* is a parable of the straitened role of belief in a secular age. It is also one of the comic masterpieces of our time.

H.G. Wells

Christina Alberta's Father

New Introduction by Christopher Priest

The war is over: it is 1920, the threshold of a new age. Christina Alberta – one of Wells's most endearing heroines with her bobbed hair and short skirts – is ready to plunge into the heady freedom of bohemian Chelsea. But her father too desires liberty after a lifetime at the Limpid Stream Laundry; and when a séance at the Petunia Boarding House, Tunbridge Wells, entrusts him with a message for the modern world from the lords of Atlantis, Christina's plans are dramatically affected. First published in 1926, *Christina Alberta's Father* is a novel about idealists at odds with a conventional society, a tale of change and growth – absurd, funny, sad, and totally absorbing.

Mark Rutherford

Catharine Furze

New Afterword by Claire Tomalin

Catharine's desires are those of every girl as she grows into womanhood – idealistic, absurd, passionate, barely spoken. In telling her story Mark Rutherford became one of the first male novelists to write sympathetically about the fate of women, and this book, along with *Clara Hopgood*, has been sought after for many years. It is his finest novel: Dickensian in its humour and pathos, exceptional in its understanding of a woman's troubled soul.

Gladys Mitchell
The Rising of the Moon
New Introduction by Patricia Craig and Mary Cadogan

The arrival of the circus heralds a cavalcade of doom for the townsfolk of Brentford: a Ripper is loose on the midnight streets. Mrs Bradley, looking particularly peculiar by moonlight, is for once outshone – by Masters Simon and Keith Innes, orphans and sleuths aged 13 and 11½ respectively.

Like Barbara Pym and Elizabeth Taylor, Gladys Mitchell has a wry, loving eye for the details of everyday life, for the little things that matter but often remain unspoken. *The Rising of the Moon* is more than an excellent detective story, it is an outstanding work of fiction, one to be read by intrepid heroes of any age. It is, as Philip Larkin says, her *'tour de force'*.

E. F. Benson

Secret Lives

New Introduction by Stephen Pile

Durham Square seems the height of propriety; only the rumblings of indigestion, the murmur of gossip and occasional canine consternation threaten its dignity. But behind the square's genteel façade hide secret lives. There is Miss Susan Leg at No. 25, for instance: can a woman who puts caviare on her scones be altogether respectable? Riddled with curiosity, mordant pen in hand, E.F. Benson draws aside the plush velvet drapes – and reveals in this deliciously ironic novel all the hilarious intrigues and intimacies of life upstairs (and downstairs) in one of the stateliest squares in England.

J. F. Powers

Prince of Darkness
and other stories

New Introduction by Mary Gordon

'J. F. Powers is a comic writer of genius, and there is no one like him' – *New York Review of Books*

J. F. Powers is one of the most original writers of post-war America. In these stories he tells of everyday tests of faith, of disillusion on the mean city streets, in the quiet of suburbia – but with irrepressible humour and wit. Priests reach for their beer, nuns for holiness; black men and women die in whitewashed alleyways; boys grapple with adolescence, an old man with a new job; Jewish refugees find no escape in a New World. These are tales of our human frailty and our tireless optimism: taut with anger, poignant, hilarious – and at all times challenging.